Circle of Death

Novels by Maggie Rennert

A Moment in Camelot
Circle of Death

CIRCLE
OF
DEATH

by
Maggie Rennert

PRENTICE-HALL, INC., *Englewood Cliffs, N.J.*

173387

Library of Congress Cataloging in Publication Data
Rennert, Maggie.
Circle of death.
I.   Title.
PZ4.R415Ci   [PS3568.E6]   813'.5'4   74–534
ISBN 0-13-133959-1

*To my son, Philip M. Rennert: he wasn't
lucky enough to get a mother who could sing
"All Through the Night" on key, but he
made the best of what he got.
For which, my thanks.*

Circle of Death

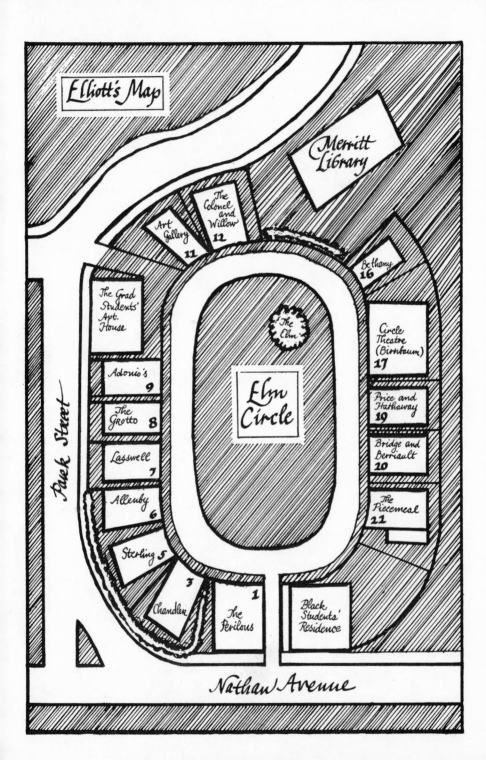

1

Elm Circle

uy Daniel Silvestri was a very model of what is loosely called the "new breed" of police officer, but he'd gotten that way by being, literally, of the old breed. In Boston and its surrounding cities and towns, members of the Silvestri family had long been sown among the public-service acres in a contour immediately recognizable to anyone who lives where local government is the major crop. Thus, a Silvestri had been a battalion chief in Boston's fire department and another was recently retired, with a silver bowl, from the post of Register of Deeds in Camford; the husband of a Silvestri daughter had risen to chief of police in North Axminster; and Guy Silvestri's mother's sister's oldest boy had been for the past ten years clerk of the City Council in Buxford, just across the river from Boston.

So Guy was not a lieutenant of detectives on the Buxford police force by accident. But on certain occasions, nepotism and the merit system may meet in the public interest, and Silvestri was clearly one of those occasions. Buxford was a college town—home of world-famous Lambert University, not to mention other less ancient but equally crowded institutions of learning—and battered by all the brouhaha typical of higher education in the late 1960's. And Guy Silvestri was peculiarly equipped, first by nature and then by training, to cope so far as anyone could.

If there is a people-bridging talent, Guy had been born with it; his ability to bring together while bringing order had been conspicuous even when he was playing outfielder for the Knee-Hi team at the Buxford Boys' Club. And almost from the day he arrived, diploma from Buxford High and Latin in hand, to sign up for the Buxford Police, his old-breed superiors told each other the boy had something—and identified it, in his personnel file, as "savvy." Whereupon, under the new-breed system designed to give a good man a break, Guy was sent to be higher-educated, part-time and slowly (not, of course, at Lambert: the Ivy League's superstar was *in* Buxford but not *of* it) at the state university's Boston branch. After that, the descriptions in Silvestri's file included such academic-world variations on savvy as "perceptive."

Because the old-breed police administrators had enough savvy themselves to recognize where all this could end, they treated with respectful caution the young comer who could someday be setting police salaries—and who, as a Silvestri, could be counted on to forget neither friend nor foe. New-breed administrators sighed happily, promoted him as fast as they legally could, and kept a wary eye out for poachers from neighboring police forces. But what all these goings on meant to Guy Silvestri was, most of the time, just overwork: both old and new breeds—beset by student riots and other phenomena vexing alike to practical experience and administrative theory—took to reaching for Silvestri as if he were ten grains of aspirin.

It was because someone superior and distraught had tried

preventive medicine that Det. Lt. Silvestri was standing around in a carefully-tended yard, on a late-March morning, at the back of a row of portable chairs. Some of them were occupied by behinds that might—but for the energies expended by Silvestri—have been "sitting-in" instead, all over Lambert University's administration building. Some of the holders of offices thus spared invasion were on exhibit on the rickety-looking temporary platform up front, where a careful tweed of black and white speech-makers sat awaiting their exactly timed turns to say something nice by way of dedicating Lambert University's black students' Residence. On the ground at stage left crouched a cameraman (white) from the single Boston TV channel hard up enough to cover nonriots, and a photographer (black) from the *Lambert Blue*. At stage right a physics major (white) working his way through Lambert applied his scientific aptitude to producing a not-too-loud broadcast of not-too-triumphant music. A Buxford patrolman (black) stood guard over the equipment and its operator, perhaps because someone thirsted for symmetry. Nothing there seemed to need protection from the members of the audience, who wore patience like a uniform.

So did Tim Whistler, president of the student Afro-American Association, though even at this distance from the platform Guy could see the disdain on the smooth tan face that somehow made the flanking whites—the president of Lambert University and the mayor of Buxford—look extra old and extra florid. But all of them were paying their dues to patience: speakers and audience appeared united in the willingness to tolerate the sort of absurdity that makes wider tolerances possible. Guy knew that young Whistler's speech, when it came, would take a cut or two at the Lambert dignitaries; but the whip would lash around their ankles, sparing their faces. And it would probably be too swift for the Buxford dignitaries to catch: Tim Whistler was gown, and gown—whether black or white—took no trouble to make itself understood by town.

3

Nevertheless, no matter what was said from the platform this morning, no adrenaline would flow in an audience stubbornly intent on exuding good will. Nearly all of Elm Circle had turned out for the occasion, precisely in order to signify either welcome or acceptance of the new Residence in their midst. Acceptance was good enough, by Silvestri's lights—which had to do with law, not opinion—so he counted off with equal satisfaction Lambert professor Hilary Bridge of 20 Elm Circle, whose elaborate welcoming of the black students might have been excessive even if he personally had enslaved their ancestors, and Ralph Adonio of the Circle's beauty salon, whom Prof. Bridge had all but openly charged with bigotry at one emotional Elm Circle Association meeting. Lt. Silvestri, present at that meeting precisely to restrain that kind of emotion, had succeeded in keeping the left wing from driving the right wing into fanaticism. And that was all it took, really: whether Adonio was a bigot or not, he was primarily a businessman. So, though he might murmur in a meeting, Adonio was not about to fight a *fait accompli*. He was right there now in his good blue suit, standing for the national anthem, bowing his head for the public praying, pattycaking his hands for speeches of giving and speeches of receiving. So Guy Silvestri was looking on benignly, pleasantly aware of work well done and trying not to be fatuous.

Apparently unsuccessfully. Because something was punctured, all right, when Elliott Sterling said softly from somewhere just behind Guy's left ear, "And on the eighth day he rested."

Guy turned. "Oof."

" 'Oof,' you say? Is that the best you can manage by way of grace under pressure?"

"I give credit where credit is due. But no tribute for malice." Silvestri kept his eyes directed at the platform, which was far enough away so his attentive silhouette was good enough.

"I'll see your oof, and raise you a cup of coffee. Come away with me." Elliott tilted his head, considering. "No, by golly. Make that 'Let me take you away from all this.' "

"Decorum," Guy said reprovingly. "Certainly when the chief of police is sitting right up there, decorum is recommended." He snatched a sidewise glance at Elliott. "Where's Kate? I see you've been properly got up for the occasion. But she didn't dress you neatly so you could roam around disrupting the proceedings."

"We only had one white shirt, so she didn't come. And I don't see why it's decorum for the chief to rise and accept thanks for what you did."

"You don't understand bureaucracy," Guy said. "Go away. I'm not a victim of injustice. So go sit down."

The tempter behind him was silent while Elm Circle politely applauded a platform advocate of the brotherhood of man. Then someone said "Lieutenant Silvestri" in an urgent whisper and Guy turned without thinking. To behold Elliott Sterling pantomiming a citizen in difficulty. A decorous citizen gesturing away from the proceedings to some unspecified point in Elm Circle, shaking his head, his hands shaping on the air something that might be small wheels, maybe stuck somewhere.

"What in the—?"

"I'm providing you with a decorous exit," Elliott said while his hands kept on indicating a citizen requesting aid. "You can be a dedicated servant of the people and still have coffee. Kate baked cookies, too." He held up his arm, pointing to his wristwatch. "This seems an appropriate gesture, somehow. Now let's see, what else?" He put a hand on Silvestri's arm and half turned away, clearly ready to lead the servant of the people to wherever some people needed service.

If anyone on the platform *was* watching, Elliott's antics could cause some alarm: there was a great sensitivity, up there, to any ripple in the peace. "Okay, okay. You win. But for God's sake walk slowly." He moved into position behind Elliott, to block the view from the platform in case Elliott thought up any more appropriate gestures. Then Guy ambled, hoping he was presenting a successful portrait of dutiful attention to something minor and rather tedious. He added a small disparaging smile when he saw one of the audience displaying curiosity: Jake Birnbaum, proprietor of Elm Circle's movie theater and a man who worried easily—though he had taken the trouble to hire Jim Waterman, one of the Circle's two student dogbodies, to babysit the closed theater in his absence. But Birnbaum turned his attention back to the platform now, his inquiring look sufficiently answered by a reassuring gesture from the departing Silvestri.

A frisky little wind carried the speaker's voice across the narrow cobblestoned alley that was the only public entry into the enclave of Elm Circle (other breaks in the Circle involved at least technical trespass). The cobblestones continued in a narrow drive that circled the grassy area (containing a bona fide elm tree), giving the residents a picturesque but tricky access to their individual driveways. The drive was barely wide enough to accommodate one modern automobile, and there were periodic feeble suggestions that the Elm Circle Association should have it widened. These suggestions were politely ignored by everyone except the ladies who ran the art gallery, who could be counted on to splutter at the mere hint of such a violation of history. By and large, Elm Circle's devotion to quaintness, and particularly its insistence on the virtues of the pedestrian way of life, was what its denizens wanted—though they grudgingly admitted that cars did have to have some way into and out of garages.

Elliott held open the side door of the Experiment Perilous bookshop—known to Lambert students as "the Perilous" —until his guest had entered. When he closed the door on the alley, the loudspeaker sound stopped abruptly.

Lt. Silvestri, exploring his new territory a few months earlier, had described the Perilous in his notes as "Elm Circle's intellectual pub." Which was close enough, but omitted the fact that its proprietor behaved as if he were one of the pub's old customers. At no time, Guy thought idly as he settled into one of the barrel-shaped armchairs and set his coffee cup down on the adjacent drum table, had he ever seen Elliott actually punch a cash register or wrap a book. "Elm Circle's first merchant," as Elliott liked to label himself, was a merchant—Guy had long since concluded—the way a gentleman farmer was a farmer. Elliott, though, was in a way responsible for the arrival at the Circle, first, of expensive-quaint purveyors of arts and crafts (many of them also gentlemen merchants) and then of merchant-merchant establishments like the beauty salon and the restaurant. Because it was Elliott, the rebel against his native Buxford Brahmin culture, who'd turned one of the two old Elm Circle houses he'd inherited into a shop—a breakthrough into commercialism that only Elliott Merritt Sterling, whose middle name was carved in stone over several sacred Lambert University buildings, could have managed without being fought tooth and claw.

But Elliott the rebel was still culture-bound. It showed when he said, "I take it This Is Farewell, right?" Guy knew him well enough by now to recognize that wrapping earnestness in overstatement was the only way Elliott could ask a question when he really wanted to know. Elliott wanted to know because, like Guy, he recognized that the easy double welcoming unexpectedly grown up between Silvestri and the Sterlings was, at the very least, a cornerstone for friendship. But "Look, let's keep in touch," or any variation on that, was too direct for Elliott.

"I mean," he went on lightly, "if it's only civil strife that brings you among us, will you now disappear from our ken? Short of the odd manhunt for an escaped lunatic, of course."

Guy helped himself to a cookie. "You're predicting an era of brotherhood and good will hereabouts?"

"Why not? I thought that's what we were celebrating." Elliott poured two more cups of coffee and set the pot back

7

on the table. "Listen, nobody around here uses 'boy' even for a boy any more. So why aren't you rejoicing over work well done?"

"I am. But quietly. It's a civil triumph, and they tend to lack drama."

"An accidental one. Lambert Blunders into Brotherhood." Elliott tilted his head as if to examine the words, and a shaft of sunlight emphasized the red in his thick brown hair—a final foxlike touch to the resemblance begun by a pointed chin and bright brown eyes. "Not drama, I agree. Farce."

Guy started to reply but got to his feet instead because there was a lady approaching and he was culture-bound too.

Kate said it for him: "What's the difference *how* it happens, Ellie, as long as it happens?" She waved away Guy's offer of coffee and took out her knitting.

"Stupidity and incompetence matter. Especially in a much-advertised bastion of intelligence." Lambert's angry alumnus all but spat out that description.

Guy grinned at Kate, his fellow believer in correcting the sin rather than locating the sinner. But Elliott was of a different school of thought, and he was already launched on an indictment of sinning Lambert. "Stay out of it," Guy advised Kate, under the flow of Elliott's outrage. "It's a family fight, really."

It was also probably the losing side of the debate, he knew. Because something you'd be hard put not to describe as stupidity had marked Lambert University's actions since, following upon certain pressures, it had decided to establish the Residence by combining and converting two old houses at the junction of Nathan Avenue and Elm Circle. The houses had long been the university's property—used for many years as guest quarters for visiting scholars and the like—so Lambert unquestionably had a right to do as it wished with them. But not the *way* it did . . .

"At Lambert, they think in abstractions," Guy said aloud. He knew the apology, if that was what it was, would be swept

away by Elliott's raging rhetoric. But it was the kindest explanation of why Lambert had marched in with big boots where
any Buxford politician would have had the sense to walk
warily. Presumably the university's theoreticians, thinking in
abstractions, had recognized that the Circle populace—
largely liberal Republicans and civil-rights Democrats—
would refrain from throwing bricks through the windows of
the new Residence; but the university thinkers (too high-
minded for politics?) had stopped there. Not until the local
chill penetrated Lambert's inner offices (via pipelines like
the Alumni Association) had anyone up there awakened to
the fact that even people who agree on what is the path of
virtue may resist being shoved down it. Elm Circle had a
record of accommodation to change: it had come a long way
from the exclusive enclave of tasteful opulence intended by
the original owners of the handsome old houses. But Elm
Circle also had all sorts of clout, and its residents thus had
no history of being pushed around.

By January of this year some realist at Lambert must have
figured out, finally, that not-throwing bricks was not enough.
The wintry air at Elm Circle was by then figurative as well
as literal. And in the chill, the Afro-American Association—
which included some easily irked students with clear memories of official hypocrisies—was inclined to perceive the ordinary headaches of wooing and waiting on artisans and
inspectors as stalls, dodges, and slithers. The vexations of
setting up housekeeping can try even happy marriages, and
the union of Lambert University with its black-student organization was at best a marriage of convenience, containing
no memory of even brief ecstasy. It could stand little strain.
Thus, if the Afro-American Association was to be kept from
applying to the communications media for a noisy divorce,
both speed and soothing would be required.

Enter then Silvestri, who didn't yet have his Master's and
so wasn't an official soother, but who was the Human Relations Office's secret weapon. What he did amounted to little

more than getting the electric wiring at the Residence approved promptly by town, county, and state functionaries while inspiring in Elm Circle—via meetings, round tables, and tête-à-têtes—a spirit acceptable to touchy Afro-Americans. Finally, accompanied by a Lambert official dressed as an Oxford don and a black student dressed as a Watusi chieftain, and trailed by TV news teams and "free press" hounds sniffing for conflict like truffle-hunting pigs, Silvestri produced both a certificate of fire safety and a populace ready to show good will—the necessary combination for civil triumph. "Sensitive," his new-breed superiors wrote in their reports. "Cagey" was what the old breed would have said, but they tended not to file reports unless something happened. And nothing had, though less because of Silvestri magic than because the black-student leader and the university representative had proved alike in (a) preferring efficiency to rhetoric and (b) squelching those in their own camps who had other preferences.

So it was all over—except for Elliott, who insisted on bookkeeping guilt and innocence. "Are you saying you see no difference between right and wrong?" he asked furiously.

Kate smiled, and admitted that she herself sometimes had a little trouble seeing it. This mild opposition only fed Elliott's righteous flame: invective roared above Kate's bent head like a flight of Phantom jets. But, Guy noted curiously, she went on knitting a blue wool something, her hands steady, her face revealing only intelligent interest in the world about her.

Maybe people who live near an air base just don't look up when the Phantoms streak by overhead? Or did she know—Guy wondered, examining the demure downward gaze that gave away nothing except a view of feathery dark lashes against the soft curve of her cheek—that these were only model airplanes, a boy imitating the sounds of war? He himself couldn't tell, but she was certainly in a better position to read the signs.

Nevertheless, Guy couldn't help himself: he had to try to

rescue her anyway. "Of course there's a difference between right and wrong," he said into a millisecond pause in Elliott's harangue. "But why use accounting methods? It's not really relevant, and besides it's not worth the trouble." Right and wrong, hell: you keep an accounting like that and you end up with a total of something-point-five on each side. Which is no use with people, who come in whole numbers. "All that really counts is, everything came out all right and nobody got hurt."

"Ah yes. Your civil triumph." Elliott grinned, suddenly looking especially foxy. "Doesn't it even allow you a 'Gee whiz, I won'?"

"Gee whiz, I won," Guy obliged.

"Mild. Very mild. Not a wow in a carload."

Guy smiled, acknowledging that civil triumph lacked kicks. It was something like the difference between the old-time doctor saving a diphtheria-stricken child and the public health doctor inoculating hundreds of children who would never get diphtheria. Probably the old doctor did get more charge out of sitting up all night in hand-to-hand combat with the disease than the public health people got throwing out the syringes and leaving for home at five o'clock. But it really wasn't much of a sacrifice to take low-calorie emotional sustenance in exchange for an absence of racial or university-vs-student turmoil. "The truth is," Guy said slowly, "I'm an organization man." He stopped Elliott's rejoinder with a gesture. "Never mind deep down in my psyche. Up front, where logic lives, I actually do think a team gets more good things done for more people than the same number of Robin Hoods do."

"Right," Elliott said. "Let's forget Mozart—a committee can do it better."

"You know that's not what he means," Kate said. She didn't look up from her knitting. "He's not talking about art."

"All right, I'll amend it. Say, a police force versus Sherlock Holmes. You'd bet against Holmes?"

"Oh, sure," Guy said. "I'll even give you odds."

Elliott sighed. "Pity. I was counting on playing Doctor Watson when you go off detecting."

"Are you going to go off detecting, Guy?" It was typical of Kate, this neat extraction of the question from the surrounding rigmarole.

Guy moved his broad shoulders against the armchair's embrace. "Right now, I'd better go off downtown, anyway," he said regretfully. It was comfortable here, where people did their fighting with words. In the other, non-Lambert, part of Buxford, brotherhood was not a word but a reality sometimes—including the scrapping and shoving for place that real brothers went in for. "But I don't do much detecting, really," he told Kate. "More filling out forms than looking for bad guys."

Kate glanced up from her knitting. "You will come back and see us, won't you? You must be off duty *sometime.*"

"Now and then." He stood, smiling down at her round pleasant face with its waiting look. Nobody, he thought, waited as quietly, without pressure, as Kate Sterling. And why not? When everything has always come to you, why wouldn't you be confident? "When I'm off duty, I'm a graduate student," he reminded her. "So I may be back wearing *that* hat—I have a paper to do for Cultural Anthropology, and I was thinking there were rich pickings at Elm Circle." It was true, though exaggerated. The Circle's relations with its two pet students—squinting down the nearest row of books, he could see one of them now, the girl the Sterlings called "Florence the Fair," sitting beside the cash register at the front of the store—had struck Guy as rather similar to those between old Southern plantation owners and their house slaves.

Elliott's interest had been immediately engaged. "Hey. Culturally, you could slice us half a dozen ways and come up with something for a paper. I'll be glad to help, Guy. A guided tour of rituals. Taboos. Just plain gossip."

Guy smiled, surprised at the rapid enthusiasm: most peo-

12

ple recoiled from the prospect of being studied. "As a matter of fact, you'd make a great sidekick for that." He hadn't realized, he thought now, how much Elliott resembled the kind of insider-outsider figure so valuable to an anthropologist studying a society. "You're a gen-u-wine certified native, and yet you spent your formative years away." And Elliott had been a Lambert student, too, before he'd gone away again. And finally come back to be Establishment.

"You admit I've got both native know-how and an immigrant eye," Elliott said. "You couldn't get a sidekick as well endowed if you advertised. So do I get the job?"

"You're hired." Guy started for the door.

"Hey, wait. I need an assignment. Sidekicks always have assignments."

Guy told himself he should have known that Elliott, whose workshop was crammed with hand-wrought relics of his various hobbies, would have to be given something to make or do. "Well, you make some general notes. And next time I come, we'll figure out an assignment. Okay?"

"When will that be?" Kate asked. "Soon?"

"Oh, a week or two." Guy glanced back at her over his shoulder and thought how easily her rosy face showed pleasure. "At most," he added, because to give pleasure is pleasing. He flapped a hand in farewell and went out.

He was back within a few days, though not for a visit.

2

Death at the
Circle

Elliott Sterling's elaborately detailed *schema* of Elm Circle—accompanied by a neatly typed thirty-page manuscript, also on the best bond paper—arrived in Guy Silvestri's office on Wednesday, April 6, after being handed around for a while because of an insufficiently specific address. Guy reminded himself reassuringly, as he glanced at what might have been a map had it been drawn to any known scale, that Elliott had shown enough restraint to send it by mail instead of by messenger. Still, when he riffled through the pages of biographical and sociological information (and some impressionistic writing, which the writer had not troubled to distinguish from data), Silvestri pondered possible means of turning Elliott off. Because, from the way it looked, there was a strong risk of Sorcerer's Apprentice here.

But a little later that morning Guy had more or less grateful recourse to the efforts of his sidekick. Because at about

11:00 A.M. Hilary Bridge, associate professor of English at Lambert University, was found dead in the garage attached to his residence. So Guy hastily dug out the still-unfiled pages of Elliott's manuscript, found the entry for Number 20 Elm Circle, and boned up on what Elliott Sterling, at least, knew about Hilary Bridge.

#20—Hilary Bridge, Jacques Berriault. These two are that rarity in ex-melting-pot America, genuine new immigrants. But don't be misled: in fact, they're both citizens of Universal University, and always were. Hilary came from England as a virgin M.A. Oxon., brain-drained over here by one of those veddy-veddy colleges that swoon at a Mayfair accent. Jacques was a French undergraduate exchange student who discovered that in America nobody distinguishes between Parisians and provincials: French is French, and is cute. He recognized his luck, and set about digging in.

Lambert is at least as anglophile as any other place, but shrewder than most: it moves in *after* the dislocations and the hassles, when the immigrant is nicely settled, housed, automobiled, citizened. Then Lambert begins the seduction, mentioning with a wink its big fat salaries and even fatter fringe benefits, murmuring when the lights are low about its billion dollars' worth of libraries. The built-in prestige of being Lambert faculty doesn't need mention, beyond the dropping of an appropriate name or two: in eloquent silence, Lambert lets the flattered little assistant prof imagine himself passing the sugar, any old day in the Common Room, to You Know Who. Actually, the sainted names on the Lambert faculty are rarely around, but the gimmick always works: if I wanted to find any academic type who's even reasonably good in his field and who has a genuine British accent, I could just sit down under the Buxford Elm and wait for him to turn up.

Hilary acquired the house at #20 when he turned

up about three years ago, and soon after that he acquired Jacques—though I believe they'd met originally during some summer beside some sea (at the
Cape? in the south of France?). The house looks as
though they've always lived in it, but that's because
Hilary feels good about "working with one's hands"
and Jacques *is* good at it. They have all this valuable
bric-a-brac, authenticated by Jacques and presumably paid for by Hilary—J. is still only tentative at
Lambert, working his way up and in. (But he'll get
there: Hilary would know if he wasn't making it, and
Hilary doesn't hang out with losers.) They're both
really minded to an art-for-art's-sake aesthetic and
aristocratic pleasures, but you know that's Out at
Lambert now; so they participate devoutly in good-
liberal causes and noblesse-obligely pony up for the
orphans—as long as the orphans aren't right around
the corner in Boston, of course. Also, nowadays when
they play bridge (with Jim Waterman and me, usually), they're apologetic about it. And lately Hilary
has been touting up the solid virtues of peasantries
and the joys of the simple life. But I had to go upstairs
once because somebody was in the downstairs pow-
der room, and I saw an electric toothbrush in their
bathroom.

Guy scanned the three paragraphs with the speed of a
student reading somebody else's notes just before an exam.
But the occasion was—as Elliott might have put it—an exercise for the team rather than for a Sherlock Holmes. So Guy
turned from Elliott's breezy prose to his own officially assigned reading, beginning with a report from Buxford's Sixth
Precinct recording a citizen's phone call. The citizen—Jacob
Birnbaum, prop. of the Circle Theatre, 17 Elm Circle—had
been instructed to return to the scene of the death and await
a patrol car.

By the time the patrol car bearing Patrolmen Donahue
and Green arrived, those assembled in the driveway of Number 20 were, according to Ptl. Donahue's further report: the

16

aforesaid citizen Birnbaum; Augustine "Gus" George, prop. of the Grotto Restaurant, 8 Elm Circle; Miss Ann Price, occupant of 19 Elm Circle; and Jacques S. Berriault, assistant professor of art history at Lambert University, occupant of the house at Number 20.

The look and sound of the scene were transmitted to Guy by the third of his sources, the verbal report of Lt. Harold "Toots" Cantor of the Sixth Precinct. Somebody with rank had been alarmed by the very brief interval between the arrival of the Afro Residence at Elm Circle and what looked like—because Hilary Bridge's garage door had reportedly been found locked from the outside and no suicide notes were found—the Circle's first murder. So Toots Cantor, who was in charge of operations, was urgently requested to share his impressions with Silvestri, pronto.

Thus Guy heard that Ann Price had been in pajamas and slippers, despite the late-morning hour. But then she was "a regular Bohemian," pronounced Lt. Cantor—who knew no more up-to-date word for it but had to say something because he was a man of the New England culture, which equates early rising with civic virtue. "But the first guy there, it turns out, was Gus George," Cantor went on, his voice betraying at least one kind of chauvinism. "He must have good reflexes for his age. He got there before the two closest neighbors." Ann Price, whose leathercraft shop was closed on Wednesdays, had been asleep in a back bedroom of her apartment above the shop; Jake Birnbaum had been working in his windowless cubbyhole office beside the theater's projection booth. Both had had to assimilate the information that someone was screaming and to conclude there was a need to go forth and see why. Miss Price's sleepy comprehension, Guy noted, seemed to have been offset by her youthful fleetness of foot, for she arrived in a dead heat with Birnbaum, who heard sooner but came downstairs at a sixty-year-old's pace.

But Gus George had had the advantage of visual aid. Standing in the doorway of his restaurant across the Circle, he'd

17

seen Jacques Berriault stagger up the driveway with the black square of the open garage door behind him. Gus comprehended promptly, if incorrectly: Ptls. Donahue and Green found the baseball bat Gus brought with him and dropped after he discovered that Jacques was not screaming for help against a marauder.

"He says he didn't know he had the bat with him," Cantor reported, in a carefully flat voice. "It's the one he keeps under the bar."

Guy found Gus George's reported behavior entirely in character. But it was clear Cantor had doubts, and Cantor was an old-breed cop and sometimes they smelled things. "Anything wrong with that?" Guy asked respectfully.

"Who knows? I mean, it turns out nobody hit this professor with a baseball bat or anything like that. And the science boys say the bat wasn't laying out there all night, no way. But—it's funny, that's all. There's a couple of things just look funny."

"Like what, for instance?"

"Well, look how Gus got rid of the other witnesses right away. Sent this Miss Price over to the Grotto for brandy and Birnbaum to call the precinct." Cantor stopped, then offered a sudden untroubled grin. "You know what's really funny? This Miss Price, the one that don't mind coming out in the street in her pj's? Well, believe it or not, when she gets over to the Grotto she hunts around the bar for a brandy glass. She brought the bottle and a *brandy* glass." He shook his head slowly. "Don't people do the damndest things when they're upset?"

Guy agreed, and then listened amiably while Cantor trotted out another instance of oddly meticulous behavior under stress in another case a long time ago. Clearly, Guy decided, Toots Cantor didn't really think anything was "funny" about the way Gus George had acted: he knew too much about the ways of people. It was something else, and Cantor would get to it when he thought it advisable.

Meanwhile, it might help if Silvestri asked the right question. "About Gus George," he said mildly. "Didn't he do pretty much what you might expect? If you find somebody dead, you call the cops. And don't most people consider booze first aid for hysterics? Miss Price and Birnbaum both said Jacques Berriault was pretty hysterical. So Gus had his hands full, and he sent the others to do the errands. It sounds just about like what I'd have done in his shoes."

"Yeah." Cantor's face under its thatch of ginger hair was closed. What could you do, his faintly resentful silence said, when you were up against one of these slick talkers?

Guy knew how it felt to know what you know and be frustrated by logic. "You got a hunch, Toots? Don't be selfish, share it."

The older man laughed shortly. "Okay. If you was in Gus's shoes, you said."

"Right."

"Well, I just don't think you'd *be* in Gus's shoes. If you see what I mean." Cantor eyed the Buxford force's golden boy, who was supposed to be so smart. "Look, you know where this Frenchy Jacques was the night before, during the time the doc figures this professor was breathing in exhaust gas? Answer: over at the Grotto. Only not at the bar—he was in a back room with Gus. Okay. Now who's the first one on the scene in the morning? Old buddy Gus again, right?"

"So? They've been neighbors for quite a while, the two professors and Gus. They're all in the citizens' association together—hell, Gus is chairman of the flag-raising committee, if I remember right. For all we know, Hilary Bridge was chairman of snow shoveling." Guy's glance fell on the reports lying on his desk. "And didn't somebody tell you Berriault and Gus George played chess regularly on Tuesday nights? Well, that's not too good a game for a crowded restaurant. So you end up with two guys alone in a back room, and what's remarkable about that?"

"Oh, for Christ's sake," Cantor said disgustedly. He stood up. "This here professor. The victim."

"Well?" According to Bridge's biography (courtesy of Lambert University's Department of English) Hilary Bridge had only last September been awarded tenure, the academic world's security prize. *Appointed Associate Professor,* the formal wording ran, *without limit of time.* The typed line flashed across Guy's memory now. "What about Professor Bridge?" he asked, quelling irony and pity.

"This Bridge was queer as a three-dollar bill, that's what about him. Everybody knows it. And all you have to do is take one look at Frenchy. So lemme ask you, Guy: *you* know any straight john that just happens to be best friends with a couple of faggots?"

"Oh."

"Yeah, oh."

Guy put both hands flat on his desk and pushed back in his chair. "You can make mistakes, going on just how things look," he said mildly, wondering whether that alone would do it. For the problem was a little delicate: Gus George didn't live in the Sixth Precinct, and the Greek church, which was the center of his social life, was also outside Cantor's purlieu—though it was a familiar, and often helpful, factor in the calculations of Human Relations. So it was not surprising that Cantor didn't know of Gus's long-standing quasi-connubial arrangement with a widow on Lambert Street, especially since, unlike the window-dressing marriages found among homosexuals, the relationship was not flaunted. So, though Guy couldn't swear that Gus George wasn't a homosexual maybe somewhere deep down in his psyche, it was a good bet that if it was there it was deep down enough not to count. Only, if Human Relations turned to gossip—

"Listen, son," Lt. Cantor said, "I'm telling you for your own good, maybe. One." He used his hand to enumerate, bending each thick finger in turn, what had to be taught. "You got a pair of fags—the quiet kind that just keeps house, but you know how that housekeeping kind fights, right?"

"Right." Guy's career might have been speeded up but it

had skipped no steps, so Saturday-night duty had once meant acquaintance with the typical high-strung, high-pitched homosexual family fight. Like Toots Cantor, Guy Silvestri had rocked on his heels in the doorways of rooms full of smashed crockery and said "Now, now" to placate shrill demands: *Officer, I want you to remove this—this person from my apartment right now. I insist. . . .* "But they don't kill, Toots. You get noise, but not homicide."

Cantor nodded, but he pushed the second finger down anyway. "Two. You got a third party that hangs around all the time, and even has a once-a-week date with the girly one. Because the victim was the man of the family, that's for sure: Frenchy's ten years younger than this Bridge and real—you know." In case Guy didn't know, Cantor assumed the traditional limp-wrist pose. Then he returned to business, his wrist firm again and ready for the manly job of supporting his numbered fingers. "Three. Frenchy admits him and his sweetheart had words Tuesday night. And four—the last one to see the victim alive turns out to be Frenchy, even though he denied it first time around. You read that, didn't you? Where the fellow from the bookstore said—"

"I read it," Guy interrupted. He left it at that, though once again he thought the scenario indicated ordinary life rather than mystery. At 8:15 Tuesday night Elliott Sterling had appeared at Number 20, by arrangement, to drive with Hilary Bridge to a poetry reading on the other side of the Lambert campus. Elliott knew about Jacques's chess date and wasn't surprised to find him leaving the house, but because Jacques was carrying a paperback book of chess endings, Elliott was reminded that he'd meant to take along tonight's poet's new book. He thought there was quite enough time, so he went back to the Perilous to get it. Yes, Elliott had said when asked, there did seem to be an air of tension at Number 20. But he suggested that he himself might have been the cause: Hilary was fussy and disliked sudden changes of plan, so he could have been simply annoyed with Elliott for delaying their

21

departure. In fact, Elliott remembered, Hilary, offering to warm up the car, had remarked rather pointedly that it would save time.

"So the bookstore fellow left them two professors there alone. With this Professor Bridge heading for the garage, right?" Cantor paused meaningfully. "And the bookstore lady—"

"Their name is Sterling."

"Okay. Mrs. Sterling says her husband came back to the store and picked up the poetry book, and this girl student that works there says so too. Right after that, the Sterlings come out—she was going home, they live in Number 5—and that's when they see Frenchy going across to the Grotto. Sterling goes back in the store to tell the student something, and his missus goes on home. Okay. But we got a different story from Frenchy—the first time, anyway. He says he left when Sterling came over to the house. Then, after he finds out they seen him, he all of a sudden remembers he didn't leave right away."

"He could've forgotten, Toots. How important would it seem then, Elliott Sterling going back for his book?" Guy recalled a sentence from the report and suppressed a smile: Mrs. Sterling had been "viewing TV," said her statement, when her husband returned to say nobody'd been home at Number 20 when he got back there—nobody answered the doorbell, the car was nowhere in sight, and the garage door was closed. And visibly locked; it had one of those old-fashioned handles that must be turned by hand—when the door is open the handle is vertical; locked, it's horizontal. The Sterlings agreed that Hilary Bridge must have gone off in a huff. Mrs. Sterling suggested that her husband go on by himself, and Mr. Sterling said the hell with it—or words to that effect. Reading this domestic exchange, Guy had found everything in it authentic to the characters as he knew them, except that he refused to believe Kate could actually have said *I was viewing TV.*

22

"Okay, Frenchy just forgot," Cantor said heavily. "You win, I can't argue with you. But you just remember what I told you, sonny."

Alarmed, Guy realized he hadn't heard what he was supposed to remember. "I'll remember, Toots," he said earnestly, and hoped for luck.

"Okay. Maybe you can make mistakes going on how things look"—Cantor's tone established that Guy was indeed in luck: whatever it was was about to be said again—"but like I said, you can make a lot more mistakes trying to be smart." He hesitated, then stuck out his hand. "See you around. Okay?"

Recognizing apology, Guy scrambled to his feet and shook hands. "Sure, Toots. And thanks." He watched the big man leave and knew himself safely promoted again from "sonny" to "son." Relieved, he went back around the desk and sat down to think.

Time to play Sherlock Holmes. Teamwork *was* better, but the team had no particular interest in protecting Silvestri's black-student "constituency," and they would be what was left when Toots Cantor succeeded in eliminating the obvious choices. Which he would do, eventually. Cantor might play with the idea of Gus George as a murderer, but it was unlikely to go very far; even a Buxford cop of spotless integrity and total intrepidity would hesitate to take on the town's Greek community, so nobody would bother Gus George unless a solid case could be made. And Guy didn't see how it could.

As for the wispy Jacques Berriault, now lying lost in medically prescribed nepenthe, only a fool would tag him on the basis of the circumstantial evidence alone. Cantor was not a fool, so sooner or later he would arrive at Point Five in his finger exercise and confront the question: if Jacques had indeed left Hilary Bridge locked in the garage at, say, 8:20 Tuesday night, why in the world would he wait till eleven o'clock Wednesday morning to start screaming? The delay made no sense for a guilty man: Bridge would have been dead in an hour, and raising a late-night alarm would both increase the number of suspects and look far less suspicious.

The only explanation of the delay that made sense was the foolish, human one Jacques had offered. When he returned from his chess game, the garage door was closed, with its handle in the "lock" position that Elliott Sterling, earlier, had taken to mean Hilary was out. But Elliott didn't live at Number 20 and Jacques did—he knew Hilary Bridge always locked the kitchen door leading to the garage just so he could leave the garage door open and thus avoid the business of hopping out of the car to fool with the door. So, for Jacques, the locked garage door signaled that the car was back in the garage, and the fact that the floodlight over the driveway was off confirmed the assumption that Hilary had gone out and come home again. All the signs—by way of the kind of household code everyone lives with and any jury would understand—indicated that Hilary Bridge was in for the night. So Jacques turned out the front light left on for him and went into the house.

Nor, since Hilary's study was at the back of the house, was there anything, such as a visible absence of light, to stir doubt that Hilary was in there. "I thought he was sulking," the weeping Jacques had told his questioners. "I said to myself, all right, if that's the way he wants it, let him just stay in his study till he decides to come out." At that point, the bitter sense of if-I-had-only-known had overcome the survivor, and questioning had to be suspended for a while. But the answers were either recorded or apparent: Jacques did not knock at the closed door, and in the morning, with the study door still closed, felt even less like suing for peace. Jauntily, even defiantly ("I whistled *Wach' Auf* when I passed the study. I thought if he wanted to come out and make up, I'd give him a way to save face. But if all he wanted was to nurse his tizzy—oh my God, *Wach' Auf,* and how could he, he was—"),
24

Jacques went downstairs, breakfasted, and left to meet his early class.

Hilary never used the car on Wednesdays, because that was the day Jacques met his afternoon class at the art museum in Boston. He came home in mid-morning this time because he wanted to do some errands in Boston before his one o'clock class, and went directly to the garage to pick up the car. He unlocked the door, raised it, and strolled half the length of the car on the driver's side before he glanced up from the keys he was sorting in his hand and saw the figure in the driver's seat. ("What I thought? I thought he was sick, I suppose. Or sleeping. No, I don't know how I knew it was Hilary. Only, who else would it be?")

Jacques had more courage than his fragile looks would indicate: he tugged the car door open and first, as the body slid toward him, sprang away instinctively; but then, he actually leaned over and touched the cold cheek. With this realization that Hilary was dead, Jacques began running—none too soon for his own good, probably, because the solidly built stone walls would have contained the carbon monoxide pretty well, and not much air had yet entered through the open door. Jacques didn't get enough of a dose to keep him from making it into the open air—where his effeminacy stood him in good stead: those prompt, unmanly screams had forced large quantities of fresh air into his lungs.

Everything about it implied innocence, Guy Silvestri knew in his bones. And Toots Cantor would know it, too: he might begin with suspicion of the pansy art teacher with wavy hair and a psychedelic ascot tucked into his pure-silk shirt, but Toots wouldn't take that line for long unless new evidence turned up. That meant there was no escape for Silvestri. His services were not required for sex and domestic strife (or, lower-case human relations) in the Sixth Precinct, but they would be when those proved not to be the answers. In fact, the Buxford police administrator who'd assigned Lt. Silvestri to hover over the homicide at Elm Circle had already had reason to suspect a need for diplomacy: Lambert University, applied to for Hilary Bridge's next of kin (the distracted Jacques had only murmured vaguely about a sister living somewhere in England), had obliged; but the university had also taken the occasion to request a word with Lt. Silvestri.

The "word," Guy discovered later that day, was hardly only that. Nobody could have taken longer to reach even the neighborhood of a positive statement than the Lambert administrator to whose portfolio the Residence at Elm Circle had recently been added. Not that the man wasn't doing his best to communicate: the unfortunate matter of Professor Bridge's death, he managed to say after Guy had spent nearly half an hour in a Lambert sanctum, contained—um—possible ramifications that the Lieutenant might be relied upon to appreciate . . . "To be quite candid, Lieutenant," began a second-round attempt to get to the point—which, after a long exercise in anything but candor, emerged as "the faint but worrisome possibility that somehow a—shall we say political?—light could be cast on the—er—unhappy fate of our late colleague." Which, in view of the brief tenancy of the Residence at Elm Circle, could cause—

"Is there any reason to believe anyone at the Residence had a grudge against Professor Bridge?" Guy didn't like abruptness any more than his old boy did, but he was damned if he would sit there being "candid" any longer. "The information I have is that he went in for signing petitions, open letters to the newspapers, that sort of thing. Big on demonstrations, I'm told."

"Well. It is true that poor Bridge, like any other faculty people, had a—um—theoretical, that is to say an intellectual, appreciation of the student radicalism which—"

"Is that all he had?" Bluntness, Guy decided, would do no harm at the moment: he was already about as "respectable" as he was ever likely to get. *Cleverer than most, even a bachelor's degree of sorts, I'm told. But of course—*

26

"I don't quite—Professor Bridge had quite possibly—um—looked into the—um—literature of revolution. As, of course, the requirements of free scholarship would indicate. But his research could hardly be—"

"Okay, let's say he was your typical English Department Maoist." This character had already driven him into playing Toots Cantor, Guy realized. And wondered where next. "In that case," he went on, raising his voice to accommodate the murmurs indicating he was, though crude, substantially right, "why would he be thought to give offense to—oh. He—er—recanted. Is that it?"

"Something like that, one might say." The Lambert spokesman seemed to be addressing his own veined hands clasped on the desk. "Hilary Bridge was not precisely an easy man to understand. He had, well, complex aspects. I believe you're correct in your evaluation"—the thin lips quirked at the edge of a smile— "your implied evaluation, I should say, of his political sophistication. But he was, nevertheless, a scholar, sir. And he had a scholar's devotions." The fine old head bowed a little, and the brief color faded from the tired voice. "Professor Bridge did develop some—doubts—about his political philosophy. Recently. After a first edition, a particularly rare and lovely specimen given to the Merritt Library by a generous alumnus—well, after the library discovered the volume had been—molested—as a so-called 'protest,' Hilary seemed—um—given pause. So to speak."

"I understand, sir." Guy had been taught at his mother's knee that it all depended on whose ox was gored, and it seemed that a rare lovely book had been Hilary Bridge's ox. "The professor made his doubts known?"

"In certain circles. These matters are—murky. But I believe the term 'counterrevolutionary' was applied, and it is—isn't it?—construed as opening the way to action. In those circles. Though they do appear to apply it rather lavishly. They—"

"Excuse me, sir. I thought you'd finished." Guy had

thought nothing of the sort. But he simply couldn't afford digressions into the rhetoric of Lambert's revolutionaries.

"Quite. Proceed, Lieutenant."

"Yes, sir. I meant to say that I quite understand the problem, and its relation to the Residence." He paused, wondering how to communicate to this ignorant old man that the circles he was worrying about were mostly not inhabited by black students. All angry people apparently looked alike to Lambert officialdom. But the angry young men at the Afro Residence, even those who wielded revolutionary rhetoric, were uninterested in the fantasy-revolution games that titillated rich white undergraduates. "I don't think you have real cause for concern, sir. I'll be glad to verify it, but I'm almost certain there's been no such involvement." Guy thought of Tim Whistler and wondered how anyone in his right mind could imagine a bright lad like that worrying about the defector Hilary Bridge.

"And no *appearance* of involvement?" The Lambert man hesitated. "It would perhaps be quite as troublesome if an impression—well, by some natural mistake, let us say, if something turned up in the course of the investigation that could, accidentally of course, become a problem . . ."

Translation: Some dumb cop could pick up one of our black students and cause a little riot. Anger swelled in Guy's throat, but he swallowed it successfully by coating it with compassion: this was an old man whose trade was hypocrisy, which nobody was buying anymore—but how could you expect him to start learning another trade now? Mercifully, Guy fed the old man the diet he lived on, giving him to understand—elliptically and at length—that no black student would be apprehended without Lt. Silvestri's being immediately informed. Guy could have told the other man that some black students were already in the clear, but that couldn't be said now. For several reasons, one of them the need to deal in hypocrisies. So Guy concluded his speech, and made appropriate departure noises.

"Thank you, Lieutenant. I'm sure I needn't tell you that we are grateful for your help."

"Yes, sir. It's quite all right, sir."

"So much going on requires—well, the most careful handling, it seems. One hardly knows how to proceed . . ."

Guy recognized that one was proceeding to deliver a new pitch. "Is there something else, sir?" This was a tough one, he saw very soon: compared to whatever was on the old boy's mind now, the transmission of the simple proposition, *If one of the black students executed Hilary Bridge for deviationism, Lambert doesn't want it blabbed to the public,* had been an elementary exercise. Halfway through the preliminaries, Guy realized that whatever the new problem was, the Residence was not its focus. Which made it the Merritt Library, he deduced: that was the only other Lambert outpost on Elm Circle.

Actually, the Merritt was only marginally connected to the Circle, by the outer edge of its extensive acreage. The great stone building—not an ordinary library but a kind of specialized archive serving the needs of the more exalted scholars—showed only its handsome back to Elm Circle and engaged in no casual commerce with its residents. Nobody used the Merritt without special permission from Lambert, and those who did usually drove in from the Beltway, screened by trees from the Library's impressive front door. Except for Lowell Lester, the Merritt librarian, and a few students employed at odd clerical jobs, users of the Library tended to come and go unseen by Elm Circle.

The Merritt proved to be the old boy's problem, all right. But when Guy finally departed, he was sure of little but that fact, despite all the listening time he'd invested. Even with the cobweb words pushed aside, all he could see was that Lambert had information from an unspecified source (maybe even an unknown one?) that the Merritt had been used for "undesirable activities." And what the Lambert man was delicately wondering was whether the Buxford police might possess an inkling the university would find handy. The police did keep an eye on undesirable activities in general (though, like most of his colleagues, the old boy had an exaggerated notion of how much snooping a small force could do even if it wanted to), but so far as Guy knew at the moment, they had no such inkling. He promised to "make inquiries" —and trusted that his failure to promise to impart all results of his inquiries would go unnoticed for the present.

Gratefully free then, he set off toward Elm Circle, where he had more than one mission. But as he swung along, actively enjoying the chance to move at will after all that sitting and saying yessir, his curiosity was still a little stirred. For it was hard to believe Lambert University was so far gone as to worry about what some anonymous tipster might have said—and yet, if they had a source they trusted, why wouldn't they have simply hauled their own man in and confronted him with the information? At least *ask* Lowell Lester whether there were or were not "undesirable activities" going on at the Merritt? Which, apparently, they had made no attempt to do.

Grinning, Guy dropped the idea. Of course they hadn't —and to imagine any scenario in which official Lambert confronted Lowell Lester, or anyone else, face to face would require an impossible suspension of disbelief. There was just nobody in those lush, hushed offices who had that much soul.

3

Tim Whistler
at Home

Because of the delicate sensibilities of the inhabitants of the Residence, none of its furnishings was anything but spanking new—which, for Guy, always stirred contrasting memories of the Boys' Club he'd attended. The decor there had featured the gleanings of attics, for which the leaders had felt grateful and the rank and file indifferent. Here, the custom-made bookshelves contributed by the Piecemeal Shop (furniture in parts) next door, and the books that filled them—a Residence committee had chosen them, by invitation, from the Experiment Perilous Bookshop—were regarded, apparently, as no more than the due of the victims of racism. All of the gifts, Guy recalled as he rose from one of the pair of spiral-willow armchairs that signified the good will of the shop at Number 12, had been received with a blank calm that verged on surliness and occasionally slid over to it. He listened to the chair creaking as if in protest at being abandoned, and he found it consoling to have this evidence that his going made a difference.

Neither his coming nor his going mattered, it seemed, to Tim Whistler, who got up lazily but lithely to speed the guest. Color blind, his willow mourned him too. "So nice of you to drop by, Mr. Silvestri." His voice was soft, but the words crisped with the accent of the New England prep school to which Tim had been sent by his father, a physician. "We're duly grateful for your interest," the young man went on, standing at attention with his pale-tan hands properly lined up at the side seams of the chino pants he wore when not formally dashiki-clad. He was a handsome lad, well read and well fed and well dressed, gifted, and practically assured of a prosperous and prestigious career. And all the racial slurs he had ever encountered, or ever would, amounted to less than Guy Silvestri and Toots Cantor had met and would meet again.

So Tim Whistler was more than a little infuriating—or he would have been except that he so obviously wanted to be. Guy, with several months' practice in managing irritation, was now more curious than annoyed. "I care how you're getting along, Mr. Whistler," he said, offering the polite deadpan of an ambassador. "In fact, I care enough even to stand around and be needled."

"Tolerance is an admirable quality, sir." Tim Whistler sketched the courtly half-bow the pseudo-diplomatic con-tretemps seemed to call for. Then he turned to lead the visitor out.

"Right," said the visitor. "But masochism is not." He followed Whistler into the high-ceilinged front hall and halted obediently at a gesture from his host. "So just for the record, friend, let it be stated that I don't enjoy being mocked." Perfect for the period of the house, an oval pier glass on the opposite wall reflected a wooden settee and the antique hat rack above it—and beyond, the half-open door of the lounge, with a barefoot, jeans-clad figure flitting through it. Guy kept

32

his glance as swift and furtive as the figure it had caught in action. Then he directed a frank, open, and earnest look at the Afro chieftain, and corroborated by it that Whistler was indeed directly in Guy's path; it was improbable that he could get to the great fanlighted front door without either permission or combat.

Tim Whistler was doing his best to control a smile. "I assure you you aren't being 'mocked,' Mr. Silvestri." He shook the narrow head whose coiffure proclaimed only slightly more negritude than the aquiline nose and thinnish lips. Applied to Tim Whistler, "black" was even more inexact than it was for most of his followers. "You want to watch out—'friend'— for the tendency to see bigotry in every innocent word. That way lies paranoia."

The parroting of some elder was so perfect—even to the Lambert accent—that Guy paid the performance the tribute of laughter. Meanwhile, he checked the mirror again. He caught nobody in the act this time, but somebody had been by again, for the formerly half-closed door was now almost entirely open. He lowered his gaze and held Whistler's eyes. "It isn't paranoia when there really are voices in the walls. And I know the difference, really I do. So I ask you, for my own benefit, Tim—why?"

"Sorry, man. I don't dig."

Tim had had practice in producing his expressionless look, but Guy had had even more practice in detecting the small movements of the eyes by which people gave information away. He whirled so abruptly that he caught the student on the stairs still in the act of giving the signal Tim had been watching over the visitor's shoulder.

"All right, I'll excavate it for you," Guy said icily. He turned and explained with the help of the mirror, which now reflected the willow chairs in the lounge. One foam-rubber cushion, covered in an African-style cloth of brilliant blues and greens, was visibly tilted, and it had not been dislodged by Guy's sitting down or getting up. "What I'm asking, Tim,

33

is why such a lack of plain logic? You're a law student. You must have *some* respect for the presumption based on evidence." Angrier than he had meant to be, Guy pointed at the image of the pillow a purposeful but hasty hand had left tilted. "On the record of our dealings in the past months, where is the smallest basis for the presumption that I came here to plant something?" He thrust his hands into his pockets to keep them from betraying him, but he could do nothing about his voice, which didn't quite scoff even when he said, "Phooey. You keep me here while your henchmen check to see I didn't leave a little package. For *my* henchmen to rush in and find sometime later? Kids' games, Tim." Suddenly weary of even his own anger, he took his hands out of his pockets. "On second thought, I withdraw the question. It's true I'd like to know why. But I told you, I don't enjoy being mocked." He took a step forward and then turned to add, with exaggerated *politesse,* "Thank you, I've had a lovely time. I take it I can go now?"

Tim Whistler stepped aside and reached for the door. "Allow me, sir." But then, suddenly, he stopped, glanced up at the empty staircase, and said in a low voice, "Did it ever occur to you that *I* don't like being conned?"

Guy laid his folded raincoat across the wrought-iron railing, freeing his hands. "Prove it. Fast."

"Oh, my. Do they know back at headquarters how easy you lose your cool?"

"They may after this," Guy said soberly. "Talk, don't weasel."

"Ha! Oh man, that's funny, man, it really is. You come here weaseling around about how deeply you care for us poor black boys—"

"Bullshit. Is mockery the only place you know to run and hide?" Guy looked at the boy who was neither poor nor black. "Try it straight. Like, I *do* care."

"Translation: 'I've always been a good liberal.' Or, alternatively, 'I'm a good Catholic and the Pope says we're all God's
34

children.' Either way, you love us. Each and every little vote and/or soul."

Auden had it right, Guy thought: he couldn't remember the poet's lines except for the final ones in a verse about what it was everybody wanted—*not universal love, but to be loved alone.* He took a deep breath and let it out slowly. "I never said I loved anybody, Tim. All I said was, I care. Translation: 'For a mixture of reasons and nonreasons, I'd like good things rather than bad things to happen to you.' "

"But whatever you'd like, you'll follow orders."

"You ought to have a better idea of how a police force operates," Guy said gravely. "You underestimate my status —I'd hardly be ordered to drop by and plant some contraband on the premises."

"Do tell. But con men are an elite, it seems to me I read somewhere. So *that* mission isn't beneath you, is it?"

What Tim had read somewhere was that con men were an elite in criminal society, Guy knew, and knew he was being goaded. But much less earnestly now, he estimated. "I could have said no," he told the boy flatly. "To either the original mission or today's." He kept his gaze mild: either Tim would know he was being told the truth or he wouldn't, but he couldn't be orated into belief. "I didn't volunteer, and I didn't give a damn whether anybody installed black students at Elm Circle or not. But once somebody decided to, I cared whether it succeeded. So I didn't say no."

Tim looked at him briefly. "Okay, I'll buy that. But when somebody said run over to Elm Circle and see whether any of them niggers knocked off Professor Bridge, you didn't say no either. What you did, you read all the statements Cantor took in his 'routine investigation' so you wouldn't have to ask the same questions again. And then you showed up to ask some more, to fill in the gaps. Only—" the honey-smooth young voice shook a little— "you didn't say that was what you came for, did you?"

"Oh. So that's it."

"You dig, man. That's one of the its, anyway."

Guy said slowly, "No, I didn't say that was what I came for. I think now I should have. At least I should've talked about it."

"Guilty as charged." Tim did not seem happy in his triumphant verdict.

"Guilty of paternalism, I think you could say. Like, I didn't think I was conning you. I thought I was being diplomatic."

"Oh, great." The scornful syllable hung on the air—until, abruptly, Tim's scorn crumpled before laughter. "You're just too much, Silvestri. You're so square you *have* to be for-real: who could imagine a put-on like that? But if you're their prize diplomat, all I can say is"—he gasped, choking on a laugh that had to be kept quiet and wanted to be a roar— "war is a sure thing."

"Come on, you're hurting my feelings." Grinning, Guy fought off the wave of laughter that threatened to sweep him along. "One little mistake, and right away you're laughing."

"One mistake? Oh, man. You're such a supreme diplomat that you were all ready to slug me a little while ago. In the first minute of negotiations."

"So? So I'm a little hotheaded. I'm still young—thirty isn't old, in the diplomacy biz. And I admit I'm a trifle inexperienced . . ." Guy let his voice trail off. "How about no war this time, please? It would look bad on my record."

"I don't know." The student's eyes held lingering merriment, but he was looking at Guy soberly now. "Disguised as big white brother, you come here to do Cantor's chores—"

"It's not a disguise," Guy interrupted. "I see how it's offensive, but a disguise it isn't: I really felt big brother. Any con involved was directed at the neighbors."

"Meaning?"

"Meaning I know it titillates the gossips when a police car stops in front of the house—any house, in any neighborhood. But Silvestri is vaguely associated with the Residence anyhow, has been all along. So the eyes behind the curtains in

36

Elm Circle don't pick up anything really valuable when they see me come up the steps here." Guy let his hands fall, miming helplessness. "And that's the fancy diplomatic maneuver that damn near started a war."

But Tim was having none of the light touch. "The police car stood in front of the house Wednesday."

"Right. But it stood in front of everybody's house Wednesday. Regardless of race, creed, or color."

"Ah," said Tim softly. "Some races, creeds, and colors require two trips though, don't they?"

Guy heard the relief in the boy's voice, under the note of triumph, and recognized the source: if you suspect prejudice is lurking in the underbrush, you feel better when you can put your finger on its exact location. "I'd like to be able to deny that," he said slowly.

"But you can't. Because it isn't paranoia when the voices in the walls are real."

"I can partly deny it," Guy argued. "Hilary Bridge taught at Lambert, and this house contains a large number of Lambert students. Which would justify some concentration."

"A technicality."

Guy admitted, "It is. And there *are* voices in the walls. But some of them say sensible things, too. Like, that there's a collection of angry young men here."

"I wouldn't think of denying that," Tim said bitterly.

"All right. But Hilary Bridge wasn't what they're angry at, I think. Not really."

"He was a clod. A fancy, faggot, aesthetic clod. But a clod."

"And not worth killing."

"Oh, probably not. He could just be left to wither away. But anyhow, he'd be pretty far down on the list. One of a faculty of five hundred—and one who could easily be muscled into line, if necessary." Tim looked up, becoming a militant staring down a cop. "Not worth risking the least of the brothers."

Guy nodded. "I'll buy that. In fact, I already have. Which

37

is why I don't want the voices in the walls to be able to say anything people will have to listen to." He smiled. "You had it backwards: I came here to cover my own rear, not Cantor's. Because after a certain point he and I are not in the same game—he just wants to catch a murderer, but I want to stuff the mouths of those voices. So if Cantor is convinced the murderer doesn't live here, he'll stay away. But I'll keep coming back for more stuffing."

In the silence, they stood as on a lighted stage. Guy picked his coat off the railing because the play, or anyway this act of it, was about over. He thought there were no more lines to say—until he saw Tim Whistler's pitying look. "Paternalism works two ways, it seems," Guy said lightly. "You know something I don't?"

"A few things, maybe. Like, listen to little black brother, baby: you stuff one of those mouths, another opens up with some new yapping."

"So what? Does it hurt you if I try?"

Tim smiled. "Hurray for the diplomat. Silvestri of the unruffled cool. Look, don't get huffy. All I'm telling you is, you can't win."

"And I say maybe I can't win right away, but I sure as hell can in the long run. Because I outnumber them, 'baby,'" Guy went on, frankly passionate. "Me. Square, solid, middle-class me. Marching on with church and state behind me, and the fashionables running ahead telling everybody that brotherhood is In and bigots just aren't sexy any more. It may take a while, but can't you see that in the end I'm bound to win?"

"Don't expect me to help you wait around," Tim said angrily.

"Who said you should? Just quit sniping at me from the bushes as I go by, that's all. Have the plain good sense to know which is the enemy. Or at least try checking it out before you shoot." Guy held out his crumpled coat. "Here. You want to look it over, so I can't dribble a trail of heroin from here to the front door?"

Tim raised both hands to his close-cut coiffure and proceeded to "Afro" it in sheer exasperation. "It takes a saint to survive your diplomacy. Did you ever think I might know what I'm doing? That I operate on the basis of evidence?"

"Meaning what? If you have experience with Buxford police planting anything on you, come right along and we'll swear out a warrant."

Tim's grin held the pure triumph of one-upmanship. "Ah'm that grateful to you, Massa. But, as it happens, it's already taken care of."

"What in hell are you talking about?"

"About what your pal Cantor was supposed to find in our yard when he came hunting a murderer. He didn't find it, because we did. Because we've got every inch of the yard patrolled. So whoever tried to pin Professor Bridge on us didn't make it. And therefore, to wit, and henceforth, we'll make sure that anybody coming in leaves nothing behind. See?" Tim laughed harshly. "And no, I don't want to go through your pockets because I already know there are no little gift packages in it. And you didn't leave any in the upholstery. If you'd gone to the can, that would've been checked out too. I don't think that's sniping at you from the bushes, I think it's mounting guard over my own camp. And I intend to go on doing it, and if you don't like it I can make an obscene suggestion or two."

"Don't," Guy said quietly. "I don't like it, but I agree that it's only mounting guard."

"Okay then. Peace—with certain conditions—brother—with certain restrictions."

Guy asked cautiously, "Do those conditions and restrictions allow for telling me what was planted in your yard? I want to know," he went on hurriedly, hoping to forestall denial, "because it's not just a piece of a frame. Surely you can see that it's a piece of a picture of the murderer. And even if you don't care who killed Hilary Bridge, you must care who tried to get you tagged with it."

"I care."

"I know." Tim Whistler had not needed to choose law as a career: whatever practical reasons he had, there were likely also to be other reasons and they were likely to be idealistic—idealism is not usually narrowly specific. Guy urged, "I can find out who the murderer is easier than you can."

"Sure you can. But can you guarantee Lieutenant Cantor won't be back, if I tell you and you tell him? Which you'd have to do, because you can't withhold evidence. So the cops who're currently out of my fuzzy hair would be back in it, right? Are you going to tell me different?"

"No," Guy said sadly.

"Man, you look crushed. Don't take it so hard."

"I don't think people should murder and get away with it. I mean, nobody slugged it out with Bridge, you know. This cat took no chances: he crept up—oh hell, never mind. But he tried to creep up on you, too, remember." Guy shook his head. "I take it hard that he's walking around safe."

"You're a cop. True blue, through and through."

Guy sighed. "All right, that's where I came in. Good-bye." He walked down the shallow steps and stood at the door, waiting because Tim's hand was on the knob. Staring at the bronzed oval doorknob, Guy was reminded of elementary school—only there the doorknobs had been engraved "Buxford City Schools," and this one was all flowers and vines. He told himself that what was depressing him was that nobody had time for ornamentation anymore: only the oldest buildings still exhibited lavish stonework and ironwork and fretted doorknobs. The thought made him feel better, and he recognized why: *whenever crushed, anthropologize,* he counseled himself ironically. Maybe one of his sisters would embroider it on a sampler for him.

Tim Whistler said, suddenly and very softly, "Listen, Silvestri."

"I'm listening."

"Somebody in Elm Circle doesn't think black is beautiful, right? Well, I don't know if it's the same somebody that left us the—memento—so I won't tell you who it is. But I'll tell you this much: did you know somebody with a perfectly good mailbox at Elm Circle goes all the way up to the post office in Trowbridge to pick up mail at a box number? Ergo, somebody doesn't want the local folks to know something. One doesn't know what, but one wonders."

Guy nodded. "One does, for sure." Obviously Tim's favored explanation of the phenomenon would be secret membership in the Klan. But people had all sorts of tawdry little secrets: any police investigation turned up dozens of them, mostly irrelevant. This could be somebody just trying to cheat the telephone company. "One is grateful," he said aloud, "and one will take appropriate action." The door swung open for him. "Keep some kind of faith, baby." He added benignly, "Whatever the evidence to the contrary," and went out, leaving Tim laughing, anyway.

4

Florence, at
Home Abroad

The tree at the figurative center of Elm Circle (actually, it was closer to the Merritt Library than to the Experiment Perilous Bookshop) was an elm, and visibly old; but it was certainly not the one on which legend and the consequent glorification of the Circle depended. It had even been said— and openly published—that the historic tree believed to have shaded George Washington while he drew up an important battle plan was never an elm at all; in addition, fussy voices were heard from time to time questioning whether the nation's progenitor had ever even dismounted in Elm Circle during his gallop through Buxford. Nobody denied these dissidents their freedom of speech, but nobody guaranteed them an audience either. Photographs of a drawing ("American History Collection, Lambert University") of the "Buxford Elm" had appeared in several generations' fourth-grade readers, and nothing said since affected that fact: the

Tree was almost universally perceived as (a) a 200-year-old elm and (b) in the center of Elm Circle.

Historic image-making was not in the forefront of Guy Silvestri's mind when he emerged from the gates of the Merritt Library enclave and set off across the Circle, taking the right-hand route around the Tree. Lowell Lester, with whom Guy had just concluded an interview not quite worthy of a sportscaster's worst, lay briefly somewhere on the top layer of the detective's thoughts—until he managed to put the memory from him. Which he did by acknowledging to himself that he couldn't stand Lowell Lester and that his feelings lacked even the forthright charm of "I do not like thee, Doctor Fell." That verse rang with honest defiance; but the trouble with the Merritt librarian was, you didn't feel better for knowing you didn't like him. Yet neither could you like him, no matter what grounds you sought: told that Lowell Lester had saved a thousand children from starvation, Guy would still have had trouble coming up with some admiration; if Lowell Lester had discovered quantum mechanics, Guy Silvestri would have been hard put to rustle up some awe. It was a sad, hopeless, guilt-making fact. And the only way to survive it was to think about something else and let God or somebody sort out the blame.

But when Guy's thoughts fled guilt, they landed in Wordsworth territory. Perhaps it was a literaturish response stirred by an hour in the Merritt, or maybe looking down on a community of souls in the rapid dusk of early spring would have inclined anyone to contemplation. For whatever reason, Guy stood still on the knoll with an elevation nowhere near London Bridge's, and he surveyed Elm Circle, whose not really mighty heart was not exactly lying still but was certainly slowing down to the rhythms of evening leisure. But Guy was no Wordsworth, so even when he started from the same feeling, he thought on a less ecstatic level. ·

And in prose—for if men are either poets or politicians, Silvestri was the latter. He believed in love but not in goddesses of love, and in ardor but not in inspiration. When moved to celebrate, he praised like a social rather than a religious man—in terms of what man rather than God had wrought. Thus, as he stood alone under the swiftly darkening sky, he saw what lay about him—a little landscape of precarious peace and uneven plenty—as the product of a society. One that proclaimed itself free and knew it wasn't always, and so simultaneously generated an impulse to change and slowed its results.

The neon sign above the Grotto—discreetly colored, because this was after all Elm Circle—flashed on over his right shoulder, announcing official nightfall and jolting him out of his meditations. But the mood was with him still when he turned in and found Elliott sitting at the bar. "I came to tell you it's an imperfect world," Guy announced. "I've been appointed by a commission to bring the news."

"A tripartite commission," amended the bartender, who at this hour was graduate student Jim Waterman. He wiped a beer glass and held it up inquiringly.

"A tripartite commission." Guy nodded, accepting both suggestions. "And what's your mission here?" he asked Elliott.

"Oh, I'm anthropologizing."

Guy sipped his beer and watched Jim, halfway down the bar, begin to mix a daiquiri for one of the two ladies who ran the art gallery at Number 11. Both Lambert faculty wives, they had been dismissed with brisk familiarity in Elliott's summary: *they're both in the mid-thirties and pretty enough, and they're fulfilling themselves, you know.* . . . Elliott wrote with more talent than charity: Mrs. Preston and Mrs. Savage could be seen as somewhat absurd, but that wasn't all they were—their earnest abhorrence of racial bigotry had made Lt. Silvestri's task of urging tolerance on the Elm Circle Association a good deal easier. But on the other hand, Lt. Silvestri now reminded himself, he was hardly in a position to reproach Elliott, not when he himself couldn't for the life of him remember whether it was Mrs. Preston or Mrs. Savage who was now beginning on the pale drink. So much for gratitude, the reward of virtue, etc.

"Of course," Elliott said, "I used to just walk over for a convivial drink. But now when I'm here, it's for a Higher Purpose."

"Right. And you stick to it, my boy. Persevere. Your first effort showed real talent." Guy realized then that it had, at that, and he might be communicating the opposite. "Really truly," he went on, trying to remember and then, gratefully, coming up with something. "Old Mrs. Chandler and the hippies at Number 3, for example. I wouldn't have expected you to see that, actually." It was true: the classification of the old lady—*Buxford-Brahmin, Mayflower-kiddies, D.A.R., the whole shtick*, in Elliott's words—had perhaps been no great coup. But then Elliott's notes had gone on to record that the dowager Mrs. Chandler's decision last year to rent her basement to a bizarre threesome had been received by the Circle not with the expected anger but with unanimous glee at the old girl's sharp trading. Mrs. Chandler was profiting outrageously by keeping her trunks in her attic instead of her cellar, and *Above all*, Elliott had noted, *Elm Circle likes a Yankee to behave like a Yankee*.

". . . as soon as I stop fluttering," Elliott was saying. "You've quite turned my head."

"On the other hand—"

"Uh-oh, I recognize that bit. Are you sure you've never taught at Lambert?"

"On the other hand," Guy persisted sternly, "I was only skimpily prepared for Lowell Lester."

"Ah. You've been in conversation?"

"Endlessly." Guy sighed. "First, up at Lambert's Circumlocution Office. Then, out of the frying pan and—listen, have you ever noticed that Lowell Lester retreats when you speak? Literally. Physically—if it's at all possible, he takes a step backward. It had me worrying about whether I had bad

45

breath. But nobody else had shrunk from me today, so I decided it wasn't me."

"I should've warned you. Sorry." Elliott grinned. "The consensus is that he can't stand encounters with people, only with books. But that's the students' analysis, based on a habit of instant-Freuding rather than evidence. They don't really know him."

"No? But they call him Ell-Square. And a nickname usually—"

"Implies familiarity, right? In this case the familiarity is only with his initials—he signs time slips and all that sort of thing. But the real Ell-Square remains a mystery to them."

"Not to me," Guy said. "I see him clearly, and I make him out a nebbish, all the way through." Couched in more conventional language, that verdict would be his report. Because if "undesirable activities" were indeed taking place at the Merritt, Lowell Lester seemed to Lt. Silvestri much too timid to be conducting them. That judgment was enough to close the matter, too, because so far as Silvestri could see, this was a Lambert hassle. And he was not a campus cop: it was all very well to do a favor for the neighbors (and perhaps particularly advisable for the Human Relations Division), but Lambert had a tendency to forget that there were other taxpayers in Buxford who had a right to call the police.

"I don't suppose Ell-Square trembled any the less," Elliott said without sympathy, "when the cops turned up on his doorstep." He slid off his stool and patted pockets until he found the one containing his wallet. "I, on the other hand, am intrepid. Want to turn up on my doorstep?"

"Maybe later."

"Well, pop in at Number 5 when you can. I'd beg to be taken along on your sleuthing, but I've got a new telescope. Actually, it's only just strong enough to pierce the pollution, but it allows me to think of myself as stargazing." Elliott paid and put his money away. "Come by my attic, and I'll let you peer."

46

Guy was less than enthusiastic about hobbies in general, and Elliott's seemed to him particularly a waste of spirit in the pursuit of dilettantism. But he made an effort. "That's right, you've got a back porch up there, haven't you. With that height, you must get a good view." He had no yearning to trudge up to what was not an "attic" but the entire third floor of the house at Number 5, enough space for a family of four to live in comfortably. Elliott was, if you looked at it in a certain light, rather a spoiled brat.

Because Guy preferred not to look at Elliott in that light if it could be avoided, he sat on over his beer, giving Elliott time to get home. Meanwhile he eyed, through the Grotto's open door, the carefully ungarish lights of the movie theater across the Circle. And pondered the implications of progress: Jake Birnbaum's Circle Theatre had opened two years ago, and, though it was Tudor-trimmed and its sign was less conspicuous than that of some churches, it had nevertheless meant a breakthrough. For it made Elm Circle a place of nighttime commerce, permanently and unarguably. The Grotto stayed open until midnight now, and last-show crowds streamed across the cobblestones for a drink and a snack while they counted the symbolisms in the latest film import. True, Elliott Sterling's bookshop had always stayed open in the evenings; but it drew people in twos and threes, and its borderline location spilled no lights over the Circle. ("What about the effect of all that light on the Tree?" an anguished voice from the audience had inquired at the Circle Association meeting two years ago. But a quick-witted chairman had stilled the rising murmur of concern by appointing a committee to bring back an opinion from Lambert University experts—and then, while the experts were still studying the question, somebody called for a vote.)

Guy decided the coast was clear and departed from the Grotto. But outside, he strolled, with his hands in his pockets and his air of purpose dimmed. He glanced over his shoulder as he rounded the Tree and judged, by the glimmer of the

47

circular bench around the bole, that preparations were in hand for the coming of spring: the bench had been freshly painted and so had the flagpole, also gleaming whitely in the early dark. Soon Daylight Saving would mean light until nine o'clock, and that was when the old-timers probably felt the weight of the Circle's conservatives' objections to the theater. For when they came out to cherish the springtime evenings, the very places on the bench that were theirs by immemorial custom might now be occupied by irrelevant persons waiting for the movie to open. Silvestri was inclined to save his personal sympathies for those elsewhere in Buxford, who had never had any springtime prospect except sitting on a stoop and inhaling the stench of a tanning factory. But it was possible to look out of someone's eyes even if you weren't about to crusade for him.

It was not possible, however, to persist in societal speculation when confronted by a vision. So when Florence Hathaway appeared—her lovely face framed in swirling honey-blond hair, she rose out of the darkness like Aphrodite coming out of the sea—Guy abruptly abandoned thought. "Hey!" he called, and broke into an undignified half-trot to catch up with her.

"Hey yourself, sleuth." She stopped, waiting for him. Florence always seemed to have all the time in the world.

Guy took her three fat textbooks, a notebook, and a thick pile of index cards held by a rubber band. He looked at the handsome leather pouch slung from her shoulder, wondering whether it was an extra-large purse or a shopping bag he could properly offer to carry for her. Finally he fell back on common sense: whatever the thing was, it was stuffed and sagging and clearly heavy, so he reached down and took it. That turned out to be the right thing to do, for Florence smiled like any rescued damsel.

"That's *heavy.*" Her voice implied only mild complaint of an unjust fate, presumably visited on her by the gods. She

48

tugged at the neck of her dress and craned to see the damage.

The cone of light from the street lamp between the Residence and the Perilous was a stage spotlight now—with Florence, like the beautiful assistant to the magician, stationed at the edge of it and dipping in and out of the light to hand him things. At this moment, she was fully in it. With full effect on Guy, who observed, with a ridiculous sense of guilt, not only the red mark on the creamy skin of her shoulder but also the luscious abundance of the flesh of Florence the Fair. Just right for an earth goddess, he decided. Without being in the least fat, she was nevertheless clearly cabin'd and confin'd when got up in modern dress. And in the absence of more appropriate costume—Guy thought dimly of floating draperies, perhaps—the sensible body of Florence was doing its best to escape: her high, round bosom swelled out of the square neck Mrs. Bethany had doubtless thought of as demure, and below the hem of the skirt the old lady had made not as short as some being worn nowadays but shorter than she would have liked, the firm white thighs of Florence celebrated their freedom.

Guy knew it was Mrs. Bethany of Number 16 who had probably made the dress, just as it would be Kate Sterling of Number 5 who made anything knitted and Ann Price, Florence's roommate, who'd made the leather mail-pouch purse (which would soon be seen all over town: since whatever Florence wore almost immediately became a student fashion, her incidental value as advertisement for Ann's leather shop must be high). For Florence Hathaway was the center of a phenomenon Guy thought of as "reverse paranoia": Elm Circle seemed to be engaged in a kind of conspiracy to feed and clothe and shelter Florence—an unplanned, unspoken community effort rather like the neighborhood rallying-round that commonly occurs when, for example, a small child is reported lost. Florence herself

49

offered no interference with that image, for she appeared to have no sense of peril and apparently considered a landscape full of caring folk just the way things were.

It was a landscape remarkably easy to live off, too, if you were Florence, for—as was also true for Jim Waterman —undemanding little jobs with convenient and/or elastic hours were provided by the Circle to help pay Lambert's tuition. For the academic careers of both Florence and Jim were unmistakably community projects. But in Florence's case there was a more personal flavor: Elliott's summary was unsatisfactory about exact dates, but it had been in her sophomore year that Florence *picked up a nihilism virus and departed unceremoniously in mid-semester*. It was not clear from Elliott's sweeping prose how much time had gone by before *Florence became persuaded that Lambert wasn't entirely futile, or could be viewed existentially, or something comforting like that*. But what was clear enough was that, when Florence the Fair wanted to give Lambert another chance, Elliott Sterling ("I had to use just a jot of Merritt clout") was not the only one at Elm Circle who'd had a hand in persuading the university to forgive and forget. Though Jim Waterman was the fair-haired boy, Florence was the Circle's baby: it had walked the floor with her and brought her through the fever caused by the epidemic virus, and now it fed and watered her and worried over her sniffles and sprains. Whenever Florence finally arrived at graduation, Elm Circle would be at Commencement, full of memories and a few proud tears.

Guy had assumed at first that all this supervision, however fond, must be somewhat nerve-wracking from Florence's point of view—rather like having several dozen maiden aunts. But the notion died abruptly as soon as he met the girl and talked to her a little, for nobody was ever more visibly serene than the fair and unhurried Florence. She trailed serendipity like a perfume, and, not surprisingly, smiles bloomed in her wake; perhaps part of it was a simple response to beauty (after all, how many communities own a honey-haired, violet-eyed, peaches-and-cream maiden clearly descended from those who frolicked with unicorns?), but certainly it was also because Florence's blithe good will, her blissful unawareness of anything but beneficence, must lift all but the most churlish heart. Nobody was ever angry with Florence, though she was always late at her various jobs: she would arrive breathless, apologetic, trailing some of her possessions—and the waiting employer, who should have been aggrieved, would turn to reassuring and dispensing kindly advice on how to manage the next crisis on the horizon. Even the Buxford police officers collecting routine alibi information at the Circle after the murder of Hilary Bridge—though clearly startled by how nonroutine matters became in Florence's case—had inclined to make excuses for her ("She was kind of mixed up, but after all she don't work nine-to-five and she works all over . . .").

Florence worked, on and off, at the Experiment Perilous Bookshop, the Circle Theatre, the Grotto, and the Merritt Library—the last, courtesy of Lambert's Student Aid Office —and also went grocery shopping for Mrs. Chandler and dusted and vacuumed for the retired chicken-Colonel who'd come to roost at Number 12. All these employers deferred to Florence's academic needs, of course: during exam weeks Mrs. Chandler ate out and the Colonel lived with dust. And in any week from September through June, bookshop customers might expect to wait beside the cash register till Florence came to a good stopping place in the assigned chapter of *Economic History of Latin America.* That they did wait, cheerfully, and sometimes even supplied helpful tips on the economic history of Latin America, was typical of the way things went for Florence.

"Well, are you going to?" Florence's voice was high and sweet, and—right now—patient. "Guy?"

He woke to the fact that he was still standing there, holding her purse and frowning down at it. "Am I going to what?"

"Search it?" She was only curious: if her bag was about to be searched, she was interested to see what would turn up.

"No. Only tote it for you, if I may. Where are you off to?"

"The Merritt, actually. But the Grotto first—I didn't have time to alphabetize all the cards and they're due back at the Merritt tonight. So Jim's supposed to do L to Z for me." Her tone was matter-of-fact: ingenious arrangements were the way she always did things, and they always worked. "Where are *you* off to? The Residence?" She turned abruptly, her violet gaze full on him and fully reproaching. "You're not hassling the black students, are you? That's just too silly, Guy—Professor Bridge wasn't your student-pal type, it's true, but nobody caught the Bridge chill unless they tried to cozy up to him. And black students didn't try. Honest. So why don't you leave them alone?" She shook her head, every honey curl reproving independently. "I wouldn't have thought you were like that, Guy. Besides, there's such a thing as a civil rights law, you know."

Guy said he knew, denied harassing anyone ever, and let himself look wounded.

"Oh, I'm a shit—do forgive me. Of course you wouldn't, would you?" She appealed as passionately as though great events hung on whether he would forgive. "Say something. Say a kind word."

The combination of longshoreman vocabulary and flower face took some getting used to, but Guy was progressing. He managed to locate a kind word reasonably promptly, and forgave her in another kind word or two.

Satisfied, Florence hugged his arm before adding herself to its burdens. "Oh, wow! For a minute I thought you'd given up communication, too."

"Too?" What else did she imagine he'd given up?

"Like Red Beard," Florence explained. "He just grunts. But the first time he came around he had this little printed card, I guess so nobody would think he just had laryngitis or something. It's not that, of course—it's because you can't

52

catch the evanescent word. That's why he just grunts, I mean."

"Who is Red Beard and where does he do this grunting? In English class?"

"Oh, you. I thought they only had witty detectives in England."

Conversation with Florence was like tracking a grasshopper, Guy concluded, while he headed her off from a critique of Lord Peter Wimsey. Eventually, he learned that Red Beard, like Libby and Bibby (or Libyan Bibby?—it was impossible to determine from the context), was an occasional visitor to the ménage of Pandora and Ken and the individual known as "Dracula" (Florence paused to doubt that his parents had actually so christened him), the trio who rented Mrs. Chandler's basement. Guy could have confirmed Florence's doubt: "Dracula" was named Susan Mary Taylor (presumably female, at least technically; Dracula was far beyond mere gender) and was nourished not on human blood but on a substantial allowance from a stockbroker father in New Rochelle, New York. But Guy refrained because the "hippies" were the Elm Circle residents he was least interested in discussing. Toots Cantor, going by the book, had already dug up a patrolman who was pretty sure the three had been in a crowd on Trowbridge Common, under his outraged eye, at approximately the moment Hilary Bridge's garage door was closing.

In any case, silence was the best way to herd Florence's conversation into a new direction. Left alone, her discourse flitted and veered, the sentences either trailing off cozily— leaving the rest to an intimate understanding apparently beyond words—or linking to each other like a parade of elephants, trunk to tail. She talked the way she walked, graceful and confident that nothing troublesome would occur in her path, and pausing to give immediate attention to anything within her line of sight at a given moment. By the time Guy steered her to a point in mid-Circle nearly at the

Tree, she had taken up half a dozen topics—and abandoned most of them for lack of promising response from her companion.

But when she glanced over toward the dark blur of the Merritt Library and sighed aloud for the work waiting there, Guy responded promisingly. "Night work at the Merritt doesn't really fit with the image. You know, scholarship and contemplation."

"That's because you're *outside.* Like, this visiting shit from Harvard—he wants his list first thing tomorrow. It's those fucking fascists you need a night crew for. They don't give a shit if the Merritt *is* a sweatshop, as long as they get what they want. And they get it, man—poor Mr. Lester trembles in his tiny boots every time they utter."

Guy glanced in the direction of the sweatshop, but now the Tree on its little plaza was squarely in the way. "Does Lester really stay around trembling this late?"

"Oh, no. I have a key. Anyway, somebody else will be working—there was practically a whole book of Arabic or something, waiting to be Xeroxed." She went on, cheerfully, outlining the chores performed by various handmaidens of scholarship.

Guy steered her toward the lights of the Grotto and decided he didn't have time to lead into his question gracefully: if he didn't catch her on this veer, she was likely to be off and away. So he asked, "Is it really only the fascist scholars Mr. Lester's trembling about?" He resisted the impulse to add a wink, a leer. "I heard there were a few other things going on at the Merritt at night. For him to have a tizzy over."

Florence stopped and stared, her face carefully blank. "Like what?"

She couldn't have been more transparent. Guy sighed, remembering with what pleasure he'd concluded that l'affaire Merritt was only a Lambert domestic quarrel and no concern of the Buxford force. Ah well, a little moment of innocence, rapidly lost; now he'd have to file a real report, because it *could* be drugs and that was most certainly a matter of concern beyond the campus. Chemistry as an explanation of Florence's serenity had occurred to him, but Jim Waterman's comment, *Florence was born turned-on,* had seemed immediately convincing. "All I know is about the tizzy," Guy told her now. He shrugged and waited, hoping for luck.

"Well, if that isn't something else. I mean, I wouldn't fall over dead with surprise if anybody told me Ell-Square was finking to Lambert. But I truly didn't think he'd be finking to the fuzz."

"Listen, it's not like that," Guy began, silently cursing himself for having sent out an advance patrol so ill-supplied. But Florence's attention span rescued him from the consequences of his folly. In shaking her head over the iniquities of tiny-booted Ell-Square, she had caught sight of something: she pointed with her chin at the white gleam of the bench around the Tree and said happily that they must sit there; very probably they'd be the first couple since it was painted, and she'd never been the first customer at anything, like the people you read about who stand in line all night when something new is opening . . . Her clear voice pattered on, questioning whether the paint was dry and deciding it was, while she tugged at the slow bulk of Guy, who didn't seem to want to be first. "Come *on,* "she urged, certainly imagining a line forming behind them.

"Maybe later." Guy had a good reason for not wanting to sit and talk under the Buxford Elm, but he needed desperately a reason that could be offered here and now.

He was rescued again: Florence flitted from the immediate controversy into an account of the one at the last Circle Association meeting. She had attended and "so did the kids, because we were all gung ho about participatory democracy right then."

"Yes? I wasn't at that meeting," Guy encouraged. He

watched her rapt face and sketching hands for a while, and then tuned in again.

". . . so every time, there's this fight when it's time to fix up around the Tree. Because Mrs. Bethany always wants petunias, and people—well, maybe they're not for petunias but they still think some kind of flowers would be nice. But the Colonel always says George Washington wouldn't ever have stopped at the Tree if there'd been a flowerbed there, because what would he do with his horse? And I have to admit it makes sense. Somebody like George Washington wouldn't turn his horse loose in a flowerbed, would he?"

Amazingly, this seemed to be not a rhetorical question. "No," Guy said. "I guess George Washington wouldn't."

She nodded. "The Colonel's always the only one on his side, but you don't have to feel sorry for him, he enjoys it so. Making his speech every year." Reminiscence overtook her, in a little silvery shower of giggles. "This time the Colonel was really grooving, though. And he wound up with this beautiful roar, like leading the troops into battle—Henry the Fifth at Agincourt, you know what I mean? He waved his arm—you know, like 'Follow me, boys'—and hollered, 'I say let's have grass, and I demand a vote *now.*'" She had been, briefly, the Colonel; now, abruptly, she was a saddened Florence. "For a minute, it was onward-Christian-soldiers, it was we-shall-overcome, it was—oh, you could feel it. And then it all fell apart."

"Why?" Guy found himself most ardently wanting to know.

"Well, the kids. They don't really know the Colonel—I mean, he's so lovable when he's sober, but you know how they are about the military. So they don't dig him, so they were just sort of nodding. And then when he hollered like that, Dracula—not meaning any disrespect, really, because deep down, Dracula's actually very sweet—but he got excited, so he jumped up and—I mean, there he was, with all that hair and all, yelling 'Amen, Lord, let's have grass.' And all the citizens just blowing their minds and—" She clapped her hand over her mouth and examined Guy above it before she removed it to apologize. "You're not offended? Please don't be. I truly forgot."

For a moment, Guy dandled active self-pity. Then it was time to grab the handle somewhere in all that, so he said he wasn't offended; but it must have been something to see, all right.

"Oh, it was. But I didn't mean—I forgot you were—"

"Look," Guy said patiently, "it's not as if I belong to some anti-grass religion. Is that the way you think of it?" He knew it was. "Listen, it's not illegal to talk about grass. But it *is* against the law to smoke it. Or buy it or sell it or give it to your friend or take some from anyone." He looked at her sternly, trading on the disapproving-father image he was stuck with. "That's the *law*. You dig?"

"It really gets you mad. I'm sorry."

Guy ordered his jaw muscles to stop clenching his teeth: it was bad for his molars, and anyway anger wasn't going to lead Florence out of any wilderness. "Honey, illegal doesn't mean it gets me mad or hurts my feelings. All it means is, if I see you doing something illegal, or any other policeman does, you'll be arrested."

"What's jail like, Guy? I've always wanted to know, really. I mean, what do you do there besides write?"

"Write?" A moment too late, he thought of the *Ballad of Reading Gaol*.

"You know, like Bunyan. Gandhi. Like them." She remembered then that he was mere fuzz. "They wrote books in jail."

"Well, you wouldn't get to. It's not like that in jail—you don't get to sit around writing literature. It's just ugly, and full of mean, bad people." Even in baby talk he doubted that he would persuade. Like most of "town" Buxford, he had seen the incredible extent of the students' naïveté; but now he thought with fleeting hatred of the likes of Hilary Bridge, who probably imparted the literary glamour of the jailbird

57

life. Guy realized that he must be communicating his unseemly passion: Florence was patting his arm, soothing.

"My," she said—and Guy remembered that before she'd
arrived at the vocabulary of Lambert, she'd been a little girl
in Nebraska and thus presumably limited to the mild exple-
tives of that milieu—"you really groove on this stuff."

He thought of saying it was a matter, pure and simple, of
written-down laws. But he let her roll on instead.

"It's perfectly legal to talk about grass, though. You said
so yourself. So come sit down, and I'll tell you another funny
story."

"No!" he cried, with much too much emphasis.

"Why not?" She examined him, a newly interesting phenomenon.

"I'm allergic." He nodded at the shadowy Tree. "Elms,"
he explained, with the happiness that accompanies the exercise of imagination. "It's okay later in the season, but when
the leaves are curled up like that—well, I'd sneeze my head
off if I sat down there now."

"Oh, sure. I understand." Florence the fair, Florence the
lovable, was prepared to smile on human weakness. She
knew how allergies were, she told him: once, when she and
Ann were living in New York, there was this girl there who
was just so incredibly allergic. . . .

Gratefully, Guy steered toward the Grotto—where anything they got into would be more advisable than sitting
under the Tree and chattering about illegal drugs. But in the
process, Florence had half-turned away, and now something
else had crossed her path: she tilted her chin in the direction
they'd come from and said, "There's Kate. Going home. Elliott must be in the shop."

Guy glanced over her shoulder at the dim light from the
window of the Perilous that faced the Circle. It was not much
larger than the picture window of a suburban home, and it
had been designed to remind the Circle of no more than that:
Elliott Sterling, pioneer entrepreneur, had been deft and

58

imaginative in showing his neighbors commerce couldn't hurt. The Circleward window of the bookshop contained, always, only a small antique table holding a lamp and a book, with a leather bookmark in it, that some reader might just have put aside: it was a tableau of an elegant, gracious household that nobody, however genteel, need fear. At night the effect was even more reassuring, for lavish draperies behind the little table were drawn when the lamp was lighted, thus shutting off from view all the bustle within the Perilous, and displaying to the Circle only that small, warm, noncommercial light, just enough to tell you your neighbor was still up.

Florence took Guy's silence for doubt. "It's Kate, really it is. I can tell by that shawl. She made it herself, of course—I don't even know if you can buy shawls like that anywhere. . . ."

Guy didn't need the shawl to tell him the small figure moving past the library tableau in the bookshop window was Kate, for lately he'd learned to recognize a feeling in his chest that turned up whenever Kate Sterling did. It was not an unpleasant feeling, but the correlation was. It's like an allergy, he told himself now while it happened again—and he knew that there were only two things to do about it in that case: avoid the allergen, or find something that will immunize . . .

". . . my grandmother had one done in the same stitch but it was sort of a dreary sick-green, not like Kate's—"

Guy heard, misunderstanding and therefore startled for a moment, before he realized Florence didn't mean she could *see* the stitch. And then the thought immunized him for a time: Kate became a figure in a pattern, a pattern he'd seen in a different context in the Sixth Precinct reports. There, Kate Sterling had been a standing figure, a spectator of others' movements on the night of Hilary Bridge's death.

"You must have good eyesight," he said to Florence, calculating that his question would make a fair test: the distance from here to where she'd spotted Kate was about the same as the distance from the bookshop to Hilary Bridge's house. "It wasn't as dark as this last Tuesday night, was it?" he asked. "After Elliott came back to the Perilous for the poetry book?"

"Oh, *that* Tuesday. No, of course not, that was earlier and it makes a difference, doesn't it? I mean, it was only ten past eight when he came in and it must be after that now, isn't it? And besides, there's the earth turning meanwhile—don't the days get longer or shorter, one or the other? But we haven't got up to the solstice yet, or have we?" Florence hesitated, accustomed to having her conversational needs supplied; but no observation on solstices was forthcoming. "Anyway, I was looking from over there." Her chin, again employed as an auxiliary hand, indicated the bookshop window. "I was closing the curtain. Really, I didn't even know I'd forgotten to, but it didn't matter—Elliott can be patient when he wants. Sometimes he does get a little shitty, but I remember he didn't so much as give me a reproachful *look*, actually. He just told me, like casually."

"Told you what?"

"Well, to pull the curtain. When he was going out. And I did, practically right away. That's when I saw Jacques leaving —but you know what time that was. Jacques must've told you."

"Yes." Guy squinted back along the tangent of the Circle. The time wasn't precise—it wouldn't be with anyone, and certainly not with Florence. And whenever it was, exactly, that Elliott was outside explaining to Kate why he'd come back to the bookshop, he wouldn't have been visible from that window. But the front steps at Number 20 would have been framed perfectly in it, then and later—though nobody had been interested in that fact because Florence had been at the cash register at the time they asked about. She'd seen what others had seen—Elliott coming back for the book— and nobody had thought to ask her what else she'd seen.

60

Carefully, Guy checked it out now: "How could you tell it was Jacques Berriault? Just glancing out like that, could you—?"

"The same way I just now knew it was Kate, I guess. And it was, wasn't it, Mr. Detective. You saw her with your own eyes."

"Yes," he admitted, smiling.

"Besides, I didn't just glance, I peered." Florence giggled. "I kept on watching him because he looked so funny." She noticed Guy's quickened attention. "He was getting bigger with each step," she explained. "First he was just a top, then he got more and more leg—sort of like a slow-motion film. It was just funny, that's all. So I watched it for a minute."

The grunting Red Beard might be right, Guy was thinking. Because the word was evanescent as all hell, even when the intent was to communicate truth. Even if truth was what Jacques had intended to communicate when he finally set his departure for the chess game in the few minutes that Elliott Sterling had spent getting a book of poems from the Perilous. But had Jacques ever said specifically *how* he left the house? Kate Sterling had said *when* she'd seen Jacques leaving —while she stood talking with Elliott in the alley beside the bookshop—but nobody had asked her for any other detail, presumably. So nobody had discovered that leaving the house seemed to mean two different things. Because Jacques's "getting bigger with each step," as Florence had seen him, was a fine description, as accurate as it was artless, of a man walking up the inclined driveway from the garage door of Number 20; but it didn't fit anyone coming down the shallow front steps.

"I only watched for a minute, actually," Florence said guiltily. "Just till his shoes showed. And then I pulled the curtain right away."

"Relax. I believe you."

"Oh. You have such a disapproving-father look sometimes."

Obscurely offended, Guy said he hadn't known that. It was a little depressing to be thus abruptly hustled toward senility—how old did she think he was, anyway?—when he was still practically a stripling. And even if he were a legitimate father image, how in the world would he ever summon disapproval of a Miss Dairyland with an A in Philosophy? For Florence might be scatterbrained, but the brain was of respectable quality: Lambert was not in the habit of bending its entrance requirements, and certainly would not have for a little nobody from Nebraska. "I don't disapprove," Guy told her. He turned her toward the Grotto again, and its square of light fell on her face—perfectly beautiful, perfectly trusting, bright with lively interest in everything and everyone. "In fact, now that I think of it, I actively approve."

Florence smiled, patted his arm, and looked past him to peer into the Grotto. Guy suppressed a grin, understanding immediately: compliments were simply not newsworthy if you were not just an extraordinarily pretty girl but a genuinely beautiful one. Beauty like that amounted to an extra dimension, which its inhabitant learned early to allow for. So flattery was not interesting and probably even adulation was routine, just a part of living—reacted to politely, but not worth thinking about.

"Hey, Ann's in there!" Florence said happily. "She's back!" She darted ahead, confident that the load-bearing male would follow with her possessions.

Guy did. And he lingered a little, basking in the general light and buzz, the hubbub around Florence. He bought her a pastry and watched her eat it hungrily while Ann Price and two other people organized her sets of alphabetized cards and prepared to launch her on her belated way to the Merritt Library. Satisfied that she would not lack for escort when she finally did leave, Guy departed the Grotto for the second time that evening.

He set off quickly toward Number 5, because he had to go there and it was pointless to argue with himself about it. But he lingered on the doorstep, scanning the arc of Elm Circle at his right. And before he rang the doorbell, he made a mental map of the light sources on that side. A streetlight at each end, one near the Residence and the other near the entrance to the Merritt—plus a rosy glow from the Circle Theatre and a night light in Ann Price's leather shop. He reminded himself that there would have been also, last Tuesday night, the light over the front steps at Number 20, the one Jacques Berriault had said he'd turned off when he came home. Guy scowled at the thought of Jacques, who was not perhaps the innocent Lt. Silvestri had taken him for. It proved, doubtless, that you could make mistakes if you didn't go by the book—but Guy felt bad about it. He didn't feel even faintly happy until he recognized Kate Sterling's footsteps coming to answer the doorbell.

5

The Sterlings
at Home

I haven't felt so good all day,"
Guy said, meaning it. Perched
on a wobbly wooden stool in the small kitchen, he was both
a danger and endangered: if he stood up, his head was im-
periled by open cupboard doors, and when he sat, his feet
could easily trip Kate, squeezing by with a load of dishes for
the dishwasher. Yet Guy was actively glad he'd come, and
he said so.

"I'm glad, too," Kate told him. "Before and after meals is
when I really feel the need of company. Kitchens are boring
without conversation."

The dishwasher was an old-fashioned model, lacking sliding trays and other conveniences, so loading it meant repeated diving down and coming up—rather like bobbing for
apples at a Halloween party, Guy decided, watching Kate.
"You're right," he said. "A woman alone in her kitchen is
probably a recent phenomenon. Maybe the mark of our

own society." Suddenly he remembered the busy, peopled kitchen of his childhood—and himself the baby of the family, perched in a corner with a cracker to keep him quiet while his mother and some of his four sisters (and on holidays, all of them) chopped and pared and gossiped and argued.

"Is there any society where people get together for the preparing and cleaning up, but eat separately? Because that makes more sense, doesn't it?"

"Well, I don't know of any, not in those terms," Guy said conscientiously. But he thought she was absolutely right: why should families gather for conversation precisely when their mouths were most apt to be full? "If you want to start one, I'll join. I do most of my studying with meals." He had a swift vision of a little girl with long dark hair reading *Black Beauty*, propped against the sugar bowl. One of his sisters, he supposed, emerging from the back cells of memory. There was no Papa in the picture: Guy's father, dead in an auto accident when his only son was four, was an honored legend but not a model; any Guy-as-Papa would have to be constructed from uncles. "If I'm ever the father of a family," he announced, "all its children will be taught to come to dinner with a book." He nodded with exaggerated solemnity and banged an imaginary gavel, establishing by mockery that the discussion was closed, That was That. But it had better end there, he was thinking: *we'll have no more of these images of families, memories of kitchens, all that dangerous stuff.* It was not wholly a matter of scruples, though he was troubled by some, certainly. But, more important, he objected to being twitched around by what he couldn't help but could control. There was no point, when nothing real could be gained by it, to a disturbance of his present peace.

"You look tired, Guy." She always did that, cutting through whatever palaver was going on to what she knew was really important. She blew at the strand of hair that had strayed into her face during her last dive, then she studied him with care. "Have you been out detecting all day?"

"Not quite." It was quite remarkable: you read about gray eyes, but Kate was the first person he'd ever seen who actually had them. Really gray—not sometimes green or hazel, but always that soft smoky gray. "What I've been up to is mostly—well, going to and fro on earth and walking up and down upon it." She didn't recognize the description of Satan, he noticed, and thought that Elliott almost certainly would have; they were not much alike, the Sterlings. Then Guy returned to spectating. A pleasant pursuit, for Kate had a tidy waist and it swiveled nicely; under a loose, rather shabby skirt what looked like a pleasantly rounded haunch followed through. The whole graceful, smooth dance was most satisfying to watch.

Kate poured detergent into the little cup. "Nothing is more wearing than fruitless endeavor."

Guy grinned at the oddly old-fashioned words and admitted without pain that it had been mostly fruitless endeavor, at that. "Everybody has teeny-weeny pieces of information. Which, when properly collected, will doubtless point to a murderer. But collecting them lacks kicks."

"Maybe there isn't any? A murderer, I mean?"

He arched his brows and asked her, keeping his question carefully mild, whether she had a theory.

"Well, not a *theory,* but—" She peered through the newly fallen strands of hair, now straying toward her nose. "I just wondered if maybe Hilary could have been only—playing games. Making a sort of gesture, because he and Jacques were quarreling. You know how people—well, if Hilary expected Ellie to come right back and find him, it could've been a way of punishing Jacques, sort of."

"But Elliott did go back, apparently within a very few minutes. There's a witness who happened to see him go up the front steps and ring the doorbell. It's in the reports."

"I know, but that was a formality, really—he'd already decided, once he saw the garage door was closed and the car nowhere in sight, that Hilary'd gone without him. So Ellie was petulant. And Hilary may have expected him to be more persistent."

Watching her, but differently now, Guy said, "There's a problem there. If Hilary had started out to play games, why wouldn't he just stop when Elliott inconveniently failed to appear?"

"I thought of that. But I figured he—couldn't. I don't know how carbon monoxide—works. Maybe he was allergic to it, and it—well, happened faster than he thought it would."

She was ingenious, but a little outdated: though of course it had been clear that Hilary Bridge would hardly have sat there in his car and let somebody lock him in unless he was somehow incapacitated, the fact that he'd been given a whiff of something—the guess, based on microscopic examination of the irritated tissue at the edge of a small cut on his face, was chloroform—had taken a little time to emerge. So if Kate had stopped paying attention after the first news stories, she could have missed it. But the detail, Guy knew, had become part of any and all local comment as soon as the information was released. In Guy's neighborhood, anyway. But at this end of town people made rather a point of not recounting all the juicy details of any local scandal—and to dwell on violence was extra-taboo—so Kate, probably only exchanging murmurs about how dreadful it was, had remained ignorant.

"Hilary Bridge wasn't allergic; he was chloroformed," Guy said bluntly, and watched her wince. Annoyed, he found tolerance coming a little hard at the moment: maybe it was bigotry, but he thought with fondness of those women in his own neighborhood who were normal and human and nosy and talked specifics rather than sociology. They were easy to talk to, because you didn't need a special language for them. "It wasn't suicide, real or phony. What it comes down to," Guy said slowly—feeling like a brute and resenting that— "is somebody rendered Bridge incapable of turning off the motor. And then somebody closed and locked the garage door, from the outside. You understand?"

She didn't: the proof of murder went by her. "Oh, poor Hilary. Oh, dear."

Over her head, Guy saw Elliott standing in the doorway leading to the hall, and nodded. A little uncomfortably, because how did you greet a man whose wife you'd practically reduced to tears? He stood up, looking around him as if the appropriate words were to be found stored in one of the kitchen cupboards.

But Elliott had them right at hand. "Really, Kate, don't take on. After all, Hilary didn't even know."

Kate looked a little brighter. "That's something, I guess. It's good to think he didn't suffer."

Guy agreed, so he let her think so. But Hilary Bridge had waked at some point and made a feeble, brain-scrambled effort—not in the direction of logic, for the car's motor had not stopped running until the gas tank was empty, but in the direction of flight. When Jacques Berriault yanked the car door open the next morning, the body was slumped against it, because a frantic Hilary had managed to get the inside handle halfway down. Particles of the upholstery material of the car door were found under his fingernails. Guy decided that though he disagreed with Elliott about the sheltering of womenfolk, there *were* details Kate could just as well be spared.

". . . the way the police think of it," Elliott was telling Kate. "As a problem, requiring problem-solving methods, not throbs."

"Like what problem-solving methods?" Guy asked. If Elliott was determined to play Sleuth's Sidekick, why, let him: at this point no harm could come of it. And the Sleuth's Sidekick might, in the process, let slip some information he hadn't yet volunteered. For if Florence had seen Jacques coming from the garage, wasn't it possible that Elliott had, too?

"Like starting to unravel the thread where it sticks out," Elliott said. "Which is the fact that Hilary felt safe, and that's

68

what really killed him, isn't it? It wasn't being trapped. That garage is solid stone, so I don't suppose he could've made himself heard, but it was possible to turn off the motor and sit there, all night if necessary, until somebody looked for him."

"Except that he couldn't. He was unconscious."

"Sure, but he got that way by trusting somebody. Somebody who knocked him out. It's with that somebody that you ought to begin."

"Meaning Jacques?" In a way it was funny: Elliott, busy being the gifted amateur of the detective stories, would be crushed if he knew he'd unwound his thread and plied his little gray cells—and after all that, ended at Toots Cantor's starting point.

If Elliott intended to answer, he was forestalled: Kate interrupted to inquire about Jacques, now suffering from shock in a private nursing home. And not doing too well, Guy had heard. He contributed that information to the discussion.

"It's the last words," Kate said. The gray eyes were cloudy, a little darkened—the color of the sky above the river on a foggy morning. "Whatever spiteful, angry thing he said to Hilary before he went out. And now," she said slowly, "it's the last words Hilary ever heard. That's what hurts."

Elliott said harshly, "Spare us the homemade drama, will you?"

Her culture was awfully hard on her, Guy noted, thinking that Kate had hardly been overdramatic. All she'd done was state the problem in personal terms, which wasn't a bad idea and anyway was what women generally did. Guy frowned as Elliott caught his eye and offered a silent invitation: head tilted toward the stairs, he seemed to be including Guy in a manly conspiracy to escape female dramatics. But then an unmistakable *please* appeared in Elliott's eyes, changing the nature of the conspiracy; so Guy changed his mind and signaled assent.

"Anyway," Elliott said smoothly, "it seems hardly fair—

we're giving the lieutenant here a busman's holiday, aren't we?"

"Oh, of course. I'm sorry," Kate said. "I didn't think." She turned away from them to close and latch the dishwasher.

"That monster makes a fearful racket," Elliott warned. "So we'll have to split once she pushes the button. Why not come up to my sanctum, Guy, and pretend to be fascinated by a butterfly? You can't deny it'll be a change, at least."

Guy went, of course. After Kate urged it on him, too, with her small face full of earnest concern for his welfare. How easily she had been made to feel guilt and then been maneuvered by it! It seemed to Guy a hell of a way to run a marriage. But that wasn't *his* problem, he told himself.

He followed Elliott up the stairs, turning over in his mind the problem that was his, all his: so long as Jacques's words were not proved to be the last Hilary Bridge heard, it remained possible that they'd been, *Professor Bridge, have you got a minute?* or something like that, spoken by a Residence student entering by the open door of the garage. The scenario fit Hilary, for he might not have been "your student-pal type," as Florence had put it, but he'd dearly wanted to be a part of what he took for the new world a-coming—if it didn't cost him too much. And no black student approaching the self-consciously progressive Professor Bridge would encounter the "chill" Florence had mentioned. So what was more likely than the possibility that Hilary Bridge, smothering any impatience he felt—and secure against prolonged discussion because he knew Elliott would be back soon—would have admitted to having a minute?

Guy barely glanced at the comfortable clutter revealed when Elliott closed the door and turned on the desk lamp in his large, high-ceilinged "sanctum." Once it may have been a morning room for a lady who wrote little notes at a little, spindly-legged desk. Or who on fine days sat out on the porch beyond, where exotic flora being coddled through a

New England winter would have been set out to catch the sun.

But if the room had once been all airiness and delicacy, nothing of its past showed now: despite graceful proportions, it was close and confined, with heavy furniture and dark corners. The massive bookcases loomed oppressively, and they had clearly not known a dustcloth's touch for some time. Most of the large armchairs were piled with books and journals, but two were free. Nevertheless, Guy chose a straight, hard chair opposite the door to the porch: it was a sullen choice, announcing unwillingness of some kind, and he knew it. But he felt sullen.

Elliott seemed to sense that. He offered appeasement by way of both light talk and alcohol—grinning with a boy's pride as he exhibited his supply of brandy, stored in a flask in what seemed to be the "chemistry corner" of the room. Guy declined: he was not at leisure, and he didn't propose to pretend he was. He watched Elliott return the flask to its place, where it promptly became invisible among others, containing who knew what. Guy felt even more sullen.

"No to drink, no to small talk." Elliott sat down at his desk. "And a distinctly hostile air besides. Unpromising."

"Problem-solving makes me hostile. Especially the nitty-gritty kind that depends on who was where, and when. Which I'm afraid this Bridge case is shaping up to be."

"I could make you up a list," Elliott offered. "Minute by minute, the way they do in books."

"Thanks, but I'll manage." Guy recognized that eager-beaver Elliott was proving too much for his hostility; gratefully, he let it slide away. "Unless you can add something that isn't already in the reports," he suggested pleasantly.

"I didn't see the murderer, if that's what you mean. Actually, my contribution—I noticed it when the man came around asking questions—was all about what I *didn't* see. No Hilary, nobody home."

"You didn't even see as much as Kate did, I gather. Why not, though? You were both out there by the corner of the Perilous, weren't you? So why didn't you see Jacques leaving the house when Kate saw him?"

"Because we weren't standing side by side, Sherlock. I'd been going *toward* the Perilous, so I had my back to Hilary's house. Kate had been coming out, so she was facing it."

"It figures," Guy conceded. And silently scratched one notion: apparently Elliott had not summoned him up here for friendly advice on how to change the story you'd told the police. If Elliott had seen Jacques Berriault coming from the garage, he wasn't volunteering it yet.

"Guy? Will I have to testify to all my negatives? I mean, will it come to a big courtroom scene?"

"Presumably. If a suspect is caught and indicted and tried. Why?"

"And Kate? Does it matter what she—?"

"It matters," Guy interrupted. "What about the courtroom scene, Elliott?" He waited, but nothing happened. "That's what you wanted to talk to me about, isn't it?" It was, clearly: Elliott sat mute, hanging his head like a naughty schoolboy caught by a monitor. Only this was grownup stuff, and Guy had had too long a day to be patient with naughty boys. So he said angrily, "As far as I can see, the only thing special about telling your story in a court is that you'd be under oath. So I'm asking you, what about it? Because some serious questions come to mind."

"No," Elliott said. He raised his head and Guy saw that the denial was true: Elliott seemed only surprised, not afraid. "Everything I've said I'd say again. Really."

"Then what's the problem?"

The shaggy reddish head moved indecisively in the lamplight. "About Kate—will she have to testify?"

"That's up to the D.A. And the attorney for the defendant." Guy put down, firmly, the flutter of alarm he felt—and the alarm *that* caused. "How can I know what either of them will do?" But he was already guessing: if Jacques was the defendant, any prosecutor in his right mind would forget Kate and rely on Florence Hathaway—what jury would fail to believe the lovely, transparently truthful Florence? "Kate can corroborate *your* comings and goings," Guy said evenly. "About your calling for Bridge the first time, and then going back. And so on." But it might not be necessary: Elliott had been seen doing what he'd said he'd been doing, and nobody disputed any part of his account. So maybe Kate wouldn't have to— Guy realized what he was up to and brought himself up short. "That evokes the same kind of question," he said sharply. "Didn't Kate see you coming back for that book of poems?" It couldn't make any difference to the case, because Florence had; but it made a difference to Guy. "Was Kate lying?"

"No, of course she wasn't. You know she wouldn't lie."

"I thought I did know," Guy said tightly.

"But she can't say it in court, Guy. It's the—the public aspect. Kate just couldn't appear in a court."

"Why not, for God's sake? Maybe she doesn't relish the spotlight, but she isn't pathologically shy."

"Take my word for it, she couldn't. It would be—inflicting—enormous harm. And I know you don't want to harm Kate, so I thought I'd just ask—" Elliott broke off, seeing Guy's scowl. "Oh, my. It wasn't anything illegal. Or even ignoble." Suddenly he sounded like himself again. "Nothing like that. Gadzooks, how rigid is thy morality."

"Very rigid. Reliably rigid, so count on it."

"I will, I do. So all I wanted to ask was, is it likely that Kate will be called?" Elliott looked down at his desk. "It's a small problem, and mine own. Quite out of your official territory. And I can solve it myself, if I know the dimensions. Without attempting to bribe a police officer."

Meaning, Guy gathered, that Mrs. Sterling could be whisked over the state line if a subpoena loomed. But why should she be? If Kate had reason to fear appearing in a court,

73

and it wasn't for the obvious reasons—which seemed to be the case, for Elliott was flustered but not lying, Guy thought —it must be something that would come out as a kind of by-product. Like a police record? Guy found the idea incredible. But he knew nothing of Kate, really. She was a strong reality, a worrisomely strong one, in his own mind. He could, and frequently did, summon up her image with pleasure— but it was a here-and-now Kate, with no past. And in Elliott's map of Elm Circle the block for Number 5 had been inscribed chastely, "The Sterlings"—which made Kate somebody's wife, but that was all. Nobody's daughter, or sister, or old school chum.

Elliott was standing, making departing motions. "I feel like an old maid who heard burglars under the bed and called the cops. Ah, well. Forgive us overprotective husbands."

Guy listened to the voice of Tim Whistler in his head, saying, *One wonders.* "No," he said. "*I* have a question now."

"I hoped you wouldn't—take advantage."

"I think it's you who were taking advantage." Guy regretted that as soon as he heard it, though: it was not Elliott's fault that Silvestri had been so clearly vulnerable on the subject of Kate. You even had to admit—Guy acknowledged swallowing the anger in his throat—that Elliott was generous, a civilized duke who didn't mind if his duchess smiled at the groom. Certainly you couldn't blame him if, seeing what he had, he used it when he needed it.

"If you feel that way," Elliott said stiffly, "of course I must apologize."

Fruitless endeavor popped into Guy's head. He said swiftly, following impulses he hoped were healthy, "Let's not do this, Elliott." Climbing anger and feelings of betrayal, adding up to huffy-polite exchanges—they could go on this way for a while, but it would be fruitless indeed.

Elliott said sadly, "I can't help it. I'm ruing the fact that I brought the question up, and I'd only be—compounding the error if I went on with it, don't you see? I'm not free to

. . . Listen, couldn't you just take my word that it's nothing you'd find worth troubling about?"

Guy saw Elliott's gentlemanly bind: he'd gone too far to get back, unless Guy let him; but by the same rules, he couldn't go ahead. "One question," Guy said. It would have to be a daring one; only an all-or-nothing risk could break the deadlock. "What is it," he asked, keeping his voice casual although nothing in his body seemed to be, "that Kate picks up in a post office box in Trowbridge?"

"I'll be damned," Elliott said. He sat down. "How long have you known?"

"It's my question-time."

"But it's creepy. Are we living in a police state? Is everybody checked up on all the time?"

Guy sighed, weary at the very thought of dealing with this favorite myth. "On the contrary," he said curtly, "all the advantages are on the nonpolice side in any contest. Including—conspicuously—this one."

"All right, you have me there. But I warn you, it's a long story. The story of my shame, you might say. And a sordid one."

Guy said, truthfully, that he was used to long, sordid stories. But, he realized while he listened, he was used to reading them in official prose. Or, if he heard them, they were usually being told haltingly, clumsily, and often with tears— not flatly, as when Elliott said that "as you seem to have found out," what Kate could not risk being asked in a court-room was her name. It jolted, though Guy had gotten nearly that far in his deductions. But what kept on jolting him, while he learned that what Kate picked up in Trowbridge was her monthly pension check as the widow of one Robert Cermak, was the sense that this was the wrong kind of story for an articulate, easy-flowing, Lambert-accented voice.

One of the reasons the story flowed so easily was that Elliott apparently believed an army of sleuths had already uncovered most of it. Guy asked few questions, and those designed only to nail down a few basic facts: "How long ago was all this? When Cermak—?"

"About five years ago. I don't know how long Kate had been married to him, but the children—you knew about the children, didn't you? They were both preschool age."

He should have known about the children, Guy thought. Kate just didn't have the look of a childless woman.

"If you mean how long had Bob Cermak been a lush, I'd say probably forever. He was a legend in the Alcoholics Anonymous group in Chicago when I came drifting in there on a tide of bourbon. And I wasn't keeping track of things too well then, so you'll have to forgive some imprecision." Elliott looked away quickly, as if late to inspect something in the far corner of the room. "Kate was something of a legend, too—knitting patiently at A.A. meetings, or waiting at home, ready to offer Cermak some more faith, hope, and charity when we rolled him home from his latest fall from grace." Elliott summoned a wry smile. "They happen, even if you have more will power than he had."

Guy nodded. "I know they do. But they don't to you." Funny that nobody in Elm Circle, which went in for polite and steady though not heavy drinking, had noticed Elliott's teetotaling. But then, Guy hadn't either—not even when he's refused that brandy a little while ago. "It worked for you, it seems. A.A., I mean. Why not for Cermak?" They had had, after all, the same wife. If Kate was one of those women you saw from time to time who unconsciously encourage drunken husbands, then why not twice?

"I hate to be immodest, but since you press me—I'm made of better stuff, I think is the answer. Bob Cermak was an arrogant bastard. A charmer, and handsome—women, not to say children and dogs, swooned at his curly smile and ready hair. You could see why he'd turned Kate's head, especially since she was very young, apparently, when she met him. But he turned everybody else's too—and with that history I guess he just couldn't get humble enough, when he needed to, to sober up." Elliott shrugged. "I read in your face that you believe jealousy sits on my tongue. Maybe. At least envy—he's dead, but he got the girl first. However"—the glint of mockery in his voice was clear, and conscious—"one may envy a man and still like him, so that's not it, right?"

Okay, Guy thought, Elliott was entitled. But he asked, "How did it happen?" because he had to. To make it easier, he looked anywhere but at Elliott, who had a job before him now in which wit wouldn't help. So Guy's gaze was fixed on the telescope, pointing out at the back-porch screen like a machine gun holding off infantry, while Elliott told how Robert Cermak had solved his problems. Kate had been trying to do just that, it seemed: after her husband had squandered everything they owned, she'd gone to work to keep the family fed. But Cermak had small faith in her ability to support herself and two children, for she wasn't a career woman and had no training. "Presumably," Elliott said drily, "he reasoned that he'd help her out. Incredible. But it may be accurate."

A tilted mirror on a stand in the porch reflected a white car somewhere in the world outside. "I'm a police officer," Guy said, watching the car disappear. "You'd be surprised what I can believe about people. Drunk or sober."

"Ah, yes. Well, try this. Bob turned up one afternoon at the home of the woman who kept the children while Kate was at work. He said he'd borrowed a car from a friend and wanted to take the kids for a ride because it was such a pretty day. The woman was aware of the family problem, but he seemed quite sober—he even sat in her parlor and had a cup of coffee with her. So she dressed the children—a girl and a boy—and sent them on their outing with Daddy. And he took them out on the highway and drove into a concrete abutment at what the cops figured was about eighty miles an hour." In the silence, Elliott said slowly, "As you're a policeman, you may want the usual report. The children apparently died instantly. Bob lived long enough to talk to

77

the police, which is where that notion that he was trying to make it up to Kate comes from. He didn't live long enough to talk to her, which I myself regard as fortunate. What else? Oh yes, he'd rented the car, it turned out. He paid with a check, which later bounced. Had enough?"

"Yes," Guy said. His mother, he knew, would mention the mysterious ways of God. In a sense, he was tempted to a similar awe: there was no limit, it seemed, to what people could recover from.

"If you're wondering where I come in," Elliott said wearily, "it was as one of a crowd. Even before, everybody had tried to come to the rescue. Kate attracts rescuers—men want to take care of her." Soberly, not playing games now, Elliott said, "You know what I mean, I think."

"Yes." Women like Kate attracted men not through helplessness, but what was almost its opposite—an air of wholly womanly competence, somehow deliciously secret and separate, quirky and full of surprises and an unspoken, probably unconscious challenge to *figure it out if you can*. Nearly all men of normal self-esteem were tempted to try. So they were in short supply always, these genuine *femmes fatales* who were quite different from the popular notion. Kate was a nice-looking woman but not beautiful, and she did nothing to change that fact: her dark hair, held back by a blatant bobby pin, just hung there, curling slightly but clearly without encouragement to do so; the startling gray eyes went unemphasized and unadvertised—and thus perhaps had even greater impact when they were finally noticed; and Kate's clothes, though they bespoke an interest in color and its harmonies, said nothing whatever about the body they concealed. "I know what you mean," Guy said. Because he had had time by now to recognize what it was that persistently disturbed his peace, and even to understand why Elliott Sterling had not been resentful though he'd apparently seen Silvestri joining what must be a long list of men smitten with Kate—all of them, like Silvestri, probably troubled by immediate unseemly desires but not likely anyway to be found hiding in a closet by a returning husband. Because with a woman like Kate, the bed would never be enough to win. What a man wanted of her was nothing less than a lifetime: she was for the big league—the hunt for the soulmate, mother of one's particular posterity, and companion of old age that underlay all seduction games anyway. And yes, if you found and won a Kate, you took care of her; like Elliott Sterling, you gave her anything she wanted, any way you could.

"It's funny," Elliott said seriously, "but I won out precisely because I was the least able to take care of her at the moment."

It wasn't funny at all, Guy thought: there must have been a crowd to pick from when she chose the handsome, feckless Cermak. So it was preversely consistent, this choice of the fellow-sufferer Elliott Sterling. But it was a pity, because Kate should be allowed to be a woman instead of a nurse.

"What I was, I guess, was a kind of wet dog. And Kate just naturally takes in wet dogs and other shivering creatures. But once she'd dried me off at her hearth"—Elliott's voice was recovering its characteristic light, brisk note—"I was in fact the best equipped to help her shed the past—I had money to take her away and a place to take her to. So she came with me."

"It's possible, isn't it, that she loved you?" It was Guy's turn to speak drily. "Why leave that out of your guesses?"

"It's always possible for Kate to love anybody, so why not me? Whatever label you want to hang on it, she was willing to live with me. To love me, if you will. But she wouldn't marry me—that was the one thing she wouldn't do."

Because, Guy thought, Elm Circle and a quiet life where people didn't make fusses healed no wounds. The black-clad, noisy goings-on by which deaths were overcome in his own world were something else: there, she would have succeeded in burying Cermak. "She wasn't ready, I guess," Guy said, because he had to try to be kind. "That doesn't mean she never will be."

Elliott smiled, his teeth gleaming in his narrow face. "No, she never said never. Someday, when she felt safe—but in the meantime she had to have one foot out the door. So she's Cermak's widow, not Sterling's wife. I *told* you this was the story of my shame." His laugh was not without humor. "The absurd little pension check she gets at her precious independent post office box is a measure of her logic. I'm— well, I'm far from poverty-stricken, as you must know. So, at the barest minimum of a wife's financial rights, she'd do hugely better by marrying me." He leaned back in his chair, examining his hands. "As I said, it's a story with no relevance to the law."

People like Elliott and Kate seemed to believe the only things illegal were the crimes reported in the big news stories. Neither of these lawless innocents, Guy concluded, seemed to have been given any pause by laws against fraud— which collecting that absurd little pension check might be if Kate was now Elliott's common-law wife, which was possible. So all Elliott saw was a small social problem: Kate was settled in in this community, and that would end if it came out that she wasn't properly married.

"I realize it's hard to think of an appropriate reply," Elliott said, "when I tell you Kate's willing to sacrifice a fortune just to avoid marrying me. But you should try. It's only proper."

"Oh, nonsense. You know it's a symbol—the name and the check both. The woman's lame, so she needs a crutch."

"Uh huh. Nice try, old boy."

"Look, you can't expect complete recovery from—so much." Guy wanted desperately to help if he could. All this would have been difficult for anyone, but for Elliott to have to tell it must have been wracking. "She just can't take a chance."

"Stop it, Guy. The truth is, she could—and you know it. If she went this far, she could've been coaxed the rest of the

80

way. The sad fact is, I just didn't provide whatever it took to get that last bit of trust restored."

It was true, and Guy knew it and was wrung with pity—and some guilt for his easy assumptions about Elliott as the man who had everything. Kate *could* have been "coaxed the rest of the way," because she was not a life-denying woman. She was soft, but not really fearful.

"I couldn't manage it," Elliott said sadly. "That final correction."

The last, ungainly word jarred, wrenching Guy out of sympathy because it was so very wrong. "Inequities can be 'corrected.' But people aren't—they're healed. When enough scar tissue forms. And you have no control over that process," he added, guilty again, this time of hypocrisy.

"Oh yes you have. Not if you insist on thinking in terms of law—that big, blunt instrument that never reaches all the personal corners. But if you have enough imagination and enough courage—"

"They won't put Humpty Dumpty together again either. There's no way back to innocence—nobody's a virgin twice."

"You can balance the books," Elliott insisted. "You can make it all come out even." He rose and led the way out of the room.

He continued the argument on the stairs and Guy let him because it was probably good for him. But arguments like that were like Elliott's no-real-use sideline attic hobbies. They had nothing to do with getting on from what couldn't be helped to what could—which was Guy's way of dealing with a sense of failure.

Elliott glanced at the kitchen doorway as they stood in the downstairs hall. The dishwasher hummed faintly, but there was no other sound. "Kate must have gone out. Maybe to Mrs. Bethany's. But there'll be a note."

Guy shook his head as though declining an offer. He said aloud that he had to get along anyhow, but he wondered silently at the strangeness of, for the first time, not wanting

81

to see Kate. He thought of his grandmother making a sign to ward off the evil eye—was it like that, a fear of contact with so much death? If so, he forgave himself: he was overextended, an emotional bank from which there'd been steady withdrawals and no deposits. He wasn't completely out of resources yet, but he was in poor shape, he decided, to hang around with the demon-haunted tonight. If he needed any society at all, it was that of Toots Cantor, who was not a simple man but was an explainable one. A man who did things for reasons, and on the record.

At the door Elliott said good night and then, abruptly, shook Guy's hand. It was an oddly formal thing to do, and without precedent or explanation. *Curiouser and curiouser,* Guy thought, standing still just outside the door and taking the chill-edged air like medicine. Finally he told himself that you just couldn't figure everything out right away, and thus let himself off the hook for now.

6

Justice for Everybody

By mid-morning of the next day, restored by sleep and a few hours in a milieu where there was a book you were supposed to go by when there was a problem to solve, Guy had checked out the recorded statement of Jacques Berriault about his parting from Hilary Bridge on the night of the murder. Or one of the statements, anyway: the taxpayers were not paying Silvestri to solve a murder case, so he didn't feel obliged to read the entire transcript of the interrogation. But a colloquy on page 5, where the questioner had been establishing the scene of the crime, would do:

Q. Now, about this door to the garage from the house, Mr. Berriault—

A. Yes, it is in the kitchen. The garage was not there at the beginning, you see. So this was the back door. But now it goes directly into the garage. In the winters, this is most convenient.

Q. Right. Now, when you left the house, was that door locked on the house side?

A. Yes, most certainly. Hilary bolted it, in addition. This he did whenever we would both be out.

Q. Did he lock it that particular night, Mr. Berriault?

A. Oh, yes. He did. I stood just behind him. I saw him. We were speaking together at the time. As we prepared to leave.

Q. Okay. Then you both came out the front way, right? Now, who locked the front door?

A. I did. Hilary went across the lawn to the garage. To start the car while he waited for Elliott—Mr. Sterling.

Q. I see. And you're sure you closed it securely, sir?

A. Oh yes, I am certain. For it is a habit with me, always to try the door after I have closed it.

Maybe a defense attorney would uncover some innocent reason for a discrepancy, or argue that Jacques had simply been confused by a leading question. Anything could happen. But there it was: the Jacques who was on record here had not come from the garage, looking like a slow-motion film to the watching Florence.

As for the garage door's being visibly and unnecessarily locked, it was neither correct nor wise for Lt. Silvestri to make judgments. But he could seek explanations. He pulled a scratch pad over and wrote down those that occurred to him:

1. Habit
2. Insurance
3. To keep Jacques from investigating
4. To explain Jacques's not investigating

He doodled a neat rectangle around the first two and another around Numbers 3 and 4, thus setting apart from each other the two kinds of explanations, simple and subtle. Neither of the "simples" eliminated Jacques: he was the only person besides Hilary Bridge himself who would have developed a

84

habit of twisting that handle on the garage door to the "lock" position, and thus the only one who might have done it unthinkingly after leaving Hilary in the garage. The second category was a little larger—suspects who were not sure of the effects of carbon monoxide and so might have locked the garage door just in case Hilary Bridge got that far in an escape attempt—but Jacques was presumably no expert and thus fit there, too. As for the "subtles," the first eliminated Jacques, but the second pointed at him exclusively. So the "subtles" canceled each other, and the "simples" left a preponderance of inference that at least did not undermine Toots Cantor's choice of Jacques as chief suspect.

Guy tore off the page and deposited it in the trash basket. So much for mathematics, which was all very well in its place; but you didn't find a murderer by averaging the possibilities. Which wisdom Toots Cantor probably owned already, but Guy would mention it, just in case.

But the first word he had that day with the Sixth Precinct's homicide chief was of a more dramatic nature. Toots Cantor came by personally to tell Guy that Jacques Berriault had attempted suicide by smashing the light bulb in his bedside lamp and sawing at his wrists with the jagged glass. The result was lots of blood but little serious effect. Except that this morning Jacques was removed from the nursing home, which was not equipped for that sort of thing, to the psychiatric ward of Lambert University Hospital, where the light bulbs were encased in wire cages for precisely that reason.

"The psycho ward," Cantor repeated. "So it'll end up with 'unsound mind' anyway."

"Maybe not. He never spent any time in a psychiatric ward before, did he?"

"No." Cantor peered from under knitted brows. "The funny part is, I was kind of coming around to buying his story, you know?" He hesitated, then went whole hog: "Fact is, I still do, Guy. Could be you were right. Going by the book, he sure looks like the one, but when you listen to him—hell, homo or not, he really is busted up. I mean, I've broke the news to widows. And to tell you the honest truth, he don't act so different."

"It's possible for love and murder to coexist," Guy said, thinking of *Each man kills the thing he loves.*

"I know, but I just thought I'd mention it. You always put such stock in—"

"Right now," Guy interrupted, "I'd put most stock in opportunity, if I were you. And, of course, motive."

"Well, what in hell do you think I'm doing? We already queried the Waterville, New York, police—that's where this girls' college is that Professor Bridge used to teach at. It was only three, four years ago, so it was worth asking did he make any enemies there."

Guy said it surely couldn't hurt. He did not say that this beating of bushes in upstate New York when the bird was in Cantor's hand was a little uncharacteristic. Jacques had never taught at Merrivale College in Waterville, New York. So any motive dug up at that small, exclusive school for the daughters of the rich wouldn't do Jacques's cause any harm, and at least Lt. Cantor looked very open-minded. Guy decided wisdom lay in holding his tongue, for now. He wished Toots luck and urged him to keep in touch.

A short time later a law-enforcement man who had also been urged to keep in touch with Buxford's Lt. Silvestri telephoned and spoke at length and with assurance. Almost immediately thereafter, Guy phoned Tim Whistler. And late that afternoon there was an apparently chance encounter between the detective and the black students' leader on Buxford's Common. They paused to converse politely, then strolled in the open, away from everyone but a couple of tricycling toddlers. Then Tim continued on his way home from the Lambert campus to Elm Circle, and Guy went his opposite way toward the out-of-town newspaper stand, where he bought some papers from upstate New York.

That evening a taxi appeared at the Nathan Avenue entrance of the black students' Residence. Logan Ayres, a Lambert junior from New Jersey, departed the building. Apparently for good, because suitcases and sports equipment and guitar departed with him—but none of the house's inhabitants showed in the doorway to see him off. A few minutes later a Logan Ayres, 20, was arrested by the Boston police's special squad and charged with possession and sale of certain narcotics. Since Ayres gave no local address, only one of the Boston morning newspapers took any notice—and that one carried a five-line story, which referred to Ayres as a "New Jersey youth."

Not all the newspapers in town had a mind to be obliging, however. That same morning Guy was notified—at third hand, through devious but heretofore always reliable channels—that the "underground" newspaper which was sold openly throughout Buxford was about to run an exposé on "the Hilary Bridge case," hinting that "repressive forces" had murdered the "activist professor" and then spirited Jacques Berriault away to keep him from naming names. By early afternoon Guy had taken three telephone calls from politicians who had also heard of the forthcoming "exposé" and two from local clergymen who specialized in the drugs-and-runaway scene. By late afternoon he had a copy of the first installment of the story. It was well written, in the excitable and exciting style currently fashionable in all journalism. The writer, untrammeled by either innate compulsion to accuracy or the control of an editorial hand, would up his piece with an apostrophe to Jacques ("somewhere behind locked doors that only cops have keys to") and a lively portrait of Lt. Harold Cantor, apparently believed to be the chief keyholder ("What could bridge the gap between a frail, gentle art teacher and this hulk of a man with a brow like Markham's 'Man With a Hoe'? Can anybody seriously expect justice for Jacques at Cantor's beefy hands?").

Not unexpectedly, Guy's final phone call of the day was from Toots Cantor, who had gotten hold of a copy of the Markham poem. Lying bravely, Guy assured Cantor that nobody took that sort of thing seriously. When he'd hung up, he swiveled around in his chair and typed out a brief note to what must be the world's only underground newspaper with a half-million-dollar capitalization. *Gentlemen,* he wrote, *I have read your query about the gap between Jacques and Lt. Cantor. What bridges it, you jerks, is the law. Yours for bringing down the Establishment, beginning with you.* He ripped the paper out of the typewriter and sailed it into the trash basket. Then he went home.

By Thursday night, then, Guy could safely be said to have been thoroughly restored to his identity. He certainly knew who he was when, at Elm Circle that evening, he approached the Experiment Perilous bookshop and saw Kate inside. He even knew, also, that what had kept him from wanting to see her again was not fear but anger.

Because suddenly he was not only seeing Kate but observing her—a little, shawled, helpless figure of resignation. She was listening to the flamboyant creature known as Dracula, and she looked old and spiritless, her head ready to bow to this or any other kind of nonsense. Guy thought of his sister Angela, who was about Kate's age and had four lively children. He didn't particularly admire Angie, whose profoundest worries seemed to be the possibility of varicose veins and the cost of a new Easter outfit—she was vain and silly, she made no difference to the world at large and possibly never would. But she was so alive, so available, so visible. Sadly, Guy walked between the rows of books toward the woman who would not finish with the past and so was not available to a future—the willfully invisible Kate, dodging the life she was clearly intended for by hiding among strangers. And even then, she lived with one foot out the door.

Kate was smiling, but she knew an angry man when she saw one: it was a wobbly smile, shy and apologetic. And Guy, seeing the appeasement and the readiness to flee, grew angrier still. He bestowed a short nod on Dracula, who was at least frankly a runaway. Dracula stared, interrupted in mid-discourse and too stoned to get back on course.

"I know Ellie told you," Kate said softly. "About me, I mean."

"I listened to a long story, if that's what you mean. It was all about once-upon-a-time."

Dracula said, "Oh, cool. Like, it's the only way. Once upon a time, there was. And now, we are." The slim, grimy hand shook a paperback decorated with something like hex symbols. "Unreal, man," the breathy, sexless voice intoned.

"Yeah. Look, go—uh—cast a spell somewhere, will you?" Guy turned to Kate. "It wasn't unreal. I know lots of stories like it, and they're all real as hell. What it was, though"—his voice sharpened—"was irrelevant. Nothing to do with here and now."

"That's too simple. It's just not so simple."

"Not if you're willfully complex." She was spinning her life away, weaving an intricate web when a single strand would be quite enough. And the pity was, it was a good strong thread—first-quality silk, sturdy, weight-bearing . . . "I'm a simple man," he told her furiously. "I like stories to have happy endings."

"Oh, Guy. Some just—don't."

"How do you know? When you're in the middle of it, you can't see the end." He waited, hoping her silence meant she knew at least that much, would admit to the error of summing up so soon.

She smiled. "Then you can't just order a happy ending, can you?"

"Nope. But I can get in there and do my damndest to arrange for one." Amazed, he found himself thinking of his father again. *I am the son of a good man* wrote itself on his mind and then he was no longer amazed: if Elliott Sterling's inheritance included a couple of valuable houses, Guy Silvestri's included a couple of pieces of valuable knowledge.

"Oh, Guy, I do wish—" Kate's voice snapped off like a twig on an icy morning. She gasped. "Dracula!"

Guy spun around like a hero in a western, and with a

similar intent. But Dracula was not marching toward them with menace. Dracula sought no confrontations, meant no harm to anyone—and looked up now, smiling innocently, when Guy said, "What in hell do you think you're doing?"

Slow motion, Dracula's gaze moved from the big rough man to the conical pile of torn paper on the floor. "I *have* to. You *said* I should cast a spell, don't you remember?"

Kate's hand moved out, staying Guy: the swift, unthinking gesture was typical, almost a conditioned reflex, of mothers of small children. It was executive, authoritative; but her voice was carefully gentle: "This isn't the right place for it, Dracula. I'm sorry, but you have to do it right, you know. Or it won't count."

Dracula looked sulky. "But that's how Red Beard did. I saw him." The childlike gaze surveyed the grownups, recorded their disbelief, and searched for substantiation. And then produced it: "So did Florence. You can just ask Florence." Everybody knew Florence. They could not fail to believe Florence.

Guy shook off Kate's hand and strode toward the sad creature, who was cross-legged before the would-be bonfire and who, though it seemed incredible enough, might actually have set fire to these paper scraps. Guy squatted and began to pick them up; after a moment, Dracula helped—either because the scene evoked nursery school tidying-up memories in a clouded brain or because this was a put-on that hadn't worked. It didn't really matter which, because nothing that could be said could make a difference. And nothing cold be done, because nothing had happened—no arson, no destruction of another's property. Guy looked at the paper tatters, which seemed too numerous to have come from only the book Dracula had been holding. Probably some of the bookshop's stock had gone into these preparations for either casting a spell or provoking a policeman. But that didn't matter either, because Kate, whose belief in some kind of

90

magic was even more pathetic than this creature's, would certainly be unwilling to charge Dracula with anything. And in any case, Pop Taylor back in New Rochelle would come up with some magic money to cover all costs—until Dracula either outgrew this or did something, sometime, the cost of which couldn't be covered.

Guy deposited the scraps in the trash basket and told Dracula to go on home—*Now!* He was not surprised when he was obeyed promptly. Then he looked at Kate, who could not be protected against this because she was so busy protecting herself against something else. Maybe Mama's God-in-His-infinite-wisdom knew best, Guy concluded: he coveted the woman, all right, but if she didn't or couldn't extricate herself from all this nonsense, he thought he could cease to envy Elliott Sterling.

"Oh, Guy, how awful. The poor child. Will he go home, do you think?"

"Probably." He hoped Mrs. Chandler's basement had a concrete floor. That was, presumably, where the reliable witness Florence had seen spells cast.

"Well. He's never been so . . . But he'll be all right tomorrow," Kate said.

Guy eyed her with open scorn. " 'That's too simple,' " he quoted. "Much too simple. In fact, the whole thing is—disgusting." Pleased, he saw that the look in her dark eyes now was certainly not resignation.

"I take it that includes me," she snapped.

"Well, does it?"

She bent her head, the brief flare of spirit vanished. "I don't like to be—what disgusts you, Guy."

"Don't be," he said, his voice unrelenting. Then he thought he'd better make it clear that there was a way out, one within her reach. "But what you coddle, you've got to take responsibility for."

"I have to—coddle—*something.*" Her voice was muffled.

"Sure," he said with pity. "But why not try something real?" Without waiting for an answer, he said good night. And then, because he had to, he said he'd see her soon.

He walked quickly across the Circle, saying *Goddammit* under his breath, ridiculously and helplessly. But when he neared the center, he remembered something more useful to do. He stopped and looked over his shoulder at Number 20—and sure enough, there was a nice little brick retaining wall, one that might have been made by a pair of professors playing Sunday workman, on the left hand of anyone coming up the driveway. It cast a shadow alongside, and the far end of it was lost to view; but even from here Guy could see enough of the rows of bricks, gradually diminishing as they approached the sidewalk, to establish a correlation with the increasing visibility of Jacques's trouser legs on that Tuesday night until finally he reached the sidewalk and the flibbertigibbet Florence saw his shoes. There was no room for doubt: Hilary Bridge's front-door light was not on now but it had been then, and it would have silhouetted Jacques when Florence looked from the window of the Perilous.

Guy said, "Double Scotch, please" before he was fairly in the door of the Grotto. He'd expected to see Jim Waterman, but it was Gus George himself who was tending bar. Guy took a seat at the far end. Gus produced the drink and the chaser, and finally a tentative, "Rough day, huh?"

Silvestri set his glass down half empty, offering a weary guess that the days would never get less rough. There was no sign of Jim. The only other customer at the bar was sitting at the ell-shaped section near the door; all that was distinguishable was a male figure, chunky and probably not young, studying a nearly finished glass of beer.

"You don't get to see Jacques Berriault, do you, Lieutenant?" Gus asked. "I like that kid. I was wondering how he's doing."

"Well, nobody stops me from seeing him. But I haven't had a hell of a lot of time lately."

"I guess. You seen this here 'Justice for Jacques' stuff the students been getting up? That just eats up more of your time, I guess."

"Not mine. The murder is the Sixth Precinct's headache." Guy eyed the heavy face then, and found it full of concern. "Nobody's been beating up on Jacques," he said gently. "You know better than that, Gus."

The restaurateur said he knew, but it was hard on the poor kid no matter how fair he got treated. Because, he added, looking at Guy with ill-disguised pleading, Jacques didn't murder anybody. For sure not Professor Bridge—not the way it was between them two.

"But they had a fight that night, before Jacques came over here," Guy said mildly. "Didn't you tell the police he was a little upset about it?"

"I said that, sure. But hell, Lieutenant, people get upset. They get in family fights, but that don't mean they kill each other."

"Nobody's charged Jacques with murder." Attracted by movement, Guy looked down the bar as the anonymous customer rose to leave. And then the entrance light picked out the round, chocolate-brown face of Detective Carrothers, who was attached to Headquarters but had on occasion been detached to aid the Human Relations Division. Guy's smile of recognition began before, a little too late, he realized his mistake.

" 'Night, Gus," Carrothers said quickly, pulling Gus George's attention away from the flustered Lt. Silvestri. Then he looked down the bar at Guy and added politely, "Good evening, sir."

Guy got the message, or anyway he thought he did. He concentrated fiercely on his drink, cursing his stupidity while he worked at arranging his face, and hoped for luck.

He got it: "You know Tom?" Gus George asked in mild surprise.

That much had been clear, alas; the quick-thinking Det.

Carrothers had seen that and tried to work with it. "Sort of," Guy admitted cautiously. "In the line of work."

"Oh, sure—he's caretaker over to the Residence now. I forgot. He just started there, not too long ago."

"That's right." It came out reasonably smoothly. But Guy thought he'd better change the subject before, without Tom Carrothers around to rescue him, he managed to mess up the whole undercover operation. He was turning out to be quite a cross for the force to bear: just the other day, he'd been shaken almost into dangerous admissions by even the guileless Florence, prattling on about the Buxford Elm . . . He smiled encouragingly at Gus George and eased away from the area of Lt. Silvestri's peculiar ineptitude. "So you figure Jacques Berriault's not guilty. Then who's your candidate? Somebody killed Hilary Bridge, you know," he argued with Gus's look of protest. "And somebody's got to find out who it was."

Gus poured himself a small glass of vermouth, agreed that criticism alone wasn't really fair, and opined that being a cop was no bed of roses. But he couldn't help much, he said. The only time he'd opened his mouth to make a suggestion, they'd laughed him right off the stage.

"Is that so? What suggestion?"

"You serious?"

"Sure I'm serious. If you've got a suggestion, I'm in the market. You're around here all the time, you've got a damn good idea what goes on every day—"

"*And* night." Gus grinned. "Well, okay, if you're not really putting me on. And if I'm not going to get somebody in trouble."

"I don't go in for put-ons. But I'm a police officer—you know enough of us to know the rules."

"God knows I know cops," Gus said ruefully. "It's not your outfit, so it's not right to cry on your shoulder, but them drug squad boys sweep this place more often than a fussy housekeeper. Ever since the hippies come to the Circle." His face darkened. "Adonio, you know"—he cocked his head at the wall behind him, adjoining the beauty salon—"he don't hold with the colored, so he blames everything on them. But your black boys down to the Residence been perfect gentlemen, far as I can see."

Guy thanked him, because it was clearly expected; the paternalism Tim Whistler didn't hear about wouldn't hurt him.

"Them hippies, that's something else," Gus continued. "I don't want you to think I got it in for them—"

"They do seem to have brought you some grief."

"Oh, well, if I got my guts in an uproar over every little pain in the ass . . ." Gus shook his head. "I'm not mad at the hippies, Lieutenant."

"But you think they had something to do with the murder?"

"Sort of. That's what I mean: Lieutenant Cantor laughed, but my idea is, *nobody* murdered Bridge. I know it sounds crazy, but if you knew how kinky some of them hippies get—"

Guy said, with real interest now, that he had an idea how kinky. And he didn't even need to make an effort not to laugh when he heard Gus's idea expounded: after the experience with Dracula tonight, the suggestion that Hilary Bridge could have died of a prank somehow gone wrong was not incredible. "Prank" was too innocent and old-fashioned a word for what Gus George meant, but could some sick experiment in fear, say, have gotten out of hand? He couldn't honestly dismiss the notion, Guy decided. The crazy severance from reality that seemed almost taken for granted, the playing about with symbolic dooms and imitation deaths— what if somebody had meant to dance on a brink and then fallen over?

"It makes you sick to think it could be," Gus George said slowly. "But it could, you know? They could've just forgot to come back and open the garage door, or something."

Elm Circle's hippies, at least, apparently tended toward self-destruction rather than turning it outward. But it was a psychiatric aphorism that the two were linked. Guy shook his head to the offer of a refill, and then he sat on over his empty glass, listening absently to Gus, who was the salt of the Buxford earth and should have felt safe—but was growing scared, Guy noted sadly. And one of the things that was likely to mean in the long run was that kind of thing Guy was tending to now—the precautionary reservation, the skepticism about the loose use of the term "hippies" for individuals who were not, after all, interchangeable—would become more and more difficult. But he could still do it, so he did, recalling that Elm Circle's hippies had reportedly been seen on Trowbridge Common at the crucial time. Which could let them out—unless the policeman who'd seen them was also identifying them loosely. . . .

"We even had a little hassle over the flag," Gus was saying. "We can't even keep it in the locker over by the Tree anymore. We have to bring it in every night nowadays, to keep it safe." He shook his head. "Seems hard to believe."

Guy said "Really?" and listened to a sketch of a minor molestation of Elm Circle's flag that had not changed anything and probably wasn't even meant to. All it had done was alarm the Circle, which had its ways and took them seriously: Ralph Adonio did flag duty on the three mid-week days and Gus did it on Friday, Saturday, and Monday, with the Colonel filling in on Sunday—and the schedule was as devoutly adhered to as the ritual of a hospital operating room. Which was silly perhaps, but nevertheless deserving of respect: when people got together to work something out, that in itself was valuable and important—certainly in the eyes of anthropology student Silvestri.

"I know you heard about the Colonel's little—problem," Gus said. "But he hasn't missed a Sunday this year."

Guy returned the grin and said patriotism maybe brought out the best in all of us. He let the remark carry Gus—and,

96

a few minutes later, old Mr. Bethany, come in for a night-cap—off on a wave of reminiscences of "the service." They were talking about different wars, but the American citizen-soldier experience was apparently a seminal one, producing a lifetime's worth of anecdotes for each survivor. Guy excused himself and exited, hardly disturbing the flow.

He cut through the alley near the Circle's only apartment house, on his way to Park Street to flag a cab, pondering a comparison between the innocent ardor with which Adonio and Gus and the Colonel took on the flag-raising responsibilities for their community and the firm efficiency with which Tim Whistler directed the patrolling of his. The difference between a comfortable society, which had already paid off for its members and was served out of gratitude, and a besieged one, surrounded by enemies and served out of hope and courage, resulted in very different specific manifestations of patriotism. But they must also have qualities in common. Whatever those qualities were—if somebody hadn't taken a close look at them already, maybe M.A. candidate Silvestri should?—they made some odd lumpings: Ralph Adonio seemed as far a cry, in terms of personality, from Gus George as Logan Ayres had proved to be from Tim Whistler. Yet one thing stood out: a kind of groupness, a membership-attitude maintained for reasons admirable or loathsome, out of kindliness or rapaciousness, but in any case different in some clear and serious way from the spirit informing the unilateral men like Elliott Sterling (and from all indications, Hilary Bridge), who, whether they acted for good or ill, always really acted separately.

It was a notion, that was all so far. And graduate school wasn't like Headquarters, were you could follow up a hunch at least a little way and see what came of it. Guy would have to know a great deal more about groupness and separateness before he could even consider doing a study on the two kinds of patriotism, or whatever. Risk-taking was simply not the academic world's thing.

But tomorrow was his day in the academic world, so if he was going to investigate the notion he could get a reading list, at least. Settling back in the taxi's rear seat, Guy decided to see what fellow grad student Jim Waterman had to say about the idea. Unless, of course, Jim had joined the Justice for Jacques movement and thus couldn't be seen talking to a police officer. The double life, Guy concluded, wasn't comfy even when it was virtuous. Resigned, he set about traveling to his virtuous bed.

7

Silvestri's Double Life

I t's only when you can see the whole story—as Guy had pointed out to Kate Sterling—that you can draw conclusions. So on Friday, April 8, when Silvestri paid a brief morning visit to his office and then took off to be a student in Boston, he was being part of a pattern and not an observer of it. He had no idea the day would be a watershed, a turning point, maybe even the end of innocence. But it was, if not the Bar Mitzvah, at least the day he began his studies for it.

The beginning events of the day took place entirely without him: Guy was not in anyone's picture when the police in Tewksport, a suburb twenty minutes by the Beltway from Buxford, received an early-morning phone call from Mrs. Ralph Adonio reporting—in a tearful voice that struggled for dignity—that her husband had not come home Thursday night. In Boston a desk officer might have advised her to take two aspirins and call back in a couple of days. But there are advantages to life in a small town: the Tewksport policeman knew Mrs. Adonio—a sweet-faced, nervously pretty little woman with two pretty little daughters—and he knew that though even in decorous, expensive Tewksport husbands sometimes stayed out all night without coming to harm, Adonio was just not that kind of husband. So the Tewksport officer believed Mrs. Adonio had something real to be frantic about, and he was moved to do what he could. One of the things he could do was to call Buxford and ask that somebody go by Adonio's place of business, where the phone had not been answered since Thursday afternoon.

An index card pasted on the glass door of the beauty salon in Elm Circle recorded that R. Adonio, with a Tewksport telephone number, was prop. of this establishment. Under that, a neatly typed line advised that in an emergency the key could be obtained from the Grotto Restaurant next door. In that climate of severe winters any snowstorm could render the Beltway impassable and so create a transportation crisis for a nonresident shop-owner just when it was also creating a roof or pipe crisis at his shop. Thus it was in any entrepreneur's interest to provide the authorities with a means of entrance less devastating than the Fire Department's hatchets, and most people who lived any distance from their place of business had evolved some such custodial key arrangement.

When Gus George was applied to for Adonio's key late Friday morning, the restaurateur felt no obligation to protect his neighbor from the incursion of a Sixth Precinct patrolman. But Gus did feel a certain curiosity. Ptl. Donahue said only that it was a routine matter and continued to hold out a patient palm, though. So Gus shrugged, punched his cash register open, and dug Adonio's key from the miscellany at the back of the drawer.

"Pursuant to instructions received," as Ptl. Donahue put it in his report, he entered the business premises of R. Adonio and "proceeded" through the silent length of the shop. It had

100

been swept and tidied for the night; like the closed blinds, the bare formica surfaces bespoke a prop. both neat and thorough. The cash register, as empty and dust-free as the other equipment, stood unmolested beside the phone on the glass counter near the door.

Turning a right-angled corner at the back of the shop, Ptl. Donahue found himself abruptly cast out of pink prettiness into whitewashed back-room utility—and there he all but stumbled over the body. Ralph Adonio lay, crumpled from falling but otherwise not visibly injured, almost parallel to the flimsy wall dividing the back room from the shop proper. The only thing even faintly disorderly about him was his tweed sports coat, which was slightly rucked up under his hips as though he'd not quite finished donning it when he fell. The white cotton working jacket for which he had exchanged it hung on a wire hanger along the side wall.

Donahue examined the fallen figure only closely enough to be sure the man was dead, and then inspected the rest of the premises enough to be sure he was alone in them. Nobody was hiding in the storeroom that began after a second right-angled turn just beyond Adonio's head. Donahue made his cautious way down the narrow aisle between neatly stacked cartons, which filled the storeroom right up to the back door leading to the alley. Having ascertained that the door was locked and no key was in sight, Ptl. Donahue retreated the way he had come, noting that in that crowded space where even a small scuffle would have major effect, nothing appeared to have been disturbed. In fact, the only thing visible that had not been tucked in and/or put away was a package from the Plymouth Linen Supply Co. perched on one of the stacks of cartons; the flimsy paper was torn open at one end, but the towels inside the package were still neatly folded. Coming out of the storeroom's tidy ignorance of death a few feet away, Donahue again suffered something of a visual shock at sight of the body. He skirted it carefully, and went out the way he'd come in.

Ptl. Donahue's call to the Sixth Precinct was like ink soaking into a blotter—only it ran farther, and in more directions, than Donahue (or even some of his superiors) expected. For Adonio, it turned out, was of interest to many people with specialized knowledge. The news soaked through branches and subbranches of all the local police Tables of Organization, and then seeped outward: the big stars among narcotics investigators were, of course, the federal men; but Boston's area squad took in Buxford, too, and there were other regional squads, regular and ad hoc. Narcos abounded in the area, and more than one group of them had had an interest in Ralph Adonio.

The problem became Toots Cantor's because a search of the body revealed an absence of keys, including the ones that must have been used to lock the back door. (It also revealed the presence of a large amount of money in small bills, but that was promptly impounded by the narcos.) When, in midmorning, Adonio's white convertible Oldsmobile was found parked in the far reaches of the parking lot at the Merritt Library, Cantor's proprietorship was confirmed. For the car's keys, on a ring with a number of others—which proved to include those for the front and back doors of the beauty salon—were lying on the floor of the convertible's back seat.

But if the physical evidence of the surroundings were such as to launch Cantor into action, the physical evidence of the body was such as to stop him before he got off the ground. Because all the medical examiner would say about the cause of Ralph Adonio's death was "heart failure." The good doctor admitted to a hunch that nature had not caused Adonio's heart to fail, but it was no more than a hunch; pressed, he said irritably only that this one would be a stinker and he couldn't possibly say when he'd know, or what.

"You mean it could be natural, Doc?" Toots was incredulous. And unless Adonio had for some reason driven his car around the Circle to the Merritt Library, left all his keys there, and come back into his shop (how? and if it was open, how did he lock it again?) to lie down and die—Toots was entitled to incredulity.

"It *could* be natural," the doctor said stiffly. "Theoretically, a massive infection could do it. Meningitis, or a wild polio. Lots of diseases, if you assume the most virulent possible form of any of them, could give you this effect. Of course, you'd also have to assume the fellow felt deathly sick and still functioned normally." The doctor shook his head. "The hell with that. It's got to be chemical."

"You mean some kind of poison?"

"For God's sake, Cantor, I don't know. Not yet I don't, anyway." Briskly, he repacked his bag, his eyes fierce because he was a man who liked to know. "If you want to understand, think of when you spray a wasp. You ever watch how it dies? There's a swift-moving paralytic effect. It clobbers the nervous system and—"

"What's nerves got to do with it? You said—"

"I said heart failure. Which is what happens when you stop the machinery that keeps the heart pumping." The doctor snapped his bag on an announcement that he had no time to deliver lectures on physiology. *They'd* know what he knew as soon as *he* knew what he knew, he told them. And added grumpily that it would take he didn't know how long . . .

Toots Cantor, as frustrated and abashed as a bride left waiting at the church, telephoned Guy Silvestri that afternoon. But Cantor's message was only added to those already awaiting Lt. Silvestri, who was a base to be touched in case of any action at Elm Circle. He had been duly notified in the first spreading of the news, but nobody cared when he was reported unavailable.

Guy was always unavailable on Fridays when, until late afternoon, he was one of a weekly seminar of graduate students, one of a larger group haunting the library, one of a multitude browsing among the Jello molds in the graduate-student dining room. Only at sunset did Guy return to Buxford's police force—to stay all weekend, as a weekend off duty is not a matter of course for policemen.

It is a matter of course for students, many of whom manage to begin the weekend on Friday because a good many faculty members do: only those of very lowly status seem to hold Friday classes. Guy was listening to Jim ·Waterman discoursing on this point over lunch in the graduate-school dining room, at approximately the moment when narco men began a microscopic examination of Ralph Adonio's car.

". . . and I might point out that hardly anyone above assistant professor has classes on Monday either." Waterman sugared his coffee and salted his stew with the absentminded speed of one always pressed for time. His Ph.D. would come from Lambert when it came, but in the meantime he did a lot of hasty commuting between this side of the river—for the state university's community relations projects—and Lambert's superior library in Buxford. "The academic scene is full of self-proclaimed dedication, but a lot of it's very part time."

Guy smiled. "I did notice a gap between fact and image. Like, most faculty don't seem to me to work very hard. But, to a man, they think they do." He considered, chewing on a roll. "It lends an air of sincerity to their complaints."

"Their feelings are valid, though, Guy."

"But you just said—"

"Valid, but misplaced. The underlying legitimacy lends support, you might say, to their illegitimate complaints." Jim was enough of a teacher already to detect noncomprehension. "Okay, example. College professors were once underpaid, but they aren't now. Though they proclaim constantly that they are."

"Oh, I don't know. Calculated in hours on the job, maybe you're right. But—"

"You're about to tell me," Jim said briskly, "about all that

104

learning they've acquired. Plus the thinking they do between the two-hour seminars once a week."

"I had something like that in mind," Guy admitted.

"Well, a plumber has to learn a lot, too. And do *you* charge for thinking about a case when you're not on duty?" Jim brandished a slice of bread in an oratorical gesture. "You see? You've been driven to spouting idiotic arguments on their behalf. Now why is that, do you suppose?"

"Because I've been brainwashed?"

"My contention is, it's because you're moved by a certain sympathy. You sense the legitimate complaint, though the substance of their particular complaint is not legitimate."

Guy eyed him with interest. "Go on. What's this underground appeal, the legitimate cry under the bad logic?"

"Ah, you may well ask. One of the most powerful of all appeals. A cry for freedom."

"I see it all now. A faculty in bondage tugs at my heartstrings." Guy kept his tone expressionless.

"You think I'm putting you on? The academic world is—if you look at it objectively, and by golly, you'd better—well, it's the least democratic society in the whole country, I should think."

"You've never been on a police force."

"So? Merit systems are not unknown to police forces, are they? Nor are other objective measures for deciding whether a man should be promoted. And if he isn't and should be, there are grievance procedures, aren't there? Like, what would happen if you decided capriciously not to promote a man, or something?"

"I suppose I'd get into some kind of trouble." Guy could think of instances where caprice had not incurred trouble, but Jim had made his point and was entitled to see it on the scoreboard. "But academic promotions are governed by procedures too, aren't they?"

"The procedures inform a guy he hasn't got tenure, if

that's what you mean. But decisions like awarding tenure aren't required to have recorded reasons." Waterman warmed to his argument, enough so that he even halted his brisk collecting of the empty dishes. "In what business corporation, for example, can a worker be fired for no stated reason? But if a university doesn't choose to renew some cat's contract, it doesn't have to tell him why."

Guy conceded the point with a nod. It was all largely true: a committee recommended promotion for a faculty member on certain stated grounds, but the committee didn't need to say why Professor A rather than Professor B should be promoted. "I know it's true of grants and awards and all that sort of thing. You have to be recommended, you can't just win them."

"Right. A hell of a lot depends on currying the favor of the right people, or at least not irritating anyone who might drop a negative word when your name comes up some time. It works the other way too, of course—as witness the charmed life of our Florence."

Guy looked puzzled. "You mean because she dropped out and came back? But Lambert is notoriously tolerant of students who do that."

"Sure. But not if they come back and then turn around and do it again. Yet Lambert managed to take care of Florence the double dropout. Somebody up there did, anyway—though this time they couldn't arrange scholarship money for her." Waterman grimaced. "Hell, *I* don't object when the Fates smile on Florence. Who could, for God's sake? It seems she had a real bad, sick year somewhere back there—I gather from Ann Price—and the kid bounced back, but it took her more than one bounce to do it. Okay, good for her, right?"

"I have a feeling Florence's biography isn't really the point of your remarks. But what's the pitch? What's the pretty girl being used to sell this time?"

"Oh, wow, you *are* the suspicious type consumer. Okay, but I'm not up to any tricks, really. It's just that Florence's case makes the point clear—the name of the academic game is favor, not law."

"The scene does sort of remind me of kings and courtiers."

Jim finished piling his tray and collected his books. "A duchy, maybe. Each department its own little satrapy? Hell, I don't know—I'm not a political scientist. All I do know is, it's nothing like the outside world, which at least *pretends* to democracy."

"It's an interesting thought. I'm not sure where it goes, but—"

Jim interrupted, then changed his mind before he said anything coherent. Then, abruptly, he changed his mind again. "It goes right to your territory, that's where. I didn't like to mention that, but if you can't see it yourself I guess I'd better."

Guy suppressed a sigh. "Is this going to be about Jacques Berriault? Are you clamoring for Justice for Jacques? You ought to know better, Jim."

"I do. And I'm not clamoring for anything, because justice here—real justice,—might well consist of just leaving it lay. I'm not at all sure Jacques didn't knock off Hilary Bridge." He hesitated. "What I'm saying is, if he did, it was probably for a reason I can damn well understand."

"What reason would that be?"

"Well, in the light of what we've been saying, Guy, ask yourself—how in the hell else could poor Jacques ever have gotten out of Hilary's clutches?"

"Is there any evidence that he wanted to?"

"Oh, I haven't got a footprint to show you, sleuth. But look at it from Jacques's point of view—in the light of the feudal society he lives in, and assuming Jacques is no hero. I mean, Lambert is the first place he ever taught, and with one word from Hilary, it could be the last. So, if you were Jacques, would you venture to displease Professor Bridge?"

Guy eyed him with interest. "Maybe not. But does that leave no choice but murder?"

"In the real world, it doesn't. But people are used to choices, out there. Whereas—" Jim stood up and lifted his tray. "I've got to run, Guy. Poverty is hell on conversation."

"I know. It's okay."

"But think about Jacques in his context, is all I mean. Not only timid, but without a vote."

Guy said "Right" and watched Jim Waterman deposit his tray and take off at a lope. The graduate students certainly were the kitchen boys at the academic world's court. Sometimes quite literally—as when Jim Waterman had carried out the garbage for the occupants of the small apartment house abutting on Elm Circle. Jim had been janitor there for two of his postgraduate years, Guy remembered. But those financial vicissitudes had been, after all, a matter of choice: it would be hard, but Jim still could have ditched the hunt for the Ph.D. Jacques Berriault, however, was farther along and had even more time invested in the only thing he could earn a living by, and Jacques had never lived outside the academic duchies. It was true, Guy had to admit, that to the oppressed, murder was not a last resort. In fact, it might even be the next step after a quarrel.

The image of a younger Jacques, flattered and almost certainly tempted by the artistic beauties of Hilary Bridge's home, stayed with Guy all the time he was making his way across the campus to the parking lot. Jim's suggestion added up to an ingenious explanation of the murder of Hilary Bridge—if not as tempting, perhaps, as Gus George's had been—and it also represented a triumph for the intuitional, or non-detail-accumulating, approach to detective work. That was more satisfying than matching alibis to determine who could have been where at which minute. The only thing that could be said for the latter was that it worked; any time the former could be shown to, Guy would embrace it with enthusiasm.

He was educable, he told himself with cheerful approval while he steered through the traffic toward the bridge. In fact, he could even learn more than Jim Waterman had intended to teach. Driving slowly through the narrow streets on the Buxford side of the river, Guy considered, a little wistfully, how nice it would be to have justice not abstract but custom-tailored. So that it would be defined as Jim (and apparently Elliott, who might have seen what Florence had seen but was a strategist, as the artless Florence was not) preferred to define it—to mean a satisfactory answer for someone you were sorry for.

But how wise you'd have to be to run the world that way. You'd have to be able to judge, right away, whether Hilary Bridge had been enough of an oppressor and Jacques enough oppressed to sanction overlooking murder. The need for that much instant wisdom had not seemed daunting to Jim, but it daunted Guy, he decided as he drew up beside Buxford police headquarters. He believed in playing a hunch, but not without due respect for everything else—perhaps, he concluded, because he just couldn't manage a Watermanian degree of confidence in his hunches. He left the paraphernalia of scholarship in the car and went into the dreary little building where intuitions were strictly unofficial.

An hour later he was wondering ruefully whether the Adonio case represented his punishment for being tempted to play Hercule Poirot. Because this one was all plot and no character. And it was rife with bureaucratic angles besides, bearing promise of endless reports to read and remember —all stuffed with the kind of abundant detail that was interesting only if you liked contemplating how all the little wheels turn inside a watch. Some of the precise, detailed, attested-to certainties already in the reports had been on file for more than a year. And there were enough of them to make your head swim: though Guy had not been entirely unaware of subterranean activity—of the kind that had provided the tip-off about Logan Ayres of the Residence, for example—he still felt as though he'd blundered into an ant-hill.

A very angry anthill. For an enormous number of the man-hours of those who specialized in illicit drug dealing had gone into what was now a case against a corpse. No one had more readily believed Mrs. Adonio's assurances ("He's *always* home by eight on Thursday nights. He reads the girls their bedtime story") than the drug men, who knew all about the Plymouth Linen Supply Co. packages which were delivered on Wednesdays and contained more than towels.

It might be ironic that the pickup man who'd slipped in by the back door of Adonio's shop to collect this particular Thursday night's consignment had been unaware of the body lying beyond the turn of a wall a few feet away, but it was no surprise to the men who knew Adonio's habits best: *they* had known for some time that a net thrown over the beauty salon on a Thursday night would scoop in a messenger and the week's consignment. But that would be all they'd get— and Adonio would be home in Tewksport reading *The Wind in the Willows* and safe from any charge that had a chance of sticking. It was because a decision had been made, and a way devised, to zero in on the well-protected Ralph Adonio that each and every bill in the bundle of cash on Adonio's body (which was now proof, if it were needed, that the drug pickup man had not known of the murder) had been carefully marked by the undercover man who'd left the money for Adonio on Thursday. And that was where irony really began to hurt: an elaborately prepared case, neat and provable and the product of long and painstaking effort, now went nowhere because all it established was Adonio's guilt.

It had not been expected to stop there. Ralph Adonio had modeled himself on the old-time hoods in keeping his family unaware of where it was that Daddy really went a-hunting, so the idea had been that a live Adonio, confronted by the case against him, might well decide to cooperate. But now the planners had lost everything: there was nobody to arrest for the completed sale, and even the pickup man—who had been left unidentified in order to be sure Adonio wouldn't detect the surveillance—was now, though out of business at the beauty shop, free to make some new arrangements.

It was because the drug squad men had reason to be very, very angry that Guy Silvestri sat in on their Saturday-morning meeting. He thought it made sense, on behalf of the inhabitants of the Residence, to be wary of disappointed men who, needing something to hang all their past work on, might be tempted to look around Elm Circle a little desperately. So Guy sat, officially accepted but in fact ignored, among the purposeful strangers.

Of course they were not that: it was precisely because these men were not strangers to Lt. Silvestri that he had declined to sit under the Buxford Elm with Florence and chat about grass—and later had not perceived the presence of the undercover man Tom at the Grotto bar as accidental. Nevertheless, as Guy watched them collect the remains of their case that Saturday, he felt alien even while he also felt respectful of their performance. He had no desire to play their instruments, but he could see that, compared with him, they were virtuosos. For example, certain of the bills taken from Adonio's pocket exhibited microscopic evidence that the money had been in contact with Elm Circle's flag, which Adonio had duly turned over to Gus George at sundown on Thursday in accordance with the custom Silvestri had heard about—and, hearing, had been moved only to the conclusion that patriotism made strange bedfellows. Not much contribution, that, to abstract justice. And pretty poor performance, considered beside the contribution of Det. Tom Carrothers.

Tom had said all along, and assembled men were joyfully reminding each other (in the absence of Tom, who was still maintaining his role as houseman at the Residence), that the way Adonio picked up the money and carried it back to his shop right under Elm Circle's nose was by wrapping it in the flag. Quick and easy, and nobody would see anything remarkable even if Adonio was stopped on the way back from his civic chore—no matter how sharp-eyed the neighbor or how prolonged the chat.

Thus, on those Thursday mornings when the goods were ready (for the Plymouth Linen Supply routeman didn't manage total regularity: General Motors slips, too, and its production line isn't impeded by several varieties of cops), Adonio notified his buyer by the way he tied the rope after he'd raised the flag. The cleat on the flagpole was quite visible from almost anywhere in the Circle, so any shopper, moviegoer, or idling resident of Elm Circle could pause by the Tree, sometime during the day, long enough to slip the bills into the wooden locker under the white-painted bench. And be as unnoticed as Tom Carrothers had been when, that Thursday, he'd substituted the marked money.

That was how the agile hunters, with the aid of Tom and of "science"—also being noisily commended now in the crowded, smoky room—had almost trapped their agile prey, and it was as exciting as a game of cops and robbers. But Guy kept feeling somehow on the wrong side: somewhere inside him, some part of him preferred the lighter, larksome schemer to the heavy-booted, plodding figure of civil order who uncovered the schemes. At least, until Gus George's notion that Hilary Bridge had died of a "prank" rose from Guy's memory and restored some balance. For what these gung-ho men, reminiscent of coaches and locker rooms, were doing in their alien lifestyle was hunting the greedy who lived off the foolish—like the young who began with the fun of it all and then had to climb painfully out of a deep, dark hole. Or die. So virtue was on the side of these hunters, even if they seemed to Silvestri more fascinated by the means than mindful of the end. Maybe that couldn't be helped, he thought uncomfortably. Maybe when you spent all your time and talents in a contest, the contest inevitably became more important than the reason for it.

However, Lt. Silvestri had not lost sight of his own reason for being there. And if the drug pickup procedure he heard outlined was so elaborate it made his head ache—a detailed, ingenious arrangement, but still material for the Appendix rather than the book—the implied profile of the pickup man increased his headache to the point of migraine. For nothing in those Thursday exercises excluded the inhabitants of the Residence: everything that applied to Elm Circle familiars, and everything that applied to the sub-set "student," also applied to them. Perhaps would be even rather willingly applied to them—and even by Tom Carrothers. Because the predilection or prejudice or whatever it was, Guy thought, did not really have much to do with color: Lambert, blundering into brotherhood, had made the black students "super-gown"—and thus created a backlash that Tom, who was clearly counted by these men as their colleague, might well share. Ralph Adonio's death had altered their timetable, making it necessary now to reel in the prey instead of giving him more rope—and *that* made it desirable that someone a Buxford jury might convict be on the hook to be reeled in. A scapegoat hunt, conscious or otherwise, looked all but inevitable in the circumstances.

Guy's best hope, he decided as he left them, was to alter the circumstances—at least to the extent of avoiding an abrupt confrontation between a frustrated narco and a sullen black student, with both of them calling on all their hostilities for protection. He worried this picture, which kept growing larger and clearer, until he got home. Then he said the hell with worrying and called his boss, who was charged by the mayor and City Council to preserve, protect, and defend "human relations" in Buxford. After a couple of hours of phone calls and of argument, persuasion, and all but blackmail, Guy won—though probably only because it was Saturday night and he could outwait his boss, who had a wife and a pair of theater tickets.

But what mattered was, he'd won. Elated, Guy called Tim Whistler and began a similar process, this time to arrange the other half of the proposition that the black students be

113

present at the drug men's meeting the next day. To cooperate if they would. To be accused, if there was any evidence that justified it. But in any case to be called in, at least on the policing of their own people.

And in no case to be kept under surveillance at the Circle any longer without their leader's knowledge. "We just can't afford that," Guy had told his boss. "They can't take it, and they won't."

"But you know those narcos. Secrecy is a religion with them. And how do we know, maybe they're right?"

"They're not, not this time anyway. Listen, if anybody at the Residence has been involved with Adonio, we've either got them for it or we don't, and we'll know everything we have on that tomorrow. When, if the kids have to hear it, they'll hear it from a black man. And if they're not in the business now, they're hardly going to start after they've been told we're watching—after all, they have no way of knowing if what we tell them about is *all* we're doing." Guy drew a long breath. "So if the idea is to cut off the drug trade at the Circle, this can help and it can't hurt. But if the narcos are looking out for their box score first, it doesn't make sense to let them do it at Community Relations' expense. All we need is screams from Lambert that we're leaning on black kids, and then—"

"Never mind. I can imagine."

That feat of imagination, by the official appointed by people who needed the votes of Lambert liberals, won Guy his point. He could bring the black boy to the meeting tomorrow, and nobody would get salty about it; Guy had his boss's word for that.

Tim Whistler took longer to persuade. He also had to be dealt with in person, his initial outrage absorbed and his angry sarcasm parried in a face-to-face encounter.

During which Guy lost his temper eventually. "For Christ's sake, will you quit acting like a kid?" he blurted.

"When it comes to juvenile behavior, the cops—"

114

"I know, I know. But that's no excuse. Do you want to lose a war because you're too busy slugging it out in the barracks?"

"Will you tell me please, oh honored elder, just how you figure those pigs are in my barracks?"

Guy tried breathing deeply. It worked. "Who do you suppose winds up most often at the paying-and-paying end of the drug trade? Yeah." He looked at Tim. "Fourteen-year-old kids in some ghetto."

"I don't need a lecture on the evils of racism," Tim said softly.

"No, but you need a lecture on who's the enemy. Look, no matter how these officers act or talk or anything else, what they're up to will keep that stuff away from those kids. And *sure* they're not doing it because they care about the people at the Residence, but is it good or bad for you if you've got a busy joy-peddler in your midst? Was Logan Ayres an asset or a liability to your cause?"

"Well, I answered that at the time, didn't I?" Tim flashed his sudden smile. "Here you are, overreacting again."

"In about one minute—"

"Police brutality," the student chanted, dancing away.

"Okay, okay. You want me to pick you up tomorrow?"

"By 'you,' I assume you mean our delegation."

"What?" Guy clutched at his hair. "*What* delegation?"

"Oh come on, grow up. You don't think I'd leave myself open to—"

"To what? Do you seriously think somebody's going to beat you up?"

"Oh, wow. Neither a diplomat nor a politician, he."

"What in hell does that mean?"

"It means," Tim said placidly, "I'm not about to get myself in a spot where anybody can say I got bought by the cops. Or any reasonable facsimile thereof." He smiled. "Yeah, 'oh!' You're slow, but you do dig. Eventually."

"How many is a delegation?" Guy asked wearily. He told

himself to keep punching; with any luck this could be his last fight of the day. "I come marching in there with a squad of you kids, all breathing fire, and I might as well leave town."

In the end, he beat the number down to three: any less than that was politically impossible for Tim, Guy had to concede. He left then and went straight home to bed. Admittedly, some strict constructionist might think he ought to notify his boss that there would be a delegation of three, which didn't quite fit with the image of Lt. Silvestri shepherding a single lad—a little like Youth Day at City Hall. But it was awfully late, and whatever Guy intuited about his boss's image of tomorrow's proceedings, no number had actually been specified in their phone conversation. Besides, the way had already been smoothed, Guy was sure. And people ordered to swallow the presence of one black student would manage to swallow two more. Guy hoped.

He was deep in the velvet hopefulness of sleep when the telephone yanked him out of it. A silent scream of protest in his head echoed each clang of the bell, inches from his ear. He stopped the pain by picking up the phone. "Hello?" He tilted his watch to try to see the time.

"Hello, is this Guy Silvestri?" It was a girl's voice, a voice with a smile.

"Yes." He made out the time at last: twenty minutes to four.

"Were you asleep? Did I wake you?"

"Oh, no. Actually, I was just waxing my skis." He listened to that and decided he couldn't really be awake yet, but the unconscious was truly a remarkable thing. Then he heard the silvery laughter at the other end of the phone. "Florence? What's the matter? Is anything—?" Elm Circle again? Ridiculous. It was one of Buxford's quietest, most sedate neighborhoods. He blinked awake and said, "Florence?"

"It's me. I *am* sorry. You know I am, don't you?"

"Yes."

"But I had to talk to you, and right now."

"All right. Talk."

"Alone," Florence said.

Guy refrained from pointing out that if he hadn't been alone, he probably wouldn't have answered the phone. There's nobody here."

"And no—you know, you're not taping this or something?"

"No. I'm not."

"You give me your word, Guy?"

He could hear that she was very much in earnest, but he wondered whether she was also sober. "Word of honor. I don't even own a tape recorder." He waited a moment. "What did you want to talk to me about 'right now'?"

"Well, I reckoned I never would if I waited till morning, because it's so—I know you'll think it's weird, but couldn't you just trust me? I mean, maybe it sounds like a silly question, but I have my reasons, I truly do."

"What sounds like a silly question?" he asked patiently.

"Well, let me ask you this first. You know about Ralph Adonio, don't you? I mean, *all* about him?"

"Not all," Guy said. "Not as much as we'd like to, I guess."

"But will you answer if it's something you *do* know?"

"I don't know. Probably." There goes that, he thought without regret. Let the drug squad collect its own tips. Silvestri had responsibilities, but one of them was to himself.

"All right, then. Are you listening, Guy?"

"Yes." He sat up a little. She sounded as though she'd made up her mind, at last.

"Okay, what did Ralph Adonio die of?"

Guy said nothing for a minute because he was trying to think: surely something must be in the papers by now, or at least on the TV news? But he'd been too busy to find out. All he knew was, there'd been no press at the conference this morning. "I don't think it's—established—yet," he said finally. "The last I heard, nobody could say without more tests."

"Aha!" Clearly, she was triumphing over someone. "Is that the truth?"

"It's the truth as I know it, Florence." He wondered who

117

had just been proved wrong. But there was no sound of anyone with her. And her voice, though strange at times, did not contain the unmistakable note of playing to an audience. "Why, did you hear it some other way?"

"Could Adonio have been—like, poisoned?"

Guy's eyes narrowed. "He could've been. That's one of the possibilities, I gather."

"Thanks. You *are* a doll."

He asked genially, "Hey, don't I get a turn to ask questions?"

"You don't know which ones to ask," Florence said with sudden, surprising clarity. "You're all confused, aren't you? Poor Guy, you've got a dead man lying there and you don't know what bit him."

"Did something bite him, Florence?"

"Well, symbolically. Like, he got it in the neck, didn't he?" She giggled. "I mean really."

"Which do you mean, Florence?" Guy tried a note of sternness. "Symbolically? Really? And if there's nothing else, it *is* late—"

"So's Mr. Adonio." She giggled again. "The late Ralph. No asp in his bosom. No poison dropped in his ear while he slept, either. But you're getting warm-er," she sang out.

"I am?" Guy asked softly. "Where should I look now?"

"I told you, he got it in the neck. Right in the back of the neck."

Suddenly Guy heard a faint new background sound. "Florence? Where are you?"

"I'm at this party," she said rapidly in a gay, high voice. "Us kids is really whooping it up, you know? Why don't you come on over to our barn dance? Live a little—it's Saturday night."

Guy waited, listening: if he was right, he'd know it in a minute. Then he heard the male voice, unrecognizable but young by its timbre, becoming louder. "Oh, don't be so *mean,*" Florence said, not to Guy.

The boy's voice was clear now. "Good God, do you know what time it is? Hello?" he said into the phone. "Who's this, and did she wake you?"

Satisfied that the matter was in good hands, Guy hung up quietly. But he couldn't go back to sleep yet. He fumbled on the bedside table until he found a pencil. The only thing handy to write on was his school notebook. He opened it to the back and scribbled, substituting scrawls for the last parts of words, everything he remembered of what Florence Hathaway had said. It was time, he concluded foggily, to get a little systematic about Elm Circle.

8

The Rule of Three

By Tuesday morning Guy had recognized that something was happening to him. It was a thing he had seen before, in other times and contexts: you wandered over bumpy roads in darkness, and then something not in itself very important turned up and there you were, up and over and on a smooth road built to go somewhere. Guy didn't know where yet, but he had a welcome sense of going.

By that time he also had a second entry in the back of his notebook, made after the black student/drug squad confrontation. About that, he should have had more faith, and the notebook duly recorded that self-reproof. For at the Sunday meeting Guy saw what he had forgotten to take into account—that the detectives and Tim Whistler's delegation were all single-minded men, though senior and junior models, and once an outside force set them down in each other's presence, there was a fair chance they'd recognize their common character. The fair chance grew to more-than-fair in the fact—mostly, Guy concluded, because Tim Whistler was an aristocrat and even when he did a thing under compulsion, he did it gracefully.

Thus Tim had created a small initial breathing space, had stood in the middle for a moment, refusing to be either Us or Them right away, and succeeded in being, briefly, an unknown in a situation where too much was lined up and labeled. It didn't last long; but once it was thus demonstrated that the space between the lineups would support life, one of the drug squad gave it a whirl, too. Eventually, both sides were exhibiting a tendency to discover Guy's presence with faint surprise. He departed, leaving any remaining bridge-making necessary to the black detectives, who bridged by example. Writing it up later, Guy added a parenthesis for his own edification: unfair as it might be, the indications were that hypocrisy and paternalism worked best for peace. Tim Whistler, pretending to be the victim of racism he for the most part was not, to advance the interests of those who were, had been capable precisely because he was unimpaired; if he'd actually been a survivor of a childhood in Harlem, nothing constructive might have come of the meeting.

The middle-of-the-night phone conversation with Florence Hathaway had to wait for attention until Monday morning, when Guy filed an Information Received report and took a copy over to the Medical Examiner's Office to add a verbal amendment. The fact was, Guy told the doctor with some diffidence, the informant was known to Lt. Silvestri and was, though perhaps a little erratic, apt to be unexpectedly wise in far-out matters. And so, if they hadn't already done it, a close inspection of the corpse's neck area. . . .

The fierce little doctor called him later in the day. "Listen, Silvestri, we can't be expected to go over every inch of every cadaver with a magnifying glass."

"No, sir."

"Well. It was there, all right." The old man abandoned ill temper, as he always did when he was really interested. "Of course, we'd looked for needle punctures. But this man was clearly no junkie, so I assumed the stuff had been ingested." The voice paused. "Cantor was relieved to hear about this. It makes it solid homicide, though I guess you *could* commit suicide by jabbing yourself in the neck. But why would you?"

"Would you have to be a doctor to know where to jab?"

The doctor snorted. "In this age of blab-blab-blab? Hell, if you sent away to Doctor Hassenfeffer's newspaper column for the booklet on migraine—"

"But are those popular things adequate as sources?"

"They sure aren't, if you're talking about real disease. In fact, they can be dangerous as hell if they get some poor slob diagnosing himself when good diagnosis would make a difference. Listen, I could tell you cases—"

"Yes, sir." Guy rolled his eyes. It was also dangerous as hell to trot up a man's *bête noire,* if you didn't want him to mount and ride away. "But you feel even crude information would have been enough for—"

"Oh, that? Sure. The popular stuff doesn't give you a course in the circulatory system, but they don't add or subtract arteries and veins. As far as I know." Denied the chance for real discourse, the doctor was prepared to be brisk. "Besides, if you've ever had migraine, you know where the blood vessel back there is, all right. Big fat baby. It pulses strong enough to register on a seismograph."

"I see. Well, thank you, sir." Return thanks rumbled in Guy's ear. "Oh, one more thing, Doctor. Do you know yet what the drug was?"

"Not me, Buster. I said right away it would be a stinker. In that biochemical league, I'm hardly even a bat boy. You better ask Lambert—I dropped it in their lap."

"Yes, sir. Where at Lambert would I be likely to get—"

"Well, I started with Chemistry—Dr. Feinberg, Emil Feinberg, is head of the department—but it could be anywhere by now. Even the army, maybe." The doctor's voice warmed with interest again. "Because it's a form of one of the nerve gases, is my hunch. The military can't count on sneaking up and jabbing the enemy. But it's quite similar stuff, with the same paralytic effect."

"I take it it won't be easy to identify."

"I can't see how it would be. There must be thousands of possibilities. And then of course," the doctor added, with the calm of a bureaucrat noting the heaped contents of some-body else's In-basket, "there's always the natural compounds, don't forget. Because some snake venoms will give you the same effect."

Guy left the doctor entertaining, with ill-suppressed glee, the prospects of confusion at Lambert University ("and if they have to approach the chemical-warfare people, oh brother!"). It was clear that Toots Cantor had better start his investigation of the Adonio homicide with some nonmedical aspect.

Monday night was a school night for Guy, so he turned his attention to a far-off tribe of tiny brown men whose idea of shelter was a slight rise in the hostile ground they bedded on. He listened to the lecture, but the tribesmen and their hunting habits seemed especially irrelevant that night. Sometime in the pale hours of early Tuesday, however, he woke from a semi-nightmare in which an angry pygmy, screaming, "I'll teach you to reject me, Hassenfeffer," chased not Dr. Hassenfeffer but Lt. Silvestri and finally brought him down with a blowpipe dart in the back of the neck. Guy woke, but not in panic, for he had also been in the dream in another capacity: dressed as Hercules, he'd been standing by, taking notes on a dried snakeskin.

On Tuesday Jacques Berriault's lawyer met with Lt. Cantor in an effort to "normalize" his client's status. Things were piling up, so if the police had seen the light of Mr. Berriault's innocence, some order should begin to be brought out of chaos. Some of which was caused by the fact that Hilary

Bridge's sister had not been able to come from England: probate was a clumsy business at best, but when it got international, it could boggle the mind. Thus, the sooner Prof. Bridge's worldly goods were inventoried—a task Jacques Berriault's advice could lighten—the better for everyone. And Jacques himself was finding life intolerable around here at the moment. He had a friend who had a cottage down on the Cape, which was still free of vacationers this early in the spring. If Jacques could be sprung from the by-now-foolish restriction against leaving the county. . . .

A sympathetic Toots Cantor got and gave the necessary clearances—and dropping in to tell Lt. Silvestri, added a private opinion that the Justice-for-Jacques hoo-ha was mostly what was making life intolerable for the poor little guy. Silvestri refrained from observing that even to serve as an agitprop-prop apparently required a certain stamina. He said, instead, that the second murder at Elm Circle should incline anyone to indulgences for Jacques, who'd been in a locked hospital ward the previous Thursday night.

"There doesn't have to be a connection," Toots said.

"Come on. You know the odds against two homicides at Elm Circle being a coincidence? I don't, but any defense attorney will start by looking them up."

Cantor sighed. "My wife is waiting for another one. She believes in the rule of three—when you get two calamities, you got to get a third one."

Mrs. Cantor was not the only believer in that particular magic. The Sunday before, the *Boston Star* had managed a prompt but lumpy feature, clearly tossed together by whoever happened to be around in the office on Friday. What had come through the inflated language, set in even more than usually pied type, was a vague but insistent hint that Doom hovered over "once-tranquil Elm Circle, until recently an exclusive hideaway from the troubled times."

The possibility that it was the troubled times that had disturbed Elm Circle's peace was under discussion in Silvestri's office. "It's hard to believe Hilary Bridge never dabbled in some Saturday-night chemistry," Guy said thoughtfully. "So is it possible he got his dabble from Adonio?"

"No way. Adonio was out of the retail business long before he set up in Elm Circle. And anything this Professor Bridge got into, it would've been recently." Cantor shrugged. "He wasn't a secret addict or anything like that."

That figured: if Hilary Bridge had smoked or swallowed anything in order to see pretty pictures dissolving on the walls, it would have been once or twice, probably. And only when it became fashionable—not back in the days when Ralph Adonio was in personal contact with the consumers of the goods he sold. "The times are all wrong," Guy began. And then he stopped, snagged as if he'd walked past a bramble bush, by the fact of how exactly, neatly *right* the times in fact had been. "If it wasn't whoever picked up the drug consignment—"

"It wasn't," Cantor interrupted. "If he killed Adonio, why would he leave all that money on the corpse?"

"Because he knew it was marked? I know the narcos say nobody could know. But what else could they say, without admitting a leak?"

"Very good." Cantor looked absurdly like a music teacher whose pupil had gotten the cadenza just right. "But you can forget that angle, Guy. If the pickup man was tipped, he wouldn't come at all. The stuff would still be in the laundry package."

"So it was business as usual." Guy let Cantor's encouraging *Right* hang on the air between them and thought about how much knowledge of usual business was needed to arrange things so the pickup man slid in and out of the beauty salon, oddly innocent of the murder. One thing that took was an overall view of Ralph Adonio's double life, a view not possible to anyone who inhabited only one half or the other. An observer's view . . . Guy stopped, trembling on the edge of the possibility that a narcotics squad man had found waiting and watching just too frustrating. The notion was numbing: *all* those men, and each with skill and practice in evading notice, added up to implications of Herculean labors.

"You know," Toots Cantor said thoughtfully, "it's like the pickup man was sort of fitted into a slot." He shifted in his chair, visibly uncomfortable. "This kind of thing is not my bag . . ."

Guy heard what was wanted, and supplied it. " 'But'?"

"But either this character was just too damn lucky to believe in, or else it had to be planned like a commando operation."

With all the risks allowed for, Guy thought. Including the heavy probability of being seen by somebody who'd remember a stranger— His thoughts twitched, something almost audibly clicked into place, and he saw the face of the observer who was particularly skilled at being invisible in Elm Circle. Who would be surprised to see Tom, handyman from the Residence and patron of the Grotto, in the alley behind the restaurant—and the adjoining beauty shop?

Cantor said sharply, "Okay, let's have it." He shook his head, aborting Silvestri's protest. "I'm too old to play games with, son. I know you got something. And I hope to God I don't have to tell you who you're working for." Something—a kind of alarm, a kind of disgust—struggled in his heavy face. "It's one thing to be den mother for the black boys. But if you're gonna start putting them ahead of—"

"No. I'm not." Guy told himself he ought to be angry. But he couldn't be: there was too much hint of heartbreak in the implied accusation—*How sharper than the serpent's tooth* was what was thinning the voice of Toots Cantor, afraid of having no posterity after all. And there was too much respect in Silvestri for this man who went by the book but could, it seemed, write a chapter on intuition, too. "I did think of a possibility," he said slowly. "But you did your mind-reading trick too soon, Toots."

"Meaning what?"

126

"Meaning, I also thought of something that knocks it out."
That wasn't quite true—and now, he had a healthy fear of
the perceptions of Cantor. But what Guy was about to say
was true, so he hurried on. "Look, I do want to keep the Afro
Residence out of it, sure. But only if the kids are innocent.
I do know whom I work for." Cantor was looking shamefaced
now. Guy brushed away the stirrings of apology and went on
quickly. "So let's get that problem out of the way, once and
for all."

"I'm not following you," Cantor said warily.

"I mean, if I can show you the Residence students couldn't
have killed Adonio—"

"All of them? You talking about clearing the whole pack?"

"All of them. If I can clear them for Adonio, are you willing
to let them off the hook for Professor Bridge?"

"Wow! I don't know, Guy. The odds are against two murderers, like you say. But it could happen."

It could indeed, Guy thought bitterly—if, for example,
Det. Tom Carrothers had taken advantage of the odds to
piggyback the murder of Adonio, knowing it would be tied
to the Bridge case. "Okay, it could happen. And if Hilary
Bridge had been killed by a jealous lover in a midnight quarrel, and Ralph Adonio had been shot from ambush as he
traveled his clockwork route from Elm Circle to Tewksport
—okay, then I'd have to buy it, odds or no odds. But neither
one was a *natural* killing, if you know what I mean."

"I know what you mean."

Design was the word hanging in Silvestri's mind. An outside reason linking the hairdresser and the English professor—the sense that that link had to be there was so strong
that Guy simply could not bring himself to yield up the name
of Tom Carrothers to the possibility of official suspicion. Not
yet, anyway; not until he was sure he had to. But at the same
time, Silvestri was not a Sherlock Holmes betting on his
hunches; he was a team man, with no right to throw out a
possibility because it ran counter to his hunches.

"What you're saying is," Toots said slowly, "if we put all our money on the one-murderer line, you can cross off twenty-odd suspects. Is that it?"

"*And* get rid of my own problem." What he was offering, Guy was aware, was unification: *I'll be your boy again.* And it would be as unscrupulous as an ad man's use of Freud except that the would-be seducer himself had just as much wistfulness as he hoped to evoke. Guy was discovering with some surprise how much he wanted to trade lobbying for the Residence for being, pure and simple, Cantor's boy.

"Well, okay, that's what you get out of it. That part's fair enough. But what's in it for me, is what I'm wondering."

So much for getting high-flown in the presence of an honest man, Guy told himself wryly. "What can you lose, Toots? If you don't buy it, you can always go the other route. But right now, you're not going anywhere anyway. Take it," he advised. "It's a good deal."

Cantor grinned. "I guess it is. I get the benefit of your 14-karat brain working for *me*, right?"

"Oh, come on, I—"

"Okay, okay. You won't have one eye on your Afros after this, that's all I mean." The Homicide man stood up. "All right, it's a deal. Start proving."

"Not this minute, Toots. I need two things." Guy dismissed Cantor's suspicious rumble. "No catch. Just—I need Tom Carrothers. Can you set up a meeting?"

"I guess. But it'll take a couple of days—he's supposed to be an ex-con getting rehabilitated by all them Lambert kids. So we can have his so-called parole officer call him in, but he'd have to give the parolee a little time to get off work and so forth. Now, what else does your miracle take?"

"About the night of the Adonio murder. Can you give me a rundown of all the innocent-bystander views of Adonio that night? Or do I have to look it up?"

"Not unless you have to have split-second timing." Cantor crossed his arms over his chest, pursed his mouth for a minute, and then began. "We got the woman in the art gallery. Around the Circle from the beauty shop. She saw Adonio closing up—well, lowering the venetian blinds on the front window of his shop. Everything just like usual. I forget what time exactly, but it was whenever he always closed up."

"Could she actually see him at that distance?" Guy asked.

"Not good enough for a courtroom, if that's what you mean. But she saw a man in a white coat, doing what Adonio always did, right at the time he always did it. That good enough?" Cantor saw that it was, and went on. "Then we got this fellow has a shoe repair store on Park Street—right about where that alley behind Adonio's place empties into Park, but across the street. You got the picture? Okay, he saw Adonio's convertible coming out of the alley. It stood there, waiting for an opening in the traffic on Park, while this shoe repair guy was locking the door of his store. A little after eight, he says. His usual quitting time is eight o'clock."

"Did he see the car leave the alley?"

"Yup. Adonio turned right, heading up Park to the Beltway entrance. And before you ask, Adonio was all by himself—the shoemaker waved to him when he first come out and seen the car. Then he finished locking up, and Adonio waved back when he made the right turn. It's pretty solid, Guy."

"Yes. There's a streetlight on Park at the mouth of the alley, right?"

"Sure, but there was plenty of light anyway—car headlights, stores, Park Street's no country lane. And besides, Adonio's white convertible sort of stands out. I mean, it ain't just another Lambert University VW."

"Okay." Guy offered a moment's ironic thought to a society in which a nonforeign car is conspicuous. But it was true: at the Lambert end of Buxford anyone who sported Detroit's vulgar product—and shined and fussed over it besides—did stand out in the crowd. "Anybody else?"

"One more, a beaut. Sixth Precinct patrolman, name of

129

Patullo, making the rounds of the closed stores in the Circle. He tested the back door of the beauty shop and it was locked, all right. Also, like usual, the car was gone from the alley by that time. Eight-thirty." Cantor uncrossed his arms. "You're lucky. It's not a lot of minutes to account for. But still" —he shook his head— "twenty-odd college kids can cover a lot of ground in that time."

"I know." Guy decided that wisdom lay, at the moment, in changing the subject. So he asked whether the prophetic Mrs. Cantor, believer in the rule of three, had offered any hint as to the nature of the third catastrophe.

"She did not. Like the other kibitzers," Toots said shrewdly, "she don't have to make sense. Or bother with evidence." He took off then, noting without malice that, pending revelations and miracles, he had chores to do.

Guy departed the office, too, soon afterward. For when the rule of three failed, by early afternoon, to produce anything requiring the suspension of peacetime plans, he felt free to keep a private, long-standing appointment at Marshall and Dallas, the only Boston department store purveying official Girl Scout equipment.

Guy Silvestri's Christmas present to one of his nieces had been not only the immediate Girl Scout canteen but also a contract to provide whatever other impedimenta were needed during the year. A list had since accumulated, and a shopping trip had been set up under the terms of the contract. But Uncle Guy was more prompt this afternoon than the Girl Scout, who was supposed to take the subway to Boston right after school. So Guy was waiting, a little uncomfortably because he was the only male idler sitting in the lounging area on a balcony above the buzzing street floor of Marshall and Dallas—when, abruptly, the familiar odd feeling in his chest signaled the presence of Kate Sterling.

She looked strange in that collection of respectable ladies—like another respectable lady, but from a foreign place, one with different customs. Yet there was no apparent reason why, for the simple British tweed topcoat she was wearing had been bought in Boston and could have been worn by any true descendant of the dowager Mrs. Chandler. And yet the blue-green color of the coat and the gray of the eyes evoked, in combination, not Boston or anywhere else with streets but the sea, a seafarer's sea on a misty day: her dark hair, slightly disordered, might have been tumbled by a damp wind as she stood on a headland, peering out to sea . . .

Guy came to his senses and fumbled to his feet, trying to ignore the stares of the surrounding ladies, and the first thing he did was to knock a parcel out of Kate's hand while he was offering her his chair. Whereupon he caught the scornful-tolerant eye of the lady in the next armchair and knew, instantly and with a dreadful certainty, that she was a reader of women's magazine stories in which men are always great big bumbling children. Kate's own gaze, he saw, was not scornful-tolerant; but it was suspiciously grave, and thus immediately rendered him as endearingly bumbling as any magazine-story hero: he even managed to step on Kate's foot before he finally succeeded in giving her his chair.

Kate suggested, too kindly, that they repair to the coffee shop. Listening to the rattle of paper bags being collected somewhere behind him, Guy told her he couldn't. "I'm waiting for somebody," he said, with his mind on the chances of grabbing the adjacent armchair if it should indeed empty. "I'm afraid I—" He saw Kate's reaction and heard the departing lady at the same moment. And, winning something at least, he snagged the armchair. He hunched there miserably and tried to think of a way to answer Kate's "Oh" that wouldn't sound like an explanation and would still be one.

"Well, I'm finished here," she said brightly. "Ships that pass in the night, and all that."

He said helplessly, "No, don't go, please. I've— I haven't seen you in a while."

"No." She laid her gloves in her lap, smoothed them, and then studied them as if she were reading their palms. "Guy,

131

when you have a minute sometime—well, we can catch up on things then, can't we?'"

The change of direction in the middle of that sentence couldn't have been clearer if it was neon-lighted. Guy craned his neck, wishing he could be sure he had a minute at least to find out what she'd really meant to say. And then he had no minute but, he saw with immense relief, at least *this* would get cleared up. "Here I am," he called. "Over here."

Eleven-year-old girls tend to be either too skinny or too plump, and this one was on the too-plump side. But everything else about her was almost exactly down the middle—including the breathless voice in which greetings and excuses tumbled over each other. ". . . not my fault, Unky. I got *right* in the subway, but then I had to wait and wait—you should *see* the crowd on that platform." She giggled softly. "I feel sorry for the one in charge of the subway if he wants people to vote for him."

Guy stroked the silky hair sliding in deep waves down her back and thought how beautiful she was even if she *would* vote for anyone who made the trains run on time. He said he hadn't minded waiting and it was all right. Then he turned her around and presented her, with all his pride in all her perfections perfectly visible, to Mrs. Sterling. "This," he said, patting the smooth, olive-skinned cheek, "is Mariana"—he caught the glare from big dark eyes—"I mean Marian Ferraro." Inspired, he added gravely, "The lady I was waiting for."

Above her polite greeting, Kate's eyes registered the child's pink flush of pleasure and applauded Guy. "Is this a regular shopping date for you two?"

Guy explained his requisition-and-resupply function, but he got no help from his niece: she was leaning over the railing to look down into Marshall and Dallas's book department, which was tucked under the balcony. Finally, Guy noticed. "What is it, honey? You want something down there?"

132

She hesitated, then decided it was worth a try. "Could I just go look, Unky? I know you're busy and all, and you have to go back to work. But I could just see if the new Sally Simpson is in yet. *Sally Simpson and the Astronauts.* It wouldn't take a minute, honest."

Hearty Uncle Guy gave her permission to go and take as long as she needed. Only she was not to go anywhere else in the store without telling him first—because he was no coward, but he was not brave enough to face her mother if he lost Marian in Marshall and Dallas. "Promise," he finished sternly. "Girl Scout honor."

She sighed and glanced at Kate, who shrugged and spread her hands. Satisfied that this was one of those cases of that's-how-men-are, Miss Ferraro delivered her promise, patted her uncle's arm reassuringly, and went off about her business.

Hypocritical Uncle Guy settled back in his chair, avoiding the eye of his companion—who quite probably had been in a position to say whether *Sally Simpson and the Astronauts* had yet arrived in the area's bookshops. So he missed whatever change in Kate's look went with the change from her polite voice to the one that said, "Oh, Guy. She's so—marvelous."

"I know." He tried to remember how old those little children would have been by now.

"So busy, and full of her affairs. So—*sure.*"

Guy glanced at the scene below. Marian was sitting on the floor, turning the pages of a book; he hoped Marshall and Dallas wouldn't send anybody to bother her. "The world is full of children, Kate," he said slowly. "This one's a lucky one—fat and sassy, supplied with a full complement of parents and siblings. Not to mention Grandma, a slew of aunts, and me." He didn't want to be cruel, but he wanted it understood that Mariana—citizen of Buxford, fan of Sally Simpson—was nobody's symbol or substitute. If he also wanted to make something else understood, a kind of self-advertise-

133

ment, a statement of possibility—he was unaware of it then.

"That's—sort of what I wanted to talk to you about," Kate said.

Whatever "that" was, Guy knew the true antecedent of the word was shared guilt, was the fact of conspiracy. But he recognized the original ending of the sentence that had begun, pre-Mariana, with a wish for a minute. He said, "Now is a good time," and waited. He would deal with the rest later.

"Well, it's just—look, you were right about—a lot." Her gloves, consulted again, must have advised haste: she continued quickly, on a note of getting-it-over-with. "But you were wrong about me, Guy. I thought it didn't matter—"

"It matters," he said.

"And then I thought I couldn't do anything about it, anyway. Because there was no way to say—anything—without being—I don't know—unfair to Ellie, I guess. But now—" she glanced down at the absorbed reader below. "I think I have to be fair to myself, too. And maybe it's more important. That you should know I'm not—what you thought."

"What are you, Kate?" He waited. "Tell me. Please."

"I'm not—afraid. The way you thought. When you found out I didn't marry Ellie." Suddenly, she looked into his eyes. "That's what I wanted you to know. I got over that: I was all set to dump the past and marry again. But then—well, there's something wrong with Ellie, Guy."

"My God, don't." It wasn't until later, much later, that he saw how his own lack of innocence, rather than any logic, had caused him to jump to the conclusion. But right then, all he saw was that no man should know that about another.

"No, not what you think." After the first moment, it began to strike her funny. "Don't be so—primitive."

It struck him funny then, too. "I told you I'm a simple man." But he was thinking again now. And if the problem wasn't "primitive," it might not be a problem but an excuse.

Even if it was what a simple (or guilty) man thought of first, it could still be a cop-out. "What is it, then?" he asked, not sympathetically. "Not putting the top back on the toothpaste? Snoring?"

"Guy, don't. I'm not—doing that. It's real. Even if I don't know what to call it."

"Then describe it," he said boldly. He would know if it was a phony. And he had to know.

"It's things like—well, the way he's been treating Florence lately. Chivying her, snapping at her all the time. And before that there was the business of Lowell Lester."

"What about Lester?" Guy concentrated on looking impassive.

"I don't know how to—" She consulted her gloves, but they were offering no further help, it seemed. "It looks like—well, Ellie's been conducting some kind of—campaign—against poor Mr. Lester. I realize that's hardly a crime, but—"

Guy, who realized it might be a crime, waited in silence.

"—it's so *ugly*. Such a nasty way to be." She was twisting the gloves in her hands now. "When I saw it, that there was this thing wrong with Ellie, I wanted to get away. Just go. I mean, that was the idea originally. That I could."

"I thought it still was," Guy said. "That's were I went wrong."

"Maybe you didn't, after all. Because I still couldn't say 'for better or for worse,' could I?" She sighed. "Selfish."

Or self-respecting, Guy thought, and decided not to say it. It was safer to let her figure out for herself that, in her case at least, any unwillingness to sacrifice herself for some messed-up man was a healthy sign.

"But I couldn't just leave him, either. Not when I knew that could make him worse. And there was a chance it would get better, because it wasn't something big and frightful. Just—mean. I thought, well, people get things wrong with them, but they can get fixed—"

135

"You asked him about it," Guy guessed, watching his niece.

"Yes. When I found out Ellie had complained to Lambert. That was the beginning."

"Complained? Oh. About the Merritt Library?"

Elliott couldn't have known about the accidental revelation, over some of Lambert University's sherry, from someone who assumed Elliott's wife was in on Elliott's secrets. Listening to her account, Guy saw how neatly this fit in with the Lambert administrator's worrying about "undesirable activities" at the Merritt. Elliott Sterling wasn't an official personage but he wasn't an anonymous letter-writer either; he was not only an alumnus but a Merritt. What he said would be given just about the weight the Lambert man had accorded the "information received" he'd spoken to Silvestri about.

It was not hard to extract specific details from Kate, whose intent was to describe not Elliott but herself. But Guy's very success was causing him some suffering. And he kept seeing Kate's air of defeat and resignation, the night he'd struck out at her over Dracula's muddled head, as what it really was—a fighter being shot down in a mistaken uniform. By Silvestri, the observer who forgot to allow for the effect of his own presence on what he was observing. . . .

Partly as a change from kicking himself, he returned his attention to Kate's account of the anti-Lester "campaign." Elliott had dismissed her direct question, insisting she'd heard wrong or gotten something confused; and at first she'd retreated. But then she continued to see signs—little digs at Lester, she said under Guy's deft questioning, that weren't responses to anything but just planted. And in company where it would count: Kate had been particularly distressed, once, when Elliott hinted to Hilary Bridge—"a dear man, but Ellie knew he was a dreadful gossip, everybody knew it" —that Lester simply didn't have the backbone to keep the Merritt from being abused. Guy remembered the reported damage to a rare and lovely volume that proved too much

136

for Bridge's dabble in revolution. If Elliott had meant to make trouble for Ell-Square, he'd surely picked the way to do it.

Did it add up to a "campaign," though? Kate could have been simply seeing the backbiting that was intrinsic to the academic culture, in which she was after all a newcomer. But then, backbiting for what purpose? Elliott could hardly be after Lester's job. And there seemed to have been no encounter between the two men, either of the professional kind or the neighbor kind, that would inspire spite.

". . . a psychiatrist," Kate was saying. "But the suggestion only got him upset. And I got scared, because no psychiatrist could do anything if Ellie was so opposed, but a fit of depression is always dangerous for him. Alcoholics have to keep things on an even keel as much as possible . . ." Her voice trailed off. "By that time, we were into the winter, too, and Ellie always gets to feeling low then. So it wasn't the right time to stir things up any more." She sighed. "I suppose I was unfair to poor Mr. Lester. But you can't be fair to everybody, it seems. Or I can't, anyway."

Guy saw his niece close her book and stand up. "I'm glad you decided to tell me about it."

"It doesn't—change anything, though. I'm still—right where I was. You know what I mean, I—oh," she said, clearly relieved, "Marian's waving to you. Look."

Guy stood up and waved back. "Don't worry," he told Kate. "Everybody's unfair, all the time. And some of us are smart alecks besides. I want to say more about that. But I've got to—"

"I know." Kate was smiling, waving to the little girl, too. "Tell her about the great buy she can get on Sally Simpsons at the Perilous, will you? Free home-baked cookies, too, for friends of friends of the management." She turned the smile on Guy. "Run along to the Scout Shop, Unky."

Because he had to, because what you coddle you must take responsibility for, he ran along.

But what ran along in his mind, while he weighed the merits of the latest model Girl Scout backpack, was how remarkably easy it was to be unfair to Lowell Lester. In the real world, slander could bring penalties, if it could be proved. But in Ell-Square's world, a charge of betrayal of trust was as good as proved the moment it was even implied. For there, authority would dump you without letting you face your accusers—and the students who rushed to the aid of the downtrodden would not see you as downtrodden and would dump you at least as fast. Ell-Square, it seemed, was getting the shaft from both directions: Lambert had him countenancing "undesirable activities," and Florence Hathaway hadn't hesitated to decide he was "finking to Lambert."

And Lowell Lester was not an adaptable type, by training or personality, and so was not likely to be up to the demands of cultural migration. If his ability to survive in the air he was used to breathing was impaired—even if only mild spite was the cause—the effect could be fatal. Guy took the opportunity, while Marian was in a dressing room trying on a uniform with some room to grow in it, to scribble in his notebook, "Look up L² biog." Maybe he could find some understandable reason why Elliott should want to do the man dirt.

9

Birth of a Hunter

M y God," Toots Cantor said. "Hair." He announced that he would be damned. Then he revised the prediction, settling instead for a future as a monkey's uncle. "You," he told Silvestri with something like awe. "You've got *some* kind of luck."

Tom Carrothers shook his graying head in reproof. "Only when it came to LeGrand, maybe. And even there, I don't know—you take any bunch of boys that age, one of them's bound to be having woman trouble."

"Sure. Once you narrow it down to three."

"That took reason, not luck." Carrothers looked at Guy, as if seeking an ally in the debate.

Today's philosophical hassle is reason *vs* mysticism, Guy was thinking—while he smiled faintly, letting silence stand for the modesty proper to a hero—and at Tuesday's seminar with Toots, the subject had been The One *vs* The Many. If the Philosophy Department at Lambert knew how relevant it really was, maybe it would go back to its subject instead of setting up in the draft-resistance business.

"You're sure only three of those Residence kids look—" Cantor paused, hunting for a seemly word.

Carrothers suggested, "White enough?"

Guy said, "Come on, Tom."

"Okay. Yes, I'm sure, Toots. The only ones without Afro hairdos are Whistler, Cannon, and LeGrand. And Whistler's the president and Cannon's chairman of the program committee. So they were both nailed in place that night, right there in plain view at the head table all during the dinner and the speaker, from seven o'clock on."

That's what was not really luck, Guy decided. Not that he'd reasoned that way at the time, but probably he should have: a democratic society tends to elect its moderates. So if Silvestri had any kind of analytic skill, he should have been able to predict that high, wide Afro coiffures would not show up among the student officers.

". . . and the damn thing was compulsory," Tom was saying. "Even for me. The speaker was one of those white student revolutionaries, so I was particularly asked to come and get my consciousness raised." His round face was carefully expressionless. "That cat wasn't what you might call a spellbinder, though. So three kids snuck out. But that's all—I know because I snuck out myself at eight, and I wasn't halfway out the door when LeGrand come after me. We sat right across the hall for two hours while he was telling me his troubles, and"—Tom grinned—"I was telling him a skirt is only a skirt, or words to that effect. I had my eye on that door the whole time. Nobody else come out till it broke up in there, and that was easily after 8:30."

"The other two who left the dinner," Guy reminded him.

"Oh yeah. Both of them hit the sack—I looked in on them later, and you could tell they'd been flaked out for some time.

I know," Tom said, "that's not good enough, not by itself. But the fact is, both of them got Afros out to here."

"So neither of them could have driven Adonio's car out of the alley," Guy finished triumphantly, "and still been 'recognized' by the man on Park Street. He didn't really *identify* Adonio, Toots; he just 'recognized' him."

"I know, people see what they expect to see," Cantor said.

"Right. So even the silhouette of an Afro hairdo would've been something he didn't expect to see—it would disturb his 'recognition.' If not at the time, then certainly afterward, when a police officer began asking questions."

"If Adonio even wore a hat, I'd—" Cantor gave up. "He didn't? I suppose you checked it."

"I checked it, Toots."

In the small silence, Tom Carrothers said, "I'm not any crazier about this psychology stuff than you are, Toots. But it hangs together, it makes sense. And you could carry it further—I'd be willing to bet any skin darker than Tim Whistler's, say, would show up even from across the street. Considering the streetlight on Park, right by that alley." He shook his head. "If you're thinking I'd naturally go for anything that clears the Residence kids, forget it. Just for the record, if I knew one of those kids done it, I'd be tempted to strangle him myself."

"Why?" asked the only man in the room who'd been thinking that an alibi for young LeGrand was also an alibi for Tom Carrothers.

It was Cantor who answered. "That's a dumb question." His glance at Tom Carrothers was apologetic: clearly, Toots's boy was not doing him proud at the moment. "Did you forget the murder messed up a beautiful drug pinch? The fellows were just waiting for that marked money to show up in Adonio's possession." His gaze abandoned the backward scholar. "Tough luck, Tom."

"That was a Christmas present for the drug merchants,

that murder," Det. Carrothers mourned. "Any other night. Even any other Thursday night. But that one ruined us."

Guy caught himself in time, so he didn't bestow a huge, happy grin on the company and thus further embarrass his mentor Cantor. But no possible scenario wherein Det. Carrothers, maddened by frustration, decided to get rid of Adonio himself could survive the fact that all the narcos and their associates (which certainly included Carrothers) knew about the Plymouth Linen Supply package waiting in Adonio's back room that Thursday night. Tom Carrothers, even if driven to murder, would have picked another night. And even if he *had* picked that one, the drug courier would never have been allowed to slither in and out, still anonymous. He'd have been either in custody or dead.

". . . goddam waste of time and sweat," Tom was saying bitterly. "All for the likes of that trash Adonio." He forestalled Cantor. "I know, you don't make the law and neither do I. And I guess Professor Bridge had a right not to get knocked off—far as I know, he didn't do nobody any harm."

"If nobody but the virtuous were entitled to policing," Guy said, "the force could be cut in half." He smiled—an awkward, approval-seeker's smile, for which he disliked himself, and also by way of apology for stating the obvious, which also didn't endear Silvestri to himself. But he had to say *something:* wasn't there anyone, even among the good guys, who didn't take the processes of law sort of on approval, to be applied when they suited the occasion?

Tom Carrothers said, "The boy's right" in a precise, teacherish voice that made Guy wince. "It's just that—well, it burns me up, it really does." Then emotion dislodged the conscientious concern for bringing up baby. The voice now was Tom's own, dark and angry and earnest. "We stayed away from that pickup man, gave him plenty of room, because we figured to do better getting Adonio. Okay, it was a gamble, and we lost—though I still think it was a good bet. But now we're set way back: that cat's not doing business

142

there anymore, but he's sure at it *some*place. And now, when we need to scramble just to get back to where we were at, a hell of a lot of manpower's tied up on the murder. Nobody's even *thinking* about what really counts." Tom stopped, apparently remembering that there were children present. "I mean, the damage is still going on, that's what counts. It's not a matter of good and bad, Silvestri. It never was: Ralph Adonio wasn't the first fellow ever set out to make an illegal dollar, you know, and I'm in favor of leaving it up to God to decide was he a bad man or not. But dope's not like the numbers or a bookie joint somewheres. Drug money is blood money, every time. And what I mean is, Adonio ain't making it anymore but the other fellow still is, and there's no reason in the world why he'd stop without some cop stops him."

Guy nodded to indicate that he had the straight of it now, then sat quietly, half listening to an exchange of reminiscences between two men who understood the late Ralph Adonio too well to hate him. Tom Carrothers' incorruptibility was understandable because he was a black man who wanted to make a point about black men, and in that sense was not really free to be crooked. But for Toots Cantor it must take a stubbornness verging on perversity. Did Mrs. Cantor berate him, Guy wondered, because she would never have a fine house in Tewksport like Mrs. Adonio?

Carrothers was standing, making departure noises. "If I don't get back pretty soon, those kids could figure the parole officer's harassing me. It don't take much to get them up tight. LeGrand, he was fussing about me being called in when it's not my regular day. Takes even less to set him off, right now." The detective's grin held a world of wordless wisdom about the crusade-proneness of young men with recently broken hearts.

"You got to go out the Maple Avenue side, right?" Cantor used the arms of the chair to lever himself upright. "I'll walk you as far as my office."

The Maple Avenue side, Guy knew, was where you'd come

143

out of the building if you'd been upstairs in a parole officer's cubicle; if you went directly downstairs from Silvestri's office, it was just possible you'd run into a Lambert student paying a traffic ticket. He watched the two middle-aged men who thought of everything usher each other out. And when he sat down at his desk again, it was with a mind to devote himself to detail: he wouldn't go so far as to say he was responding to inspiration, but somehow theorizing held less appeal for him now.

He needed facts, though. He opened the file drawer and lifted out the folder labeled "Whereabouts," the reports by the Sixth Precinct team assigned to find out where the residents of Elm Circle had been during the early Thursday evening when somebody was killing Ralph Adonio. The prospect of rereading this stuff held little charm for Silvestri. Maybe that was why, when he caught sight of the unlabeled folder at the back of the drawer—the alien, unofficial folder he'd stuffed in there himself—he decided now was the time to give it some more attention. He took from it Elliott Sterling's meticulous map of Elm Circle and spread that on his desk, making room by removing a number of things with more right to be there. Then he began reading Elliott's manuscript, which described the scene and characters in limbo and in innocence, relatively speaking: each in his place at home in Elm Circle, a good neighborhood where nobody got murdered.

CULTURAL PATTERNS IN ELM CIRCLE: A SUMMARY

Guy suppressed a smile as he read that. Elliott Sterling had not been a Lambert student for some years now, but the twig had been bent, it seemed—he had produced an exquisitely academic title. Fortunately, though, Lambert had apparently had no other permanent effect on Elliott's prose style.

> #1—That's the Perilous, and it has no more culture of its own than a busy call girl. Compare the blatant plate glass window on Nathan Ave. and the

decorous face it presents on the Elm Circle side. All things to all men, and shameless about it.

#3—(There is no #2, or #4 either: they're both buried in double lots. Mine. Descended to me from my Uncle Joshua, who would have felt smothered in a single lot.) Here dwelleth the dowager Mrs. Chandler, Buxford-Brahmin, Mayflower-kiddies, D.A.R., the whole shtick. When you see the old girl out for her constitutional every day of the year, come rain or snow or atom bomb, you realize it was the *softies* who went west and crossed the Rockies in those covered wagons. The dowager is the only person I know who can sit up straight in a sling chair. But don't think of her as all ramrod and teatime, because there's a family history of adventure: when she was only a lass (if you can imagine that), she and Mama sailed round the Horn with Papa on his whaling ship. You can find the story in various anniversary issues of the *Lambert Blue*. She grants the occasional interview, but only to the student newspaper. She knows perfectly well that they then turn around and sell it to news magazines, etc.; it's her way, she says primly, of contributing her bit to Lambert . . .

The Circle's hippies, yclept Pandora and Ken and Dracula (I'm told by Kate, who always knows things like that), dwell in the dowager's basement, which became an "apartment" with the installation of a cut-rate john. If it had been anybody else's basement, a the-hippies-are-coming panic would doubtless have sprung up, but nobody got upset about Mrs. C.'s; I think it's generally believed that even the Roman Empire wouldn't have fallen if the dowager had had it under her eye, so ordinary decadence hasn't a chance. Besides, she's overcharging those kids mercilessly, which reassures us about Our Way of Life: above all, Elm Circle likes a Yankee to behave like a Yankee.

#5—The Sterlings.

#6—No active culture at the moment. Prof. Allenby is on sabbatical, and they've gone to Canada. They didn't rent out the house because they pop back every so often for the odd week. What Allenby professes is psychology.

Guy caught himself and shook his head—what was he reading *that* for? The Allenbys had not popped back from Canada at any relevant time, so who cared? It would make some sense, he decided, to distinguish from the rest those entries with some relevance to Adonio's death. He picked up a pencil and put a check mark beside "#5." He started reading again, then stopped and put a check mark beside "#3" before he returned to the manuscript.

> #7—Here begin the marts of commerce. Although Miss Lasswell, who runs the jewelry shop, would wince: she refers to herself as a "lapidarian," which ought to tell you all you need to know about *her.*

Well, it did, Guy thought. Especially taken along with the fact that Miss L. lived in a house *she* had inherited from *her* uncle. It was on the other side of the campus, and she returned to it in time for tea every day: her clientele, which tottered into Elm Circle leaning on a cane or just sent its chauffeur, did not need to wait till after work to bring in great grandmother's brooch for cleaning. This kind of not-very-commercial commerce made things rather easy for Guy, he noted with relief. And there was additional reason to skip Number 7: Miss Lasswell's lapidary emporium was a jewelry shop to the Sixth Precinct, which patrolled it more regularly therefore—although probably only a thief with a taste for Victorian lavalieres would be likely to break and enter.

> #8—The Grotto. Gus George doesn't live among us either, but he's definitely part of the Circle's own culture. Still, old Gus isn't *quite* assimilated: e.g., he's a bit too obliging and volunteer-y for our Buxford Brahmins—and I myself admit to flinching (unobserved, I trust) occasionally when greeted with Armenian ebullience.

Ha, thought Silvestri. Serving shish kebab doth not an Armenian make. Sloppy sidekicking there, Elliott.

The dowager does better, though: *she* knows when a respectful yeoman is pulling his forelock, and she delivers an appropriate greeting and sails on. I'd guess she admires Gus George almost as much as he admires her.

#9—Beauty shop. Thanks to the black student hassle, you've had your own opportunities to observe Ralph Adonio. But you should keep in mind that, up to that Circle Association meeting when he shocked us liberals, Adonio was nearly as much a carpetbagger at the Circle as, say, Miss Lasswell. Not quite, because he does lave the locks of local ladies (not Kate, who does her own); and in fact, that's how he really got the message that if you want to do business in Elm Circle, you'd better be for brotherhood. I haven't got a purely innocent reaction to Adonio, because Jim Waterman's been spreading a little sociological talk over bridge tables, etc. So I've come to understand that where Adonio grew up, the appearance of a black family on the block was likely to mean subsequent gang fighting. And I do see that if you're busy beating your way from those narrow sidewalks to the wide lawns of Tewksport, you may not also have time for trimming your rough edges . . . But that's as much tolerance as I can summon. The truth is, I don't really *like* Ralph Adonio, and I don't think most other people at the Circle do either.

(#10)—An imaginary number, represented by the parking lot of the apartment house. Which should be mentioned, though its address is Park Street, because it is, after all, the Circle's only recognition of the student population. Anyway, Jim Waterman, who's certainly part of the Circle's culture, lives there—he used to be the janitor, in fact. This year he's moved upstairs into one of its six little two-room domains, each sporting brick-and-plank bookcases and a crooked-neck desk lamp; they run to sober graduate students, with perpetual poverty and drawn faces at the ends of semesters. Elm Circle used to take a firm no-students position, but cooler heads murmured that if we fought the apartment-house owner on the student issue, we might well lose—and then who knew what sort of students we'd get? This way, he exercises discretion in renting, and we get the kind who don't consider coexistence a form of sellout . . . There's a sort of unspoken agreement between the apartment house and the Circle that one party per semester is okay. So, twice a year we're treated to a 2:00 A.M. uproar of motorcycles starting up and merry good-byes in the parking lot. The music must be earsplitting, but fortunately only closed shops are really nearby . . . The only other general observation I can make on the culture of the grad students over there is that they must eat all night: their kitchens are in the back, and the lights seem to stay on there very, very late.

Guy smiled, contemplating not without a certain envy the gaps in their knowledge suffered by the sons of the rich. Elliott Sterling, it seemed, had no idea that in two-room apartments shared by three students, you ended up studying in the kitchen. Nor, Guy realized, his smile broadening, was his amateur-anthropologist sidekick aware of how much of the observer's culture could be read from his observations: what was Mr. Sterling of Number 5 looking at from his window "very, very late"? Insomnia first, then general nosiness, was almost certainly the answer, Guy concluded—comfortably, because it was desirable to have a sidekick with human flaws—while he made a check mark beside Number 8. His pencil hovered briefly over the apartment-house paragraphs before he decided against it and returned to reading.

#11—The art gallery. You met the two ladies who run it—Mrs. Preston and Mrs. Savage, both Lambert faculty wives; they're both in the mid-thirties and pretty enough, and they're fulfilling themselves, you know. And maybe even making some money: the stuff they sell downstairs isn't bad, but the upstairs gallery is lined with proofs that love of art is not enough; yet the art-hunters buy with equal enthusiasm from both departments.

#12—Downstairs, the willow furniture shop. The merchandise is creaky, but if you like sitting on plaited straw, etc. The proprietress is a sweet-faced woman who looks a little like Kate except with fair hair that she doesn't do by herself. Her name is Mrs. Johnson (like the dowager Chandler, but for different reasons, she is never called by her Christian name) and she's a widow with two teenage children to whom she toddles home (an apartment in Boston) every afternoon.

The upstairs is the domain of the Colonel—whom you couldn't have missed, at the Association meetings—and there were hopes at one time that he and Mrs. Johnson would meet in the middle of the stairs, so to speak. But the consensus is, it wouldn't be fair to her children anyway—though it is also believed that the love of a good woman would probably straighten the Colonel out . . . The whole thing lends a pleasant bitter-sweet note to the local gossip. And hope remains alive: teenage children *do* leave home in a few years, after all . . .

(#13, 14, 15)—What occupies this numberless space is the *back* of the Merritt, but even the back door of the Merritt is a lavish one (that's not where they put out the garbage) and there's handsome parkland to stroll through if you go in from the Circle. Which nobody does, actually, except the odd student hired for an odd job at the hourly minimum wage. People usually drive in from the Beltway (which is hidden from the Merritt by all those marvelous poplars) to the parking lot, which is off on the side of the building, and then trek back to the imposing façade.

It *is* imposing, and it occupies a substantial hunk of Circle real estate—but, on second thought, I suppose it doesn't really belong in this report. It's not, in any real sense, part of Elm Circle: all it does is raise the tone of the neighborhood, and give me a little reflected status. But it doesn't interact with the rest of us.

Lt. Silvestri, putting his check mark beside the parenthetical Merritt Library, was not at all sure he agreed with Elliott's last comment. His pencil hovered over Numbers 10 and 11 briefly, then he abandoned Mrs. Johnson and the Colonel; he had a hunch he could do the same for Mrs. Preston and Mrs. Savage, but they were after all Lambert faculty wives and thus by no means "carpetbaggers" at Elm Circle, so he afforded them a reluctant check mark. Then he went back to Elliott's summary.

#16—The Bethanys. That's the narrow wren-brown house wedged between the Merritt's parking lot and the movie theater. And I know you noticed the Bethanys at Association meetings: they're exactly the kind of intelligent, conscious listeners that speakers aim their remarks at. They're also both too eastern-WASP (he's from New Hampshire, she's from Maine) to be ethnically interesting—but how about as a study in old age? Especially since they're not slowly starving on Social Security, so they represent other aspects of aging in our society . . . In Elm Circle's society, it's a gentle process: Mrs. Bethany is involved with Kate and others of the women in projects for clothing or adorning our Florence (see #19), and Mr. Bethany is in fairly regular attendance at the ad hoc seminars, around the Tree or at the Grotto bar, on what the world might be coming to. But after that, people get on with their work, with spanking their children, with committing their adulteries—and the Bethanys presumably just go home and remember the past. Or discuss their children, who live in Colorado and New Mexico, and in whose lives the B.'s are also peripheral. The use of their leisure for travel might well be an answer, but I don't think they have enough money: he's a retired civil servant and she used to work, apparently only intermittently, as a nurse. There *is* Social Security, so presumably they have just enough to live on decently. If they're careful. If life is tidy, narrow, and wrenbrown.

Guy had noticed the Bethanys, all right. They were both physically frail enough so that it wasn't to consider a check mark that he paused in his reading. What stopped him was Elliott Sterling, for whom he felt, first, the purest admiration—how swiftly and competently Elliott had communicated his compassion for the old couple!—and then a great sadness for the waste Elliott's dilettante life amounted to. What charm and perception and maybe talent, all on top of a Lambert University education, added up to was only, like this report, an aside . . . Guy shook his head and went on taking advantage of his sidekick's perceptions.

#17—Circle Theatre. Like the Perilous, it's what you might call culturally equivocal: right now the Circle Theatre's fare goes in heavily for the obligatory closeups of people in bed together; but if Bambi comes In again, that's what we'll be seeing . . . Jake Birnbaum is Elm Circle's only Jew, so far as I know—we've progressed far enough from the original Anglophilic anti-Semitism so people may be Jews without its being generally known or speculated about. Jake apparently isn't a very devout one, as he eats at the non-kosher Grotto. But he belongs to Jewish organizations, and once a year he gives a benefit to raise money for Israel (well-subscribed in the Circle, partly because Birnbaum is entitled but also because the hard-working, early-rising Israelis, periodically snatching up their rifles to defend the land they farm, are clearly simpatico: the Bethanys, for example, come of people very like that). Jake is a widower, and seems to like it that way. In theory, he lives with a married son who teaches Computer Sciences (whatever they are) in Boston, but in fact Jake camps out a good part of the time, in a little bed-sitter he's fixed up behind the theater's office. He's a man of few demands, and of low visibility. But he can be counted on when it comes to cooperative projects, etc.

Guy checked Birnbaum's name without hesitation: a low-visibility, solitary type who managed to live exactly the way he wanted to, and who also displayed firm and consistent loyalties, was always a possible suspect. There was no visible motive, but still . . . Lowell Lester, Guy thought, would be capable of some subtly cruel anti-Semitism. And Elliott Sterling, who was more fiercely compassionate than you might think, could have decided to wreak vengeance on behalf of Birnbaum. It was only speculation, and it didn't touch the questions of Hilary Bridge and Ralph Adonio. But to check on Jake Birnbaum's whereabouts seemed, at the least, desirable.

#19—Ann Price and Florence Hathaway. The girls live above Ann's leathercraft shop—or, actually, Ann lives there and Florence the Fair lives with her. Ann bought the building, and the business, in order to resettle Florence and reinstall her at Lambert. Ann is one of those products of expensive colleges who reject the whole thing after graduation and find themselves via some kind of arts-and-crafts. Which is what Ann was doing when she met Florence, then a brand-new dropout from Lambert. When Florence came back the first time, Ann opened a shop down on the Cape; but after Florence flopped again, Ann apparently decided she'd have to be right on the spot. The second time around she'd bought the house in Elm Circle and was there to send Florence off to school with a clean handkerchief . . . Ann is a little like Kate, in the sense of a tendency to croon over fallen sparrows, but an older Ann is much more likely to end up like the dowager Chandler—dauntless, righteous, energetic, and tough. Her devotion to Florence sounds a bit homosexual, maybe, when I put it down on paper this way. But I'm pretty sure it's not. Florence the Fair is a girl you go out and win empires for, whereas Ann is the kind of girl you feel comradely about—but she's a girl, in any case. And there are those who think Ann's sentiments about J. Waterman are more than comradely.

Florence? Well, she represents one of Lambert's finest moments (as usual, compelled by outside pressures). For Florence the Fair was, if you can believe it, the brainiest kiddie in her high school class, somewhere in Nebraska (or Kansas? Lots of prairie anyway, and where the fathers of girls like Florence are farmers). She was awarded—sight unseen!—a scholarship complete with special funds for everything right down to bobby-pin money. She did well, better than most freshmen, but in her sophomore year she picked up a nihilism virus and departed unceremoniously in mid-semester. Lambert was frantic, and you can see why—to have a chance to demonstrate liberalism toward both Nebraska and women in one specimen, and a specimen that looks *that* good!—and so, apparently, were the Hathaways, who had thought a course in animal husbandry at the state college was capital-L learning and certainly never aspired to holy Lambert, mother of Presidents, etc.... Anyway, when Florence became persuaded that maybe Lambert wasn't entirely futile, or could be viewed existentially, or something comforting like that, there was general rejoicing—and all her scholarships and perks were restored.

But alas, Florence not only learns, she learns too easily. Along came another glib futility-talker, this one said to be armed with chemical aids, and off went Florence again. That time Lambert stood on its dignity a little when Florence wanted to return: I myself had to use just a jot of Merritt clout, and I know of others who helped, too. In the end she was readmitted, but only in the lower ranks—without a living stipend, with a requirement to take Economic History all over again, and for all I know with a penance of seventeen Hail Marys . . . My hand fails me, my eye grows dim, I cannot go on—not if I'm expected to describe the culture of Florence the Fair. She is eclecticism gone dotty, a good mind half-listening most of the time and then suddenly zooming in on whatever happens to be going on. Usually some irrelevance, to which she then devotes the meticulous attention of a Talmudic scholar . . . Oh, the hell with it. The only thing I can say about Florence's culture is that whatever it is will probably be every other kid's next month.

Number 19 got an automatic check mark, of course, if only for housing Florence. But what caused Guy to hesitate was the next paragraph, headed "#20." With a pang, he remembered having read it through on the morning of Hilary Bridge's death. Maybe, he thought wryly, he should have read the whole thing then . . . He skipped the speculation as well as the text and went on.

#21—Piecemeal Shop, furniture in parts. This is an example of what the prophets of doom warned about if we allowed commerce into the sacred precincts of the Circle: Piecemeal is a step beyond even, say, the Circle Theatre, because it's a branch of the big outfit in town and a faceless manager runs it. I'd feel very bad if I really thought this was the inevitable consequence of what I began with the bookshop, but I don't because it's really dear old Lambert's fault: once the university decided to do over those two guest houses to make the Residence, they didn't give a damn what went next door. So #21 was promptly zoned full-commercial and the Piecemeal people snatched it up. I must admit the Piecemeal, with its absentee owner, does represent a qualitative change of some kind—maybe you can use it in some decline-of-a-neighborhood paper—but to tell the truth, it's quiet, closes early, and doesn't attract much noise or produce smells. And unless Lambert decides to sell the Merritt Library, we're safe from any more: everything else at the Circle is owned by people, who're more reliably cooperative than the university.

#22–24 are of course nonexistent, since the front door of the Residence is on Nathan Avenue rather than Elm Circle. And heaven forfend that I should tell *you* about the culture of its inhabitants. But I thought to point out that the two houses it replaced were not equal: #22 occupied two lots. Which is why your black students have such a big yard on the side adjoining the Piecemeal—and which is nice for me, as I'd rather have them playing badminton over there than just across the alley from the Perilous.

Finis. Any questions? Observations? Comments? They will all be dealt with promptly. (Animadversions will be shrugged off equally promptly.) I remain, sir,

y'r obedient servant,
E. M. Sterling, sidekick

Guy sighed, shuffled the pages into a tidy pile, and set about finding Sixth Precinct reports for the people who lived or did business in—he glanced through the pages, noting his check marks—3, 5, 8, 11, 17, and 19 Elm Circle, and the numberless Merritt Library. He soon discovered that neat organization wasn't helping him much, as people had thoroughly messed up all symmetries. Patiently, he pried out what he needed for Number 3.

At the relevant time, he found, the dowager Mrs. Chandler had been lending her august presence to the preparations for an important do at the Congregational Church. That let her out. The other inhabitants of Number 3 would have been among the most popular choices for murder suspects in any election. Even the liberal Circle had begun to murmur, after the second death in their midst, that nothing like this had happened before They (in this case the hippies, but sometimes also the black students) moved in. But Pandora and Ken and Dracula, it turned out, owned as solid an alibi as their landlady's. Only it wasn't the church but the state that removed them from suspicion: the Circle's own hippies had been in attendance since 5:30 that Thursday afternoon at a demonstration designed to rouse the conscience of a public emerging from the subway station in lower Buxford—and it was certain employees of both Boston and Buxford law-enforcement agencies who said so. Some of them in uniform, others in beards and sandals, they had participated in the demonstration until the last trickle of homecoming wage slaves dried up, and then in the discussion and critique that followed. So this time it was not just interchangeable "hippies," but Elm Circle's own specific artificial-flower children who'd been under official gaze until safely past the relevant time.

As for the occupants of Number 5, they were swirled through Elm Circle on that Thursday evening like the chocolate in a marble cake. Elliott, it seemed, had fancied shish kebab for dinner and Kate had not; thus, she'd stayed home, eaten a snack, and done some household chores. Fortunately they'd involved putting clothes into a washer and then a dryer, for the machines provided perhaps the most solid idea of the spans of time involved. Everyone was vague—although neither of the Sterlings quite matched the floating-in-space of the existential Florence, who was on the scene because she'd been keeping store at the Perilous meanwhile. Just when "meanwhile" began was not entirely clear: Kate had waited for Florence, who was supposed to arrive at seven but had not, for it was known that Elliott had left for the Grotto at seven, and he was gone by the time Florence came. Kate's time thereafter was sometimes unattested to, but there was corroboration for some of it and other batches were corroborated indirectly: She'd been over at Mrs. Bethany's between her attendance on the two machines and then again after the laundry was finished—and one of the things she'd washed and dried was a piece of cloth that old Mrs. Bethany had given her only that afternoon, part of a

156

new project for clothing Florence the Fair. Kate did not finally return from her visit to the Bethany's until about nine o'clock, and for the two hours or less before that, a series of happy accidents seemed to provide a patchwork alibi. A believable one, too, given Kate's catch-as-catch-can habitual housekeeping.

In the same time, Elliott had been moseying around, which was in character, too. After dining only theoretically alone at the Grotto—for various other patrons had stopped by his table and Gus George joined him for coffee—Elliott walked with Gus across the Circle to the movie theater, where a Greek film featuring Gus's favorite actress was playing for the fourth week. Elliott had seen it once and declined another go-round; he left Gus (who'd seen the film three times) standing in front of the Circle Theatre in conversation with the proprietor. Mr. Sterling told the interviewer—doubtless with polite regret—that he had no idea what time it was when he wandered back to the Perilous. For one thing, he'd returned via the Nathan Avenue door, because he'd wanted a look at the window display there; and he reported conscientiously that he'd gone out for another look, or maybe even two more, before he settled down in the little "parlor" corner at the back of the Perilous. Florence, either busy or studying, remained up front and did not notice either her employer's entry or his reentries. Elliott did offer one certainty about time, though: he'd glanced at the clock when Florence sought him out because she wanted to leave, and it was then 8:30 P.M.

All that leisurely sauntering around not only took care of Elliott Sterling, it also served as partial corroboration for both Gus and Florence, and indirectly for Jake Birnbaum. The movie proprietor was a relief to Lt. Silvestri, too, because his was the first of the interviews to include some solid times. Birnbaum set his conversation with Gus George in front of the theater at 7:45. The show was supposed to go on at 7:30 and actually began about five minutes late, and Birnbaum

157

had just emerged from the box-office booth when Gus and Elliott appeared.

It was a point of *politesse* that, in the end, took care of Guy's doubts about both Gus George and Jake Birnbaum. For Gus offered to pay, Birnbaum refused to consider it, and Gus therefore took a seat in the back row in order, as a matter of delicacy, to avoid occupying a paying customer's possible seat. Therefore Gus was a perfectly visible silhouette, conspicuous in the half-empty theater and the wholly empty back row, all the time Birnbaum was doing his chores. And at one point the theater owner leaned over just behind the rapt fan Gus George and watched a scene with him; Gus turned, smiled, and then restored his attention to the Greek actress . . . All of which disposed of any notion that Gus George could have slipped out, relying on his previous visits to establish his familiarity with the film, and been at Ralph Adonio's shop to commit a murder. He had no way of knowing when Birnbaum would choose to keep him company. And Jake Birnbaum had chosen a moment when the murderer of Ralph Adonio must still have been in the beauty shop. So, unless you wanted to assume collusion between the two men—which Guy did not, as it was just too unlikely—that took care of his tentative check marks against both Number 8 and Number 17.

Ann Price of Number 19 offered further corroboration of Elliott Sterling's story—she had found him in the Perilous at 8:30 when, after waiting dinner for Florence for some time, she went over to the bookshop to fetch her roommate—but had nothing absolutely rock-solid for herself. Various people had dropped in at the shop and the apartment above it after seven o'clock, but none of them was certain exactly what time it was. However, Guy was equally short of possible motives for Ann Price to commit two murders, so the intermittent gregariousness of her evening would serve well enough to remove her from active consideration. For Florence, much the same situation pertained: once she arrived at the

158

Perilous, she'd been almost constantly under the eye of somebody or other, and customers, passersby, and friends could be checked out. But why? Guy shrugged and, not without relief, discarded contemplation of the occupants of Number 19.

The report on the occupants of Number 11, the art gallery, was brief and neat, and Guy thought he could detect a certain gratitude in the writer, the same Sixth Precinct cop who'd had to struggle through an interview with Florence. For Mrs. Preston had gone home early because she had out-of-town guests. And Mrs. Savage had closed the shop by herself at about seven and taken the subway to Boston, where she'd met her husband for dinner and the theater.

That left only the Merritt Library—or, more precisely, Lowell Lester. Guy examined the report with a certain nonprofessional curiosity: what did Ell-Square do on a Thursday evening, anyway? He found out, with precise times. For apparently never in the memory of living man had Lester caught any bus but the one that passed near the Merritt Library a little after seven and carried him to within a block of his apartment in one of the old buildings on the other side of the Lambert campus. The bus driver knew him, the regular riders (some of them nearly as regular as Lowell Lester) knew him; from the comments noted by the Sixth Precinct inquirer, it seemed likely that the police would be notified any day Lowell Lester *didn't* take that bus.

The rest of the librarian's Thursday evening—dinner at home alone, a session of balancing his checkbook, and an hour of practice on the recorder—was not directly confirmed. But the lady in the next apartment had heard the recorder, and she also heard the bath water running when the hour of practice was up . . . It was not what you could call mathematically impossible, Guy decided, for Lester to have gone home and then turned around and gone back, whizzing between his apartment and Elm Circle with split-second timing to set up appropriate noises at home and

159

evade the drug courier at Adonio's beauty salon. But that called for casting Lowell Lester as a kind of James Bond, complete with technology and panache—and even a mind intent on avoiding psychological-type detecting boggled at that.

Grinning a little ruefully, Guy summoned himself back to order and returned to the map. He stared at the Merritt Library block—from which the librarian had doubtless not issued forth to feats of derring-do. It was a pink rhomboid, neatly lettered, with one parallel backed up almost to the lines indicating the Beltway ramp. But Elliott Sterling, if he apparently had little idea of scale, was conscientious about detail: the space between the Merritt and the Beltway ramp, Guy realized, was meant to allow for the leafy road running between the library's bordering trees and the elevated ramp. A small, little-used road—and if you were on Park Street and apparently headed for the Beltway, you could cut off to the right just before the ramp entered the Beltway. Ideal for misleading a watcher on Park Street. And an excellent place to abandon a car, Guy noted.

He backslid then, seeing not reports but a white convertible and its sighing-with-relief driver who'd not, after all, been accosted by the Park Street cobbler. The little road was only a few yards beyond the Merritt, adding nothing to the problem of walking back to Elm Circle even if one's time was short.

So why, then, was Adonio's car left in the Merritt Library's parking lot instead? Because the idea was not to abandon the car but to plant it—or something in or near it? If Ralph Adonio's wife had reported his absence Thursday night, and if the Buxford police car routinely passing the Merritt parking lot had therefore already been given a missing-persons reason to watch out for the white convertible, then what other incriminating thing would have been seen once the lights and the flurry of police around the Merritt began to happen? The murderer did not have a real-life picture, but

160

rather an expectation of everything clickety-clicking along efficiently—not to mention a prowl car apparently inhabited by bright, observant eager beavers just looking for complications on a routine job—but this was the way a mind not accustomed to allowing for human factors might design things. In real life the innocent always bumbled things, hesitating, backing and filling. So the schedule was messed up: by the time the car was actually found on Friday, Lowell Lester had been at work for some hours, and able to remove or cover up whatever was supposed to have been revealed.

The guilty were more reliable: whoever would come to the beauty salon for the drugs could be counted on not to come a minute early. So the man coolly helping himself to the keys that had been in Adonio's coat pocket—perhaps even in his hand?—and stepping around the body would have known exactly how much time he had. Locking the back door and getting into Adonio's car would be no problem: it was dark in the alley and it would be easy to be sure no one was in sight before coming out. But then bumbling innocence appeared—when the Park Street cobbler spotted the car, it must have been sheer hell. Because the traffic moved slowly and you were stuck at the mouth of the alley, where you *had* to wait. With your blood pounding and your mouth going dry, because suppose the cobbler decided to come over for a chat—or worse, to ask for a ride? He had plenty of time to cross the street, and if you couldn't pull out of the alley before he did, there was no way to avoid discovery . . .

But the man across Park Street didn't want a ride, and the traffic opened, and "Adonio" waved back casually—jauntily, probably gay with relief—and turned right onto Park Street, apparently heading as always for the Beltway and Tewksport, and awakening no suspicion. Guy sat back in his chair, slumping away from two kinds of tension—the one borrowed from the man driving a white convertible and thinking *Okay so far,* and the one that came of Silvestri foolishly trying to tell himself algebra would solve a murder. If he wrote down all the numbers, then subtracted, canceled like terms, and solved for x—could he really come up with the man who had set the problem in the first place? Guy knew now he couldn't, because he knew now how that man thought. The real problem was not knowing but showing, and it would hardly be solved by trudging along within a design specifically planned not to show. What was needed was not to follow a murderer but somehow to get out in front of him.

Guy shuffled the reports back into their folder and hunted through his desk drawers until he found a manila envelope to carry them home in. Because somewhere in them, maybe, if he read them over and over, not looking for anything in particular, he might come on the unintended fact—some irrelevance, some human bobble the theoretician hadn't allowed for. That was the only way he could think of to get outside the design, to come up with something that could be used to pry it open. He was folding the map of Elm Circle when the telephone rang. He hesitated, wondering whether he'd need the map, and then thrust it in with the homework because it couldn't hurt and wasn't worth wondering about. Then he picked up the phone and said "Silvestri" in a voice that revealed more anger than he'd known he felt.

"Golly gee," Elliott said. "Should I have flung my hat in first?"

"Oh. I'm sorry. I'm feeling churlish."

"And I'm feeling guilty. Because I'm disturbing the busy with butterfly matters. Is it illegal to call you at the office for nonoffice purposes?"

"I don't know, but it's a relief." Guy realized he had been scowling and was not scowling anymore. He felt absurdly grateful to Elliott. "What's your frivolity?"

"Well, this is a social buzz. I mean"—Elliott hesitated, and then went on rapidly—"you haven't been around. I suppose for some good reason, but in case it isn't, I didn't want things to just—wither away. If you follow me."

Guy said gently, "I follow you," because he knew how hard

it must have been for Elliott to call. There'd been that revelation about the Sterlings' past, and people got frightened when doors were opened too abruptly. Maybe, it occurred to Guy, people got scared at the other end, too: it was a little frightening to know too much about somebody else. "Any absence you noted," he said, allying himself with Elliott against all chasms, "is not voluntary. I *like* your little establishment, you know. The murmur of the millstream, the milkmaids in their flowered dirndls. It's enough to lead the most dedicated of public servants astray."

"Okay, but when you're not serving us, how about coming over to our bucolic glade? That was what I called about. As you've doubtless detected."

What Guy had detected was that Elliott was ill at ease, and he would get more so—and thus more frivolous—the longer this went on. "Invite me," he said, and, already guilty of long pauses, added extra warmth to his tone. "Name a time when I'm not slaving in your service and I'll come and drink your liquor."

"Gad, how staunch. This afternoon?"

"I can't. I've got school." Guy grinned. "And I don't want to cut because today we take up a nineteenth-century Frenchman who's a favorite of mine. He found a tribe that simultaneously rewarded fertility and practiced infanticide, and it blew his mind."

"Wow! I'm impressed. But their system must make for full employment, right? Are they extinct, this tribe?"

"No," Guy said happily. "But the Frenchman is." He stopped listening while Elliott marveled about the things you learned by being a sidekick, and he thought instead how satisfying Elliott was when he stayed within his own culture—saying nothing seriously and everything gracefully, awkward only when forced to be direct. He tuned in again when Elliott suggested tomorrow sometime. Guy agreed, with pleasure, to come by tomorrow afternoon.

But he thought of Elliott again when, by scrambling after

163

school, Guy made it to the Merritt Library in time to forestall Lowell Lester's departure. In the abstract, it was hard to think of Elliott's lightness turned to bludgeoning poor old Ell-Square; but when you were faced with the fact, when you were actually sitting there getting the my-good-man treatment, it got understandable.

Lester had a right, Guy reminded himself conscientiously. It was getting on to the sacred hour of seven and this policeman, though apologetic about it, was likely to make the librarian late for his bus. And not, apparently, for any good reason. Looking at himself through Lester's eyes, Guy had to admit he was being a strain on patience. He hung in there grimly anyhow, because he couldn't think of any other way.

There'd been nothing amiss at the Merritt, Lowell Lester said with a dismissing courtesy, on the Thursday night in question. And he'd discovered nothing whatever wrong on the Friday morning. If he had, he would have notified the authorities.

"Yes, sir. It's just—perhaps you wouldn't bother if it was some nuisance thing? Like a defaced book, in a minor way." This wasn't questioning but something far less permissible, and Guy knew it. He tried tugging on his own halter. "I mean to say, so much of that sort of thing goes on. One might simply have it repaired and let it go that."

"Ah." Lester put his fingertips together. He looked as though he would certainly say something more. But nothing more got said.

Guy rose, defeated. "Well, I guess I've been seeing ghosts." Faintly elated then, he saw the church steeple of Lester's fingers quivering. "Maybe somebody's hexing me, eh?" *Bingo.* It was a pretty poor throw, and very nearly random. But it had hit something, or anyway chipped a corner of it.

The librarian held onto his desk even after he'd stood up, as though it helped him to touch something solid. "Clearly there is a certain—malevolence—in the air these days. After

164

all," he added, his voice gaining strength, "we have had two acts of violence in very short order, have we not?"

Guy grasped the game, then: Ell-Square, who dealt in hints, had perceived Silvestri's clumsiness as a subtle thrust and was riposting with you're-guilty, a heavy stroke in his circle. Guy looked suitably guilt-struck, listened to a short sermon on what an oasis of quiet Elm Circle once was, and departed—empty-handed in any real sense, but with a solid hunch that Lowell Lester had dealt with some "malevolence" and probably expected more. Though it was useless to push him on the subject, for all he did then was fight back with his own weapons.

Guy got his car and drove around the outside of the Circle, behind the movie theater and the adjoining houses, and parked far down on Nathan Avenue, out of sight of both the Residence and the Perilous. He walked back to the Residence.

Tim Whistler was in a hurry, he said. "Not a diplomatic excuse, Guy. The truth. I've got a date."

"I believe you. But this'll only take a minute."

Tim looked at him curiously. "Well?"

"I want information, and I can give you the guarantee you wanted in exchange, when I asked you for it before."

"What—? Oh, that." The boy rubbed his freshly shaven chin. "Wow. I don't want to welch. But maybe I should have my lawyer. I know you're not trying to trap me, but I'm not interested in making a damaging admission."

"Dammit," Guy exploded, "I *told* you, I *need* this. Can't you ever trust anybody, for God's sake?"

"I'm a fox," Tim said seriously. "Why should I trust a hunter?"

Guy stared, taken by surprise, wanting to say *I'm no more a hunter than you are* and then, half-frightened, wondering whether it was true. But what he needed at the moment was agility, not self-knowledge. "Okay, we'll do it this way. I'll ask you a question and you nod or shake your head. So my numerous hidden microphones won't pick up a thing and I'll have nothing to back me up, whatever I say you said. You dig?" Guy took a deep breath. "Was it a scarf the brothers found in the yard the night Hilary Bridge was killed?" He waited, thinking of Florence, who had not been asked what there was about a man walking up a slanting driveway that had made her so sure it was Jacques Berriault. But Florence had recognized Kate in the dusk by Kate's shawl . . .

"Right on," Tim said, abandoning distrust for admiration.

"An arty-type ascot, the kind—"

"*One* question. No bonuses. And I do have a date."

"Okay." Guy turned to go. A bargain was a bargain. "And thanks."

"Goodnight, bloodhound." Tim came to the door. "You work too hard, you know?"

"I know. It's a sex substitute."

"Oh wow, a witty bloodhound. And"—Tim smiled—"one who is not, shall we say, barking up the wrong tree."

Guy said goodnight gratefully and hurried out to his car, because he had a date, too. He did not always trade information for information, so he hadn't bothered to advise Tim Whistler that people over thirty sometimes try their luck of a Friday night, too.

10

The Friendly Hunter

Saturday morning Guy rose obediently when his clock clamored. But it was earlier than his brain wanted, so only a few of its minor-league cells were functioning while he put together his unvarying breakfast. And he was still far from fully awake when he took out the folder brought from the office and began plodding through its brief sketches of the life and times of Elm Circle.

Maybe that's why, with all the words plopping evenly onto the surface of a lamentably open mind, something not stated—an implied fact, unaccounted for in an apparently explained character—suddenly stood upright in the limp field of details. Guy shook his head like a dog coming out of water, and then he hurried to the telephone. There he smoked three cigarettes without ever chain-smoking, while he cajoled and persuaded and suggested and hinted. He got what he wanted and hung up, secure in the knowledge that while he was shaving and dressing, machinery was turning—though perhaps squeaking, and certainly moving reluctantly—at Lambert University.

A few hours later, in the deserted Saturday offices at Lambert, he got what he wanted again: the Lambert man looked up from a mound of computer printout and said, "Not for three years now. But of course"—his hands were full of the computer paper, so he indicated with a nod the folder labeled "Waterman, James P."—"there *was* the departmental prize. That was only a few hundred dollars, though."

Guy read, carefully, the hand-printed legend on the folder imploring one and all to refrain from removing it from the office of the department chairman. He said "I see." But his voice said he did not see, not at all.

"Well, it does seem rather too bad, doesn't it?" the other man said uncomfortably. "But after the federal money finished, naturally there was a hiatus until he could be funded from some other source. And when the matter came up for review then"—the worn tweed shoulders of a Saturday-leisure jacket moved in a suggestion of a shrug—"the grades in the interim had been, well, discouraging."

Although, shortly before, Jim's grades had been good enough to win the departmental prize? Guy didn't indulge himself in the futile question. If a student earned prize-winning grades while a federal endowment was paying his tuition bills, and then his grades dropped sharply when he had to earn the money himself, the only real question was why anyone should think that "discouraging" rather than understandable. "Was there any warning?" Guy asked. "Did Waterman have any reason to anticipate a need to earn the tuition?" He thought there had probably not been any such reason: nothing about Jim Waterman suggested fecklessness, grasshoppering through the summers without thought for the winter's hungers; if he'd been caught with an empty larder when the cold began, it would be because of something sprung on him suddenly. Guy took a stab at the answer:

168

"One would think," he said mildly, "in fact it would be reasonable to assume—wouldn't it?—that he'd get an instructorship when the federal scholarship was due to run out?" It was not strictly relevant, the reason Jim had found himself suddenly short of money. Only, if you have to take responsibility for what you coddle, then let the Circumlocution Office admit responsibility for what it had apparently first coddled and then turned out into a cruel world.

The administrator inspected the wall behind his visitor's right ear. "One can't say, of course, what any individual might expect at any given time."

"No, sir." Large and obdurate, Guy waited.

"But there was, as it happens, a revision of departmental practice just then." The man sighed, inclining his head as if to the fates. "Of course in any innovation involving some cutoff date, an individual arriving at the barrier at the wrong moment, so to speak, may—suffer. Most regrettable, you'll doubtless agree."

Guy caught himself as he was about to incline his own head graciously. With an effort, he produced a stiff nod instead.

The Lambert man stirred the computer paper, looped back and forth on itself like molasses candy. "These choices must be made, I dare say. And of course financial aid must be awarded on the basis of excellence. *At* the time of decision. It would be capricious to go back into the candidate's record for previous, irrelevant years."

Unable to manage a respectable comment, Guy simply stared. Whoever said the university didn't prepare students for real life? Surely you couldn't get much better preparation for the real-life bind where only the man who could prove to a bank that he didn't really need the money could borrow money from the bank. The only catch was, a university was not supposed to be like a bank: it pretended, at least, to less chilly indifference to individual factors, less emphasis on tidy bookkeeping.

The troubled man at the other side of the desk had been

at Lambert since the days when it had resembled a bank rather less. Perhaps because he had needs arising from that fact, he had been studying the papers again. "Now look here," he said suddenly. "These grades, the more recent ones, are fine. Quite creditable." Relief brightened the lined face. "Naturally I can't speak for the Department. But I should think there would be a very good chance of reinstating financial aid if he reapplied for it." Inspired, he studied the record again, and found more safety and solace. "I don't see any indication that the student applied for aid at a later time."

"No, sir. I don't believe he would have."

The Lambert man sighed and pushed back from the desk. "Well, then. It would appear the young man solved his financial problem, after a bit." The beautifully modulated voice descended to something like a chuckle. "An inheritance, perhaps. Or the equivalent: sometimes aging aunts, and the like, see the advantage of sparing their heirs income taxes." The blue eyes, innocent and refusing to be dislodged from innocence, surveyed the policeman with satisfaction. "I've seen that happen, often." Guy stood up, and the Lambert man closed the folder. "Well. It does look as though everything's shipshape there, does it, Lieutenant?"

"Yes, sir," said Guy, betting silently that when anybody looked, they'd find Jim Waterman's aging aunt had paid off his undergraduate loans, too.

"I'm happy you thought of this way of examining the question," the old man said graciously. "At the cost of only some minor administrative—um—eccentricity, we are able to keep these researches from—too much attention." He led the way to the door. "And discretion is terribly important. We shouldn't care to embarrass the boy by some careless disclosure, should we?"

The face of Tim Whistler flashed into Guy's thoughts, and he tasted suddenly the shared bitterness that can also be called brotherhood. While, aloud, Det. Lt. Silvestri gave deft

170

assurance that Lambert need not worry (on behalf of its student's sensitivities, of course) about official discretion, he was saying a silent *Right on* to Tim, who had squeezed Lambert hard and would do it again.

The odds for buttoned academic lips was the first thing Guy was asked about by the man he phoned when he'd left Lambert's empty loveliness. "I wouldn't call it a sure thing," Guy said. "But relatively, it's a pretty good bet. Because the leak would have to come from the top."

"You don't think the biggies talk?" the voice scoffed.

"Sure they do. But ponderously. I couldn't make a real guess, but you can probably count on having three or four days."

"That'll do fine: we already got a partial fingerprint, and now that we know where to look . . . Thanks, Silvestri. If you don't mind me asking, though, I'm curious how you figured it was this Waterman. Did you maybe—"

"I didn't talk to him, if that's what's worrying you," Guy interrupted. He wondered whether this bunch ever trusted anybody, even each other. "It was a matter of taking an abstract view—of the kind of person it had to be, I mean." A combination of intelligence and maturity, you might say: someone who had wit enough to handle complicated details, and was also sensible enough to abjure identity-seeking and go along with being a cog in a machine when necessary . . . Abruptly, Guy realized that if he said these things, he would sound like a job reference. "Mainly, I was thinking in general terms about money," he said instead. "It occurred to me he was spending a lot of money, but we'd missed it because he was also poor. Not like Adonio, with his expensive house and car."

"It's a different type of mind," the voice suggested—cautiously, as though such a grand assertion might leave one open to criticism but one must try, anyway. Something about the tone reminded Guy painfully of the Lambert administrator. He cut off the rest of the man's thanks and hung up.

Then he got his overplump laundry bag out of the back
of his car and carried it, and a textbook, to the nearest laun-
dromat. Nobody interrupted his studies while the washer
and dryer fixed him up for the coming week. And when he
went on to the supermarket to stock up on everything except
frozen foods, because the bundles would be sitting in the car
for a while, he met nobody he knew in any of the aisles of
goodies. Silence and strangers ordinarily constituted a real
holiday for Guy, who spent too much of his time during the
week in discourse and involvement with other people. But
today, isolation bothered him: he realized with some shame
that right now he had a great wistfulness to run into Tom
Carrothers.

But he didn't, not even when he'd found a parking place
on Park Street and entered Elm Circle via the parking lot
of the small apartment house that backed up to the Circle.
He peered into the Grotto as he passed, but the bar stool near
the door stood empty, spotlighted by entering sunlight; the
dark beyond looked empty, too, which made sense for a
bright Saturday afternoon hinting of spring. Elm Circle
might well be having a drink about now, but it would be on
a golf course.

Or in its back yard if it was an amateur gardener, like
Elliott Sterling. Guy was about to ring the bell at Number
5 when he heard the familiar voice being funneled through
between the wall of Number 5 and its right-hand neighbor.
Guy ran down the steps and turned in between two budding
forsythias, then stopped to fumble with the catch of the ironwork gate, which was stiffened by generations of winters.

". . . remind you that the way of the lemmings, young
lady, is also a lifestyle, if you must use that disgusting word.
But when you choose that, remember it ends with a glub-
glub in a very cold sea," Elliott announced. Dramatically,
and at full volume, his voice rose, reaching for the second
balcony now. "In fact, that cozy solidarity you wallow in, that
gang-bang nihilism, isn't a lifestyle but a deathstyle."

172

"Hallelujah," Florence shouted. And Guy, agreeing silently with her mockery, had his way with the lock at last. He debouched into the garden—or what would someday be a garden but now looked rather like a news photo of tornado damage—as Florence was saying, "Love that Puritan ethic. You really climb, man, high and wide and outa sight." She turned then and saw Guy. "Wow! Like, save me, Sir Knight. This is some kind of dragon here."

Guy threaded his way past a havoc of cut-off and dug-out flora, on which gloves and trowel and clippers lay like boots on the necks of the conquered. Beyond, Elliott, apparently exhausted by all this molestation of nature, was sprawled on a redwood lounge in that imitation of taking the sun peculiar to New England—where, at the merest hint of clement weather, everyone rushes outdoors to engage in a mass-hypnotic pretense of California.

"Rescue me instead," Elliott said. "I'm a victim of my own altruism." He gestured at a small table behind Guy. "Do you thirst? May I—?"

"I'll do it myself, thanks." Guy examined him curiously, noting the pale skin still blotched with color, and decided at least some of Elliott's anger was real enough. And it certainly sounded convincing: listening, Guy had recalled that "chivying Florence" was one of Kate's examples of something wrong with Elliott. But, Guy decided now, either Kate took a remarkably comprehensive view of chivying or Elliott had been worsening since then. Still, it had been turned off so fast, with Guy's own entry . . . The anger was real but deliberately exaggerated, he concluded while he was greeting Florence. It was a portrait of a man out of control by a man in control.

"Yes, altruism," Elliott was insisting in the face of Florence's sneer. *"Somebody* ought to speak up, before your decline becomes irreversible. Look at her, Guy," he roared, blooming abruptly into fury again. "Just *look* at her."

Guy did. And Florence the Fair could not be anything but

fair, but he had to admit that she was limp-beautiful now instead of creamy-beautiful, and it was a shame. He remembered the middle-of-the-night phone call and wondered whether frantic frolics that went on till 4:00 A.M. were her only recreation from the business of scrambling for bread and tuition. Didn't she ever get to skip about in the sunshine? "You do look a bit peaked," Guy told her gently.

Florence grinned cheekily. *Camille* is the In look. Haven't you heard?"

But Elliott was not about to yield the floor permanently. "Indeed she does look pale and wan, fond lover. And do you know why?"

Guy knew he would be told why, in any case. He turned his attention to the table while the tirade raged. The waiting tray offered evidence that Elliott, out ahead of the pack as usual, had not only proclaimed spring but was fantasizing all the way to the tropics: the liquid refreshments on display were reminiscent of a tea plantation in Ceylon. Guy rolled his eyes at the temperate-zone heavens, which featured a peekaboo sun and a lot of scudding cloud. In a breeze brisk enough to raise whitecaps on the river, he fixed himself a gin and tonic and took it to a chair that had come up out of the cellar the moment the first crocus poked through the earth.

". . . and that our Florence has further forsworn such dull delights as sleep and vitamins. Thus daily dimming further an already dim wit," Elliott concluded elaborately. He flung out an arm in an orator's gesture—an old-time political orator on the Fourth of July. "What you see, my friend, what you yourself have seen here for yourself is the result of a diet of witches' brew and—"

"What witches' brew?" Florence interrupted shrilly. "You talking about what Gus cooks up at the Grotto?" She shook her head and said to Guy, her tone establishing that they were the only two sane folk present, "He's a method actor. Only the method is from silent films."

Guy smiled, because she was right, in a way. The word was

Schrechlichkeit, and it was conspicuously not part of this time or this culture. Particularly here in the garden Joshua Blaine Merritt, no lover of *Schrechlichkeit,* had left to his nephew, presumbaly in the solid faith that anyone born to a Merritt would know how to behave even if he'd been raised in Non-Buxford.

In the unaccustomed role of spokesman for maturity and moderation, Florence was not exactly underacting either. "I'd better go back and spring Kate," she announced demurely. "Much as I'd love to stay for the rhetoric-fest. But Duty is—"

"The stern daughter of the voice of God," Guy helped her out. Deadpan, but firmly. Because he was not sure he could take much more of Florence's maturity.

Elliott laughed, with much noise and little tact. When Florence had fled (still stubbornly in character and wearing a look clearly borrowed from old Mrs. Chandler), he said into the sudden silence, "I suppose I should apologize for the performance. Unless, of course, you're an opera fan?"

"Well, I *was* wondering why you do it. I mean, what's she up to, really, that's worth all that?"

"You have a damn good idea what she's up to."

"All right, the young have their rituals. But she's not shooting heroin, Elliott. If she dabbles in a little nonsense and it costs her some sleep—"

"Dammit, that's only what it costs *her!* Sure Florence draws back from the brink—but every time she goes dancing on it, half a dozen other kids fall over."

"Oh." Elliott was right: it was true that Florence set trends. "Well, it's a problem. If you lead, you have to take responsibility for your followers. But people who lead without especially meaning to . . . I don't know that it's fair to—"

"The hell with what's fair. It happens all the time, and with disastrous results. And the cops don't stop it, do they?"

"It's not a crime. To fail to be your brother's keeper."

"And it certainly doesn't get punished, does it?"

"Not by the state, anyway. Not the way you mean, I guess."

"Then the Florences never learn they'd better not do it again." Elliott laid his head back and closed his eyes, a portrait of a man who'd won his point and was now at peace. Guy watched him, thinking that Elliott was no more relaxed than the sun was the kind you could bask in, and wondered how anyone knew whether Florences learned.

Elliott opened his eyes. "So. My methods are admittedly a little lurid, but my intentions are honorable. I take it you don't mind if I try?"

"*I* don't mind." Florence hadn't minded either, Guy thought. Not really—it was as though she sensed that Elliott's fury, however excessive, was not intended to draw blood. "But I don't think much education's being accomplished," he added. Because, though under the harangues you could almost hear a beseeching note, the whole performance still didn't resemble either a teacher or a parent: Elliott made almost no attempt to be fair, to weigh actual acts or specific derelictions. What he did was no kind of adjudication, Guy decided, but simply a kind of hysterical warning, like a sheep dog barking at the edges of the flock.

"I hope you're wrong," Elliott said softly. His face was very pale.

Kate asked from the back gate, "Wrong about what?"

Nobody answered her, but she didn't seem to mind. And, Guy saw in the few seconds between Kate's words and her joining them, Elliott's color had come back and all the strings of his muscles seemed to have been untied. In Kate's presence, Guy admitted, some of his own knots tended to loosen, too. He accepted the fresh drink she made for him and began to talk and listen with an enjoyment he'd only been pretending to before. She laid a kind of peace on the afternoon. It was expensive, but worth the cost. Guy sighed and said he was glad he'd come.

"You should've come before," Elliott told him smugly. "I remember recommending this spa. Repeatedly."

"Ah, well. When I think I was actually close, only yesterday. And then I had to spend my time stifling yawns in the presence of L. Lester."

"My God! I hope they give you hardship pay."

"Why are you both so unkind?" Kate said. "The poor little man has never so much as spoken a cross word to you, Ellie."

"I don't care, he infuriates me anyway."

"Why?" Guy asked. "I'm not smitten by his charms myself, but he doesn't set my adrenaline flowing."

"Well, he starts mine gushing." Elliott seemed anything but full of adrenaline; he looked very nearly asleep. "There's no use discussing it. It would amount to useless talebearing."

"Don't feel you need to hold back on my account," Guy said mildly. "I know most of the tales, I think."

"There you have it, in a nutshell—you know, but nothing changes because you know."

"What is this, some kind of Lambert-student wah-wah about the grownups? Or just about the shortcomings of the police force?"

"Certainly not the latter." Elliott opened his eyes. "Because Ell-Square hasn't got the guts to call the cops."

Suddenly, unmistakably, Guy was slapping some kind of controls on himself: it was as though his Early Warning System had picked up a radar blip and abruptly, automatically, an alert had been announced. But not yet a scramble . . .

"Lester would have a rough time if he got too unpopular with the students," Guy said cautiously. "And he knows calling the cops would mean just that. Maybe it's hard for you to accept that kind of pressure as an excuse, because you're so free of it." He regretted that immediately: Silvestri, like America, was committed to never striking the first blow. "What I mean is," he added quickly, mending, "not everybody's a hero, that's all."

"*Argumentum ad hominem* is beneath you." Elliott was cool and severe. "And I've already considered your last point.

I found it wanting. For one thing, it makes nonheroism a handy excuse for any cold-hearted son of a bitch."

"So does Christianity, in other circumstances. Or for that matter, any other open-hearted ideology. They all contain possibilities of abuse." Guy felt like someone playing chess against two adversaries simultaneously—which could be done, but he was not a master. So he made a fending-off move against the opponent he knew well, the fox-faced angular fellow whose game was leisure-time dialectics for a pleasant afternoon—and meanwhile he struggled with the hidden strategy of the other fellow, the one who translated being your brother's keeper into moral vigilantism.

The phone rang inside the house just as Guy was wondering whether that "moral" really belonged in there at all. He stopped thinking then, distracted by his annoyance at the way Kate went without question to answer it. No question ever arose about this sort of thing in the Sterling household, apparently: it was just assumed that it would always be Kate who would do whatever was inconvenient.

"For you, Ellie," Kate said from behind him. "It's Professor Gamble. I said I'd see if you're in. Do you want to—?"

"Oh hell, I might as well. Excuse me, Guy. And don't think up arguments while I'm gone. Because it's my turn at bat, and I have a right to find the plate where I left it when I get back."

Guy smiled, and contracted to be fair. But that was in *that* chess game. Not in the one in which he was—to be fair about that, too—probably suffering a worm-eaten sense of being outmatched—by Elliott, who tended to see himself always as a kind of spectator at a theatrical extravaganza, but who maybe was not just spectating now. He seemed to be in the audience but he was also all over the place, moving props, joining in the dialogue on stage. What Guy couldn't figure out was whether all this was theater-of-the-absurd, in which the audience was *supposed* to participate, or whether Elliott

178

Sterling was in fact part of this production. As the director? The author of the script?

Guy had confronted that notion before, winced away from it, and decided finally—with some relief—on the assumption that Elliott was only playing I-know-a-secret. Unless Silvestri, an investigator of perhaps dubious impartiality, could find something objective—as opposed to a series of flimsy conjectures rising until the structure bumped into an impossibility—that assumption was all he was, in honor, entitled to. But he was tired of the distasteful quandary, sick of paying his dues in self-doubt and the need to examine his every thought for taint; he would accept anything, he thought wistfully now, anything at all that would move the problem one way or the other.

"Kate, listen," he said aloud. Too loudly, he heard: apparently he was even more desperate than he'd thought, for any way out. He cleared his throat and managed to ask more casually, "Did you and Elliott ever live in New York?" He wasn't sure right now what year it would have been, and anyway he didn't want to pinpoint it, just in case. So he added only, "Before you came here, I mean." A thoroughly imprecise question, because it arose from a thoroughly imprecise purpose: what Guy needed—but didn't know exactly what for, or how he'd use it—was some kind of outside-Elm-Circle link that could explain Elliott's knowing all the secrets he seemed to know.

Kate was looking surprised. "No, never. As a matter of fact, we never even go to New York for a weekend. Why do you want to know?"

"Well, did Elliott ever live there?" What Jim Waterman had called Florence's "bad, sick year" was not so identified in official records, but her dropout years were—and she had spent at least some part of them with Ann Price in New York's East Village. And Lowell Lester—whose human fear had just been dismissed with the light, disdaining *I found it*

179

wanting—was easy to follow via records. He was known to have spent exactly one year in New York, on a research grant. It could have been Florence's year.

". . . thought you knew, Ellie always lived in California," Kate was saying. "Except when he went to Lambert. And when he was very little, of course."

Guy nodded. He did know the biography: Joshua Blaine Merritt's young sister Cynthia and the Ausländer she'd married had found life in Elm Circle too constricting; the young Sterlings had taken off for the wide-open West when Elliott was only a kindergartener.

"Ellie had just come east when we met in Chicago. And then, after—after a while," Kate went on steadily, "we came here."

Guy produced appropriate sounds of gratitude-cum-apology and silently watched his frail hunch slipping away. He told himself he was a fool anyway—nothing so big and conspicuous as geography was going to help him out with a reason, more comfy than the obvious one, why Elliott knew so damned much. But if geography was no help, psychology was even worse—it put the lid on conjecture, brought speculation to a halt. Because if it was possible, on the grounds that nobody is immune, to imagine Elliott as a double murderer, it was emphatically not possible to imagine Elliott trying to frame the black students at the Residence.

And yet, that was the first thing the murderer had done *qua* murderer, and it had to be taken seriously. Just because it was gratuitous, because he had done it though he needn't have, it was a kind of identification, a basic line of the portrait that couldn't be dismissed. But neither could it be made to fit a picture of Elliott Sterling—not even by a guilt-ridden nonobjective detective (for psychology was, alas, a double-edged tool) who might be harboring a hidden eagerness to misinterpret harmless eccentricity and thus remove an obstacle. . .

You need a gimmick, Guy said to himself in something like
180

panic: forget both logic and intuition, and just pray for a gimmick. He was aware of sudden sweat on his forehead, and Kate looking at him with concern. He shook his head, warding off her question, and told himself that without a gimmick the best he could hope for in this game was a draw.

Elliott came back then, real and cranky. "Why the hell didn't you tell them I was out?" But he consented to take the tall glass offered by an apologetic Kate. "They're coming over. I wiggled, but I couldn't get out of the trap." He sipped and then smiled, a sweet pixie-Elliott smile. "You know, the gin in a Tom Collins must be entirely a state of mind. Because I feel quite lightheaded right now. Thank you, darling."

So the game was postponed. Guy yielded to pleas not to leave the Sterlings alone with the unbearable Gambles; he stayed on long enough to discover that the Gambles really were unbearable, and to see with his own eyes how infinitely preferable was Elliott's grace and wit. But it was also long enough to see himself too clearly for comfort, too—the good boy who loved his mother and had sworn to uphold the law, but somehow also managed to covet his neighbor's wife and drink his neighbor's liquor while . . . *Such a nasty way to be*, Kate had said of Elliott's "campaign" against Lowell Lester.

Such a nasty way to be, indeed. Guy pled his bachelor status, with its implications of big doings on Saturday nights, to make an acceptable early-evening exit. He went home, worked a little, ate and drank, and by the time the late movie came on the local TV station, he had managed a fair degree of peace with himself. Until he remembered Kate saying, once, that she just loved to watch old movies on TV. Then he snapped Clark Gable off and went to bed.

To Lena Silvestri's surprise, her son came over on Sunday. He was a good boy, not always phoning as often as he might but more faithful than a lot of other sons she heard about: she could tell, if she chose, some sad stories about the way young men treated their mothers nowadays. But she'd practically just *seen* Guy, and he hadn't said Word One about coming over the house till he phoned Sunday morning. She was lucky there was this little store open on her way home from church, because there really wasn't a thing in the house to feed him.

While he was putting a new washer in her kitchen faucet—he was such a lovely son!—she studied him and concluded there was something on his mind. But he didn't talk about it, or about anything except things from long ago. Finally, after he got her to tell him all over again that old story about Papa and the crooked election in the union—the time Mr. Cavallone, such a nice man and a neighbor and all, turned out to be one of the crooks—she decided what was on Guy's mind was his Papa. Deep down underneath, Guido had always been a sentimental boy.

She did the best she could to make him feel better, but of course there were some things nobody could help.

11

The Civil
Hunter

Guy? Listen, I've found something a little—odd. Maybe
it doesn't mean anything, but I figured I ought to tell you."

It meant something, whatever it was: Silvestri's nervous
system seemed to know that at once, the voices of his body
calling *Here we go!* What was going on inside him was like
what happens when a roller coaster stops being just another
little cart racketing along and becomes all looping, swooping
speed. The very rhythms of his blood first accelerated and
then settled down to a fast and steady warming, as if he had
been out for a brisk run on a cold day.

And then exaltation ended with nightmare suddenness, as
he realized whose voice he had been hearing. "Jim?" Guy
thought having a heart attack must feel something like this,
this abrupt, untransitioned stopping-in-action. But he had
not, in fact, been stopped in action: somewhere in his mind,
information was still registering, for he heard Jim Waterman

183

explaining the mission that had taken him to 20 Elm Circle. "I don't quite understand," Guy said dully, "what it is you were supposed to do." He blinked at the phone in his hand.

"I told you, the inventory is part of the whole probate bit. Jacques will have to sort the books, of course. But in the meantime, it made some sense to have me open the house and start. And I figured if I began with the top shelves, at least Jacques wouldn't have to scurry up and down a ladder."

"The yearbook was on the top shelf?" Guy said. He stared at the familiar furniture of his office, at the government-issue calendar announcing a Tuesday morning. All of it seemed, all at once, to belong to somebody else.

"All the yearbooks were. One for every year Hilary taught at Merrivale. It seemed obvious Jacques wouldn't be terribly interested—I mean, he never taught there himself—so I just stacked them all together and—oh," Jim said with sudden comprehension, "I know which one the picture came out of, if that's what's worrying you."

"Can you give me a little more detail about the picture?" Guy asked. His shock and confusion seemed to have gone up in that instant explosion. He listened now with a cool attention, recognizing that this was probably it. The gimmick. The boost that would let him get out in front of the plan.

". . . no caption or anything, no writing of any kind. Just a picture cut out of a newspaper. Originally a studio portrait, would be my guess. The girl is young. Pretty, but not enough to make you fall over in a fit of trembling, if you know what I mean." Jim hesitated. "I feel a little silly now. I mean, so Hilary cut a picture of a girl out of the newspaper and stuck it in a book, so what? If I didn't know you outside—well, I can't imagine myself ringing up the police over something like that."

"No, no, you did the right thing, Jim." Guy put his best effort into that: Jim had certainly no responsibility for the effect on Silvestri's tender guilt feelings, and he deserved at least thanks that sounded like thanks. "Whether it turns out to be important or not, I'm grateful to you." As he said the word, he knew "grateful" was understatement. Hilary Bridge cutting a picture out of a newspaper was, like the Park Street cobbler, not part of the design. Or, with luck, was more like Mrs. Adonio's delay in calling the police—a human interference with the planner's calculations. "How about the back of the picture?" Guy asked. If it came from a newspaper, there could be any amount of useful stuff on the other side of the page.

"No dice. The photo's stuck down, didn't I tell you? That's one reason I thought it wasn't exactly casual. He made a frame for it, sort of. Out of paper."

"Well, *somebody* made one."

"Oh, it had to be Hilary. You'll see—it's that elegant rice paper Hilary used. But anyway," Jim went on, forestalling objection, "Jacques couldn't have helped doing a better job of it even if he was stoned. It looks—well, like the paper valentine you brought home to your Mom from kindergarten."

"Where are you now?" The phone at 20 Elm Circle had been cut off, Guy realized suddenly. "You don't have it with you, do you?"

"No, I left it in the house. I figured it must be illegal or something, to take it out of there. I'm at school. In an empty office I found." The voice held a smile. "So this is Lambert's dime. I hope *that's* not illegal."

"One way or another, Lambert must owe it to you," Guy said lightly. Appalled, he heard how easy it was: anybody could learn to be two-faced, no prerequisites needed for the course. He went on with it, with shame for both this cool and its opposite, the working warmth of excitement. He swore Jim to secrecy about the find, at least until further notice, and said "I know" quite unblushingly when Jim boasted of a capacity for discretion. It was all a little shocking, and more than a little saddening, but it was not confusing anymore because life was often hard and never much like the Boy

Scouts. Guy thanked Jim Waterman almost as if this was a day like any other day, for either of them. Then he hung up, because they both had need to hurry.

In the silent and beautiful library of Hilary Bridge's house, Guy found the stacked yearbooks and the newspaper photo. He lifted it as carefully as if it were an archaeological find and held it up for Toots Cantor's inspection. Jim's estimate of the arts-and-crafts skill required to make the paper frame had been accurate: except for the absence of crayoned decoration, it did look like a kindergarten project.

"Nice-looking girl," Cantor said. "It's a damn good thing you got the tip, you know? If Jacques got to this first, I bet we wouldn't ever heard of it. I tell you, I seen widows do things that'd curl your hair. There was this one time, the widow grabbed the evidence—it was a canceled check—and flushed it down the john because she didn't like who it was made out to."

Guy smiled at him, grateful to Cantor for having been in his office when he was called. Grateful, but not surprised: everything was going to fall into place from here on out, Guy knew. He let Toots talk while he studied the photograph in the oblong frame cut out for it by a hand inept with scissors. The girl was smiling gravely, showing pearly teeth over a pearl necklace and the shoulders of a dark dress—not an academic gown, so it wasn't graduation that had been newsworthy. But it could very well have been an engagement—or, if this was from a hometown newspaper, just Mr. and Mrs. Somebody's daughter winning an essay prize. The girl was young, with serious eyes and long, slightly wavy hair that was probably dirty blond or light brown. Somewhere, she had dressed up and combed her hair and sat for a studio portrait. But if the newspaper had credited the photographer, Hilary Bridge had trimmed the credit line along with the caption.

"The lab can get it off that paper," Toots said. "You'll see, they'll fix it so you can read the back. Just give 'em a little time."

186

But Guy was through waiting, finished with patient gathering of facts, meditating, speculating. He switched on one of Hilary Bridge's Japanese lamps and held the photo up between his eye and the light. What was on the other side, between dried blobs of paste, was not words but part of another picture—one wider and longer than the girl's. Guy saw that he had the bottom right-hand corner of that photo —of what looked like a building, with the bottom halves of people standing in front of it . . . Toots Cantor, who didn't need to deal with a leap of excitement before he could move, found the magnifying glass belonging to Hilary Bridge's handsome leather desk set. Guy held it over the tiny line of agate type and the words, clouded by the smeary paste but legible, swam into focus. Guy managed to hold the glass steady while he translated the backward print: *Jack Connery photo.*

Toots didn't know any Jack Connery, and anyway it didn't look like any of the Boston papers. He agreed that it was probably a staff photo and so could be checked out. But it would take a while, he cautioned.

Guy laughed. There were advantages to big families, he said, and if he could get a few minutes somewhere where there was a phone, he'd show Toots. They tied up the Merrivale College yearbooks with a piece of Hilary Bridge's twine and borrowed a sheet of his notepaper, on which Det. Lt. Harold Cantor attested that he had removed the following objects from the premises and Det. Lt. Guy Silvestri attested that he had witnessed the removal. Then they locked up and left, with Toots carrying the books to the car under Guy's raincoat draped over his arm. Elm Circle might see and wonder, but it wouldn't be given anything specific to wonder about.

At Cantor's office, the probably longish job of checking the graduates' photos for each year against the newspaper clipping was set in motion. Toots rumbled pessimism again: "All them girls with that same long hair—it could be the last one in the last book."

But by that time Guy had phoned and asked for his cousin, Frank Compofelice. "Frankie C.," they called him at the *Boston Star*: Guy could hear city-room voices asking each other who had seen him. Frank was a staff photographer for the *Star*; but, more important for his cousin's needs at the moment, he also held office in the News Photographers Association. Like most photographers, he had a good memory for faces; like most Silvestri kin, he also had a precinct-level politician's habit of wide acquaintance and gift for remembering names. He was, in short, at least as good a bet as an FBI file for rapid identification.

"Connor? Jesus, there's a hundred Connors in Boston, Guido," Frank complained. "What? Oh, Connor-*ee*. Yeah, yeah, I know how you spell it. You mean Jack Connery, you're out of luck, kid. He's out in Nam. I'm sure he's still there—I ran into a fellow that ran into him in Saigon two, three—"

"Frank, listen. I don't care where he is. All I want is, what paper does he work for?" Guy listened. And then there it was again, that feeling in him like a high wire humming. "New York? You sure it's New York?"

"Whattya mean am I sure? Jack Connery's been with that rag so long he half owns the place. He's the Guild shop steward, or anyway he used to be, so—"

"Thanks. Thanks a million, Frank. I owe you for this. Oh, and regards to the family." Guy hung up, sighed, and went to tell Toots, who was after all in charge of the investigation. Then Guy set about arranging to go to New York.

What it took was a semi-political maneuver, involving calling in some outstanding "notes" for favors rendered in the past. Also a two-level communication to Guy's boss, who was offered both an official reason for diplomacy—that the New York police might prove uncooperative with a too-low rank, but anyone higher ranking than Silvestri would make it seem much too big a deal—and the unofficial suggestion that Silvestri, a valuable fellow who never asked for anything for himself, might get unhappy if somebody was to get a free trip to New York and it wasn't he. And certainly what it took, from beginning to end, was the active backing of Toots Cantor.

He eyed Guy curiously, when they had won. "The dice are hot, huh?"

"I feel—I don't remember ever feeling so sure before. You know?"

Cantor knew, and said for God's sake to get going then, and make it fast. In the doorway he turned, looking a little proud and a little foolish, and added, "Good hunting, son."

He was gone before Guy's faint sense of objection gathered enough strength for a startled "But—"

The Lt. Clemens who, after some long-distance conversation on Tuesday, had been designated to be bothered by an out-of-town officer on Wednesday sounded resigned to his fate when Guy phoned from the airport. Clemens would be available all afternoon and most of the evening, so Guy checked into his hotel and took a taxi to the editorial offices of the tabloid whose photo staff was graced by Jack Connery. Presumably, people at the newspaper would have been reasonably cooperative with any policeman who came with a rather simple request, but Guy—still with that feeling of being an arrow already in flight to the bull's-eye—avoided channels and went straight to the photo desk to present greetings from Frankie C. In the end, that may have taken just as long, what with having his back pounded by various meaty hands. But in any case time was something that had to be served, one way or another, and wading through the 8-by-10 glossies in Jack Connery's file was only a small obstacle on a course laid straight for the goal line. Pictures can be flicked past rapidly if all you're interested in is their bottom right-hand corners. And Guy had no sooner started than someone thought he remembered the building being dedicated in the picture, and Guy transferred from a survey of

189

Connery's catholic activities to a more specific file. The date of publication was established rather soon. The newspaper's library was geared to supplying information promptly: within minutes, then, Guy was peering at a microfilm of page 26 of the final edition for January 16, four years earlier.

And finally, there was the already familiar face of the nice-looking young girl—in a brief story the point of which was, in fact, the photo: the young woman who'd died of a drug overdose had now been identified by a family friend. *Joan Mary Robinson,* Guy wrote in his notebook, his handwriting betraying his excitement. He copied the name of the street, University Lane, on which the girl had collapsed and died. But he didn't bother to note anything else: with the location, the victim's name, and the fact that it was a drug case, there could be no delay in getting all the rest of the information— rather more, in fact, than was offered in the tabloid story, which was addressed to readers who already knew something about the case. Guy forbade himself to wonder about Joan Mary Robinson now, because the sooner he got moving, the sooner he'd know. He put in an order with the Back Copy department, which couldn't fill it right away but would send a paper over to his hotel. Then he thanked everybody, bought the boys in News Photo a drink from Frankie C., and took a taxi to the dirty building in a dirty street where Lt. Clemens worked.

Lt. Clemens turned out to be a tall, husky Negro who was probably only about five years older than Guy but wore a look of having seen everything; he also seemed to expect to be able to bear up if it all came round again. Clemens disappeared briefly to put Guy's request "in the pipeline" and then came back to suggest, "How about if we go out for a bite?"

Guy hesitated. He was pretty sure he should eat again by now, and the drink with the photographers really ought to be followed up with food. But the idea seemed impossible to support.

190

"You're pretty worked up about this, aren't you—what's your name—Guy?" Clemens' glance verged on the fatherly despite the small difference in their ages.

Feeling ridiculous, Guy confessed to a sense of being somehow on a winning streak. Clemens said he understood how it was, and he'd ordered coffee and sandwiches sent in. "You care what kind? I didn't think so. Okay, just sit tight."

Gratefully, Guy sat tight, struggling with more superstition—the fear that the spirit of the narco squad now had him in thrall. If it did, he decided finally, the best thing he could do was hang onto the coattails of Del ("for Delano—my folks split Franklin Roosevelt among three of us kids") Clemens, who seemed to know how to be a hunter but a civil one.

"Sorry I'm not familiar with the case myself." Clemens had the air of a man waiting with an anxious friend in a bus station. "But I know that neighborhood, all right."

"Is that what they call the 'East Village'?"

"Near it, but closer to Washington Square." The New Yorker smiled. "They're all arty in the Square, too, but they have good jobs. At New York University, usually. That address is right around the corner from N.Y.U."

"Oh, the plush-lined Bohemians. We have that in Buxford."

"I bet you do. I just bet you do." The big man leaned back in his desk chair. "The difference here is, in the East Village they wind up in St. Vincent's Hospital's emergency room when they get a skinful—either kind of skinful. Around Washington Square, though, it's more likely to be a private sanatorium."

Guy laughed, eased by a sense of being not really far from home. He looked around at the grimy walls and battered furniture, and decided he was a spoiled darling by contrast. Here where Elm Circle was a Square, public funds must need to stretch further.

"Admiring our interior decoration? I bet yours is better." Clemens broke off to distribute sandwiches and the paper

191

cups of coffee. "Up your way, they probably still have some hope that if they spend more money they can get better police work. Here, they've given up."

Guy said, around a mouthful of corned beef, "That bad, is it?"

"Well, it's reasonable to figure no police officer's going to do much better than he's doing now, no matter how much more you pay him, whether you give him a nice office or not. I guess it could make a difference about people deciding to join, but once they do, they still only have two hands and twenty-four hours a day each. And they're right full—matter of fact, if your little girl there wasn't four years ago, I doubt it would've been in the papers. Kids and drugs just aren't news around here anymore."

"Here, let me help," Guy said. They cleaned up the debris together while Del told him about Goldberg, who might or might not have been in on the case at the time but would certainly know one hell of a lot about it anyhow. "Goldie's been around for at least three mayors and five commissioners, and there isn't anything Goldie doesn't know *something* about," Clemens said. "You know what I mean?" Guy knew what he meant and said so, smiling: waiting was easier, in this home away from home.

And then the door opened and somebody handed him a sheaf of papers, and all the waiting began to come to an end. For Joan Mary Robinson had been identified by means of an ID card issued to students at—the words jumped out at Guy—Merrivale College in Waterville, New York. She had no purse, and the only other thing in her coat pocket when she was checked in, dead on arrival, at St. Vincent's Hospital was a crumpled telegraph blank—a writing effort that had been intended as final and then become a first draft, apparently. For the name and address were printed clearly, but the message was heavily revised and thus had probably been copied over. The gist of the message was clear, though: Joan Mary Robinson had needed money, and right away.

192

The New York Police Department's first-level information on the case, gathered from direct observation or generated by routine procedures, really began with the finding of the telegraph blank: up to then, the only recorded information was the name of the citizen—Berndt Edmondsen, 142 University Lane—who had called the police at 12:20 A.M. The rest came of a telephone call to the Beverly Hills, California, police and another to the home of the telegram's addressee, Leo T. Badge. That call was accepted by a Miss Natalie Hare, who said she was Mr. Badge's secretary and Joan Mary Robinson was his stepdaughter. Miss Hare would try to locate Mr. and Mrs. Badge, who'd gone off on a camping trip in the mountains. Meanwhile, she referred the callers to Mr. Badge's literary agent, Hilliard Snowe, who would do what was necessary until someone in the family could get to New York. In the end, no one in the family had gotten to New York, it seemed: an autopsy was performed ("see attached Form S24B33"), establishing the cause of death as overdose of a narcotic drug, and the body was released three days later to Hilliard Snowe, 343 Madison Ave., who had previously appeared at the city morgue to identify it.

Guy looked up from his reading when the new man came into the office. "Goldie sent him," Del Clemens explained. "This is Rufus Spencer of the *Messenger.*"

The man lounging on the corner of Clemens' desk acknowledged the pronouncing of his name, but he looked as if he would have preferred anonymity if not absence. His air of sullen impatience aroused no resentment, though, because it was so clearly habitual.

Clemens went on, looking a little rueful, "It begins to seem I'm the only one in town who didn't know this case." He held out a fat manila envelope leaking newspaper clippings at top and bottom. "It was covered rather extensively, it looks like."

"The girl's stepfather was a pretty well-known name at the time," Spencer said. His sullenness was a little dissipated: he didn't seem to mind participating if he knew more than anybody else and happened to be around anyway. "Screen-writer out in Hollywood. He'd written a lot of mystery stories, too, so you saw his name around on paperbacks and all. And of course Berndt Edmondsen." He shrugged. "Only a theoretical big name. Commentary on our great civilization, that's what that is."

Guiltily, Guy admitted that he thought he'd heard of Leo Badge but never of Edmondsen.

Del Clemens said, "A radio-astronomer, very distinguished man. But not really so overlooked, Ru. He died a couple of years ago—he was somewhere in his late seventies—and I remember the obituary in the *Times* ran half a page, at least."

A sneer replaced what remained of Spencer's air of indifference. "Oh, obits. And the *Times* yet." Having put Clemens in his place, the reporter turned his attention to Silvestri. "Edmondsen certainly was no household name, but he did add a little news interest. The big play, though, was the telegram: the kid had it in her pocket, and it was feature stuff, all right. Very touching," he said scornfully. "Seems Daddy's secretary got the wire that evening and sent five hundred bucks. So the money was sitting there, in the Western Union office, when the girl died." Spencer's look of boredom returned. "Not a dry eye in the house, of course. What with that and the brave old man, that's probably why Wetherby used it."

"And that's why Goldie sent Ru over here," Del Clemens explained. "This Wetherby is a writer for true-detective magazines. Kind of a hack, I guess, but I sometimes like his stuff myself. Anyway, what he does is, when he reads about a case somewhere that looks good to him, he gets in touch with a news guy working on it and pays him to collect everything that got thrown out for space reasons and so forth. Then Wetherby mulls over the clips awhile and comes up with a dramatic version—supposed to be basically true but kind of touched up—for any of a slew of those magazines. Ru

194

was Wetherby's contact on the Robinson case, so Goldie thought he could help us out."

"Wetherby's a vulture," Spencer said.

"Oh, come on. Wetherby's a vulture and you're not?" Clemens' smile flashed very white in his chocolate-colored face. "I've got nothing against vultures anyway. All they do is feed aboveground on what the worms eat underground."

Guy laughed, applauding tolerance of vultures—not to say the one-upping of the reporter. Ru Spencer, maker of fine distinctions, went on fishing in the folder of clippings, muttering meanwhile about the oppressive arm of the law. The legendary Goldberg, Guy gathered, was one from whom some blessings flowed to reporters; when he said "Go," they were thus inclined to obey. Spencer had been sent to flesh out the skeleton of the Robinson case for the visiting hick and he was proceeding to do so, but nobody had said he had to do it cheerfully. "Here's the telegram the kid sent." He held up a clipping and read in a flat voice, " 'Popsy dear, Sorry-sorry-sorry but please-please-please send more money. Hurry. Your wretched Joanie.' "

There wasn't a dry eye in this house, anyway: Guy saw reflected in Del Clemens' face what must be visible on his own. He wondered whether the message was fifteen words, and whether the rewriting had come of a nice girl's muddled effort to be thrifty. She was nineteen years old, Popsy's secretary had told the New York police.

"We closed the case," Clemens said. "We did get the pusher, Guy. A half-witted Puerto Rican kid sold her the stuff. A junkie himself."

Guy nodded, sharing Del's feeling that the criminal was little less pitiable than the victim of the crime. "Most of the information seems to come from Berndt Edmondsen and this Hilliard Snowe. Their statements."

"That's about all there was," the reporter said. "It seems the mother flipped and the father stayed with her, so the body was just shipped to California for burial. Snowe arranged for it, and he answered any questions anybody asked. Apparently he had orders to be cooperative. Old Dr. Edmondsen was more than cooperative—he was hounding the cops, right from the start."

The police officer who took Berndt Edmondsen's statement had thought him very upset, but coherent. The old man had gone with the dead girl to the hospital, where an observant doctor promptly ordered him admitted for treatment of exposure and shock.

"They had him stowed in bed and ordered to rest," Spencer said. "But he insisted on talking. He wanted somebody's head on a platter."

"Any idea why?" Guy asked.

"Who knows? He certainly never saw the girl before that night—he was just closing up for the night, standing in the big bay window those houses have fronting on the street, when the girl came walking across his field of view. There were snow banks along the curb and where the sidewalk met the front lawns. Well, a path had been cleared in the middle of the sidewalk, but Edmondsen didn't think much of the shoveling job—seems he'd been fussing about it earlier that day. So the unsteady way she was walking caught his attention. He thought it showed that the walk was slippery, like he'd said it would be. Anyway, she was almost out of sight—about halfway between the old boy's house and the one on his right—when she just toppled over. Just went down all of a heap. It looked funny to him, so he kept on watching."

What was probably "funny" about the way the girl had fallen, Guy realized, was that it had not been funny, had been entirely without that grotesque flailing by which people try to regain their balance. The street was well-lighted and the piled snow reflected a good deal of light besides, so the old astronomer had been able to see her clearly. When she didn't get to her feet, he unlatched his window and leaned out to call, *Are you all right, miss?*

"He insisted he saw her move." Spencer shrugged. "The doc at St. Vincent's said she couldn't have. But anyway, she didn't make a sound. And the way she was just lying there, so still—well, Edmondsen ran out just like he was, in shirt-sleeves and wearing slippers, though it was cold as hell that night. He walked slowly because of the ice, so it took him a little longer to get to her—and maybe that's what bugged him later. Because he believed if he'd got there sooner it might have made a difference: he kept calling to her, and he thought he heard her crying. The doctor said he didn't think the old man really heard anything at all."

In any case, the girl neither moved nor spoke when Edmondsen reached her. He turned her over, to look at her face in the light. *I knew right away the child was dying,* he told the police officer.

The usually skeptical Ru Spencer thought highly of the old man's judgment on this score. "He'd served in a ski patrol in the army, back in the old country. And he'd been a farm boy before that, in a place where they have awfully long damn winters and no doctors handy. So it looks like he'd know what he was talking about."

Edmondsen had used his knowledge that night. He crouched beside the girl in the snow, wrapping his arms around her to warm her; and because she appeared to be still breathing, he propped her partly upright against the snow bank to make it easier. He held her that way, hoping someone would summon help: he was unable to lift her and carry her inside, and he knew better than to leave her. No help came, though, and the girl died in his arms.

"When it was over," Spencer went on, "he went back in the house and called the cops. That was at twelve-something —you have the report. The old boy told the cops he'd watched the eleven o'clock news before he began to lock up, so what with one thing and another they figured this whole business—from when he first saw her till she died—lasted about thirty minutes." Spencer paused. "You ask me why he was so worked up, maybe it had something to do with being out in that freezing weather all that time. He was the skinny, frail kind of old man. They're tougher than the fat ones, but he was pretty sick afterwards."

Hilliard Snowe, Guy gathered, had not been sick or in any other way troublesome to the authorities. He had simply supplied the necessary background information: Joan Mary Robinson was in New York because Merrivale College's experimental program included a "do your thing" freedom from classes during January. Joanie was a sophomore who had recently decided to concentrate on English; her "thing" for January involved a new literary magazine being started by some kids in the East Village.

"These 'kids'—" Guy began.

Rufus Spencer shook his head. "Wetherby was interested in that angle. I did a little extra digging, but there were hundreds of those pads. Thousands now, but at least hundreds then. And at least fifty percent of those people were starting new magazines. There was nothing to go on, either, because Robinson met them only after she came to New York. She'd been staying in a hotel with another girl from school, but the other girl decided to take a job in a mental hospital for *her* project, so you could see she hadn't taken any interest in these kids Joanie met. Anyway, when the other girl decided to move out, Joanie decided to move in with these kids."

If that came from Snowe, he must have known about it in time to stop the girl. But maybe he'd tried and failed? "What's Hilliard Snowe like?" Guy asked.

"Well, he looks like an agent. Sort of beautiful-people-ish—the best of threads on a petted body, a rich smell of hand-blended tobacco—*you* know. He was shook up, of course, but he talked clearly enough. Shortly after the girl arrived in town, he took her to lunch. He hadn't known her long, because her much-married mama hadn't been married to his client very long. He said the girl seemed to like Leo

Badge very much—not enough for hero worship exactly, but when she said she wanted to be a writer, Snowe kind of figured Badge was shy."

"What did Snowe think of this literary magazine idea, did he say?"

"Not much, apparently. But—well, he hadn't been appointed the girl's guardian. All that was expected of him was to take her to lunch and maybe introduce her around a little. Matter of fact, he intended to introduce her to an editor who was interested in youth stuff. But just about the first thing she said was that the Literary Establishment was dead-dead-dead, so he gathered it wouldn't be regarded as a favor. When I was digging for Wetherby's bonus, I saw Snowe again and got some more about what he thought of Joanie herself. But it wasn't much: she was cute, and surprisingly well adjusted when you considered her highly unstable mother. Leo Badge was a good client who made steady money and few demands, and taking Joan Mary Robinson to lunch wasn't an unusual chore in the life of an author's agent, and certainly not a painful one. But his relations with Badge had always been more professional than personal, so Snowe had no particular feeling about Joanie. Except that she was likable, and her death left him shocked and sorry, he found it quite incredible, et cetera, et cetera."

"Did he remember the names of any of the kids she was going to move in with?"

"He said not, and I don't see any reason not to believe him."

"Do *you* remember," Guy asked a little desperately, "whether you came across the name Ann Price in your extra digging? She makes fancy leather-goods things, and she was around at the time."

"Oh, brother. Leather, woodcarving, big copper jewelry—it's all part of the pattern, Lieutenant. There's always the one who's got some kind of business—"

"Established and funded by Daddy," Del Clemens put in.

"But that's the legit element, is what Ru means. Then you get the hangers-on, the ones who *aren't* rich kiddies."

"Joanie Robinson was a rich kiddie," Guy said. "Merrivale is a very expensive school. And you notice the stepfather's secretary just wired money without having to ask permission."

"That's different." Spencer emphasized the difference with a loose gesture. "That's the *visiting* rich kids. They're the ones who usually get hurt, too."

"Right," Clemens said. "They float into town, well supplied with cash and interested in giving anything at all a whirl at least once. The hangers-on we mentioned get hurt, too, but they protect themselves better. And the regular rich kids, the ones with the subsidies, they protect themselves best of all."

"I remember one hanger-on who got hurt," the reporter said. "But I can't help you with names, because it was all nicknames. This one they called "Beauty," and she really was: remarkably pretty girl, very, very attractive. Something about her—"

"She looked like Miss Iowa, maybe," Guy said sadly. "Cornfed and healthy. Lots of soft blond hair, big blue eyes." The image of Florence Hathaway was so clear in his mind that it seemed silly to go on trying to describe her.

"That sounds like Beauty. But she wasn't looking so healthy right then. Very shook up. I got a feeling she felt responsible somehow, but she wasn't really—she hadn't been anywhere near the Robinson kid that day, because the cops checked. I remember that on account of the way all the other kids rushed in to tell me that even the cops hadn't bothered her. They all seemed to take care of her, somehow." Spencer grinned. "In fact, I finally got thrown out by the one who must've been Beauty's Beast. Homely, skinny cat with a scraggly black beard."

"Guy, the junkie we sent up did sell the Robinson kid the stuff," Clemens said. "I realize that sociologically, he's a pretty pathetic answer. But we didn't railroad him. I know because I know Goldie. He doesn't knuckle under, and anyway there wasn't that much pressure: the girl's parents weren't around, and the papers let up on it pretty soon."

"I know." Even the clean-up-the-city advocates wouldn't fire their heavy artillery from the shaky ground of Joan Robinson: they could get a better test case than a thrill-seeking college girl wandering into town. "Her parents weren't even taxpayers. I know, Del."

Spencer slid down off the desk. "Old Edmondsen was a taxpayer, though. And he was doing his best to pressure somebody, anybody. He kept yammering about something—I don't remember what, but I know it didn't amount to much. And it didn't have anything to do with the Village kids you're interested in. He knew less about them than any tabloid reader." For the first time, the reporter's face showed real concern. "It bugs me that I can't remember, though."

And Edmondsen, who certainly would remember what he'd been so agitated about, was dead. Guy felt his run of luck sliding out from under him. After all that had been dropped in his lap, he knew he had no right to a grievance; but he felt cheated anyway. "Look, I'll be around till tomorrow—I want to talk to Hilliard Snowe if I can, for one thing. And after that I'll be back in Buxford, but still available. If you think of what it was the old man was so upset about, will you let me know?"

"You haven't got everything you wanted, then," Del Clemens said.

"Not quite." Guy finished writing the telephone numbers of his home and office and handed the slip of paper to the reporter. "Please." Inspired, he looked directly at the man who so elaborately cared so little about so much. "It's *wrong,* you know, that this sort of thing just—falls down a crack. So if you can do something more . . ." He watched Spencer leave and then told Clemens that he had, among other things, a connection now between two apparently uncon-

201

nected homicides. And everybody had been great, and if Del or Goldie or anybody else needed a favor any time, Silvestri clearly owed them.

Alone in his hotel room, he made a note to inquire at Merrivale whether Joan Mary Robinson had been a student of Hilary Bridge. But he would bet Bridge had been her advisor. He could imagine with bitter ease a possible dialogue between Professor Bridge, who was "not your student-pal type," Florence had said—but who, assigned to advise a new English major, would certainly have avoided looking square—and the silly little Miss Robinson who probably wanted to be different from her mother, a woman posed beside a Hollywood swimming pool against a backdrop of assorted husbands. It would have been a tragic combination. Guy wondered whether Hilary had kept the dead girl's picture because he recognized that it was more than the usual newspaper tragedy. Possibly because Hilary Bridge had had more perception than courage.

But either way, Hilary had moved on, with his precious chattels and his civilized way of life that was easily tranplantable to Elm Circle. And Joanie had moved on to what she believed was the real, down-to-earth life of Beauty and the Beast and artists and writers too ethereal for the Establishment. And they had delivered her into the hands of the young pusher-junkie—whose Establishment, now that Guy came to think of it, was certainly the likes of Ralph Adonio.

Okay, there were connections. Only, Guy thought crankily before he got to sleep in the strange bed, there was still no visible connection with Lowell Lester. Who was not trading in drugs or delightedly bringing mixed-up little girls the good news about how much opium had done for De Quincey . . . Guy recognized that he was being petulant, like a kid snowed under with Christmas toys and screaming for the one that got left out. But the knowledge didn't help much.

Weariness did, though, He had had a very long, full day, and he escaped into sleep.

12

The Uncivil
Hunter

Hilliard Snowe proved to be easy to see on Thursday morning, but also not really worth seeing. Unless you were interested in checking on Rufus Spencer's perceptions, which turned out to be remarkably accurate: Snowe, now no longer dazed, was still "beautiful-people-ish," and he was polite and obliging and unhurried besides. But he was also, Guy decided early in the interview, not as interested in cooperating as he liked to seem.

"What it amounts to, Leo Badge just sort of went out of the writing business, you might say." Snowe's pleasant voice and amiable manner said he would really like to help but, regretfully, he just couldn't. "Badge was always a steady worker—a good craftsman who turned out books with the businesslike regularity of your full-time hack. Though Lee was a much better writer than that: he had a real talent, and the kind of imagination hacks don't usually run to. But"—

Snowe stopped his slow pacing of the office that looked a good deal like a drawing room—"when it's over, it doesn't matter what it was, if you follow me. Not at Lee's level of talent. He was no Shakespeare: nobody wrote pieces in the Sunday *Times* mourning the lack of a new book by Leo Badge. Or in the quarterlies, analyzing his Blue Period. When he wrote, they read him; when he stopped, they read something else."

And if he started up again, his agent would be waiting . . . Once the thought came to Guy, it explained a lot. Hilliard Snowe intended to guard his investment, so Guy would hear nothing about Leo Badge that he couldn't get from other sources—just in case Leo Badge turned up again and didn't like it. Apparently he might still turn up: Guy knew nothing about the habits of writers, but presumably Hilliard Snowe did. "It's understandable that Mr. Badge wouldn't work for a while afterward," Guy ventured. "But wouldn't he begin to need money? I gather he ran a pretty expensive establishment, and then his wife's breakdown—"

"She had money, I think. And I doubt that Lee was ever hurting seriously." Snowe looked bored. "You must know more about the legalities than I do, Lieutenant. But I imagine he'd have had access to his wife's money during her illness, if he needed it."

"She committed suicide, didn't she?"

"An overdose of sleeping pills. She was still under psychiatric care, but there are some cases where it simply can't be avoided. Or so I'm told."

"Not really," Guy said. "If they really want to die, they find a way eventually."

"Well, the consensus was that she really wanted to. She never was about to win any prizes for mental health anyway, and Joanie was her only child. I honestly wasn't surprised when I heard about Mary."

"I see. You were in touch with Mr. Badge at that point, then?"

"Oh yes. He still had royalties outstanding, and some inter-rupted commitments." Snowe hestitated. "It would be—un-fortunate—if this got around, but he didn't fulfill those com-mitments. As I said, he just seemed to shut up shop. He didn't cheat anybody, you understand—any advances he'd taken, he returned. But that was that, and no new work was forth-coming. After a while, he stopped answering letters. And the last time I tried phoning, the telephone had been cut off. *Finis.*" He shrugged. "Too bad, but it does happen."

"Is there anyone else he might have—"

"I think you'll find, Lieutenant, that a writer's agent hangs on longer than anyone else."

"I see. Yes, of course."

"You could try the Screenwriters Guild. But frankly, no-body's much devoted to keeping track of has-beens. Which, to put it brutally, is what Leo Badge is at this point."

"Yes. Well, thanks, Mr. Snowe." Guy got up, shook hands, and only then had an afterthought. "I wonder, do you have a picture of him I could borrow?" He noticed the reluctance, which was clear but he thought not deep. "I imagine I could get one from his publishers, couldn't I? But I'd rather not be delayed in New York. And it's only for the record, after all."

"Ah, yes. Very well, I'll get a hold of a photo and send it on to you, if you'll leave your address." The well-kept hand waved away thanks. "Please. The least a citizen can do."

Guy saw the combination of reassurance and blackmail had worked: if the photo was only going to gather dust in some files, the risk of incurring the client's displeasure was clearly smaller than the risk of relinquishing the role as sole spokesman for Leo Badge. The literary culture—or, Guy amended conscientiously, the culture that lived off litera-ture—ran to web-weaving, via delicate testings of the tensile strengths of silken strands. Hilliard Snowe seemed to know his intricate stuff: he would never be credulous enough to be tripped up by any put-on, or impractical enough to be hob-bled by any ideology. But as Guy left the elegant offices, which intimated subtly that art and not business was what went on in the premises, he thought of nineteen-year-old Joan Robinson unimpressed at lunch with the dead-dead-dead Literary Establishment.

At the hotel, he collected the back copies of the newspaper Ru Spencer did not work for. Guy read through the clips, from the straight-news "Coed Death Laid to Drugs" to the third-day feature that began, "Joanie Robinson had only three blocks more to go, but she didn't make it. Her father's hand, holding out help from a continent away, just didn't stretch far enough." Guy packed what he needed and threw the rest of the papers away, though not without a moment for disgusted contemplation of the wonders of a free press. Maybe it made no substantial difference that a student at Merrivale College, an all-girls' school, was not a "coed" and that Leo Badge was not her father but her stepfather; nevertheless, the press's freedom to be inaccurate was cause for profoundly discouraging thought . . . Guy took himself out of the profoundly discouraging city that, he realized as he peered from the bus windows on the way to the airport, he had not really visited. He had never actually left Public-Eventville, a land of overworked police officers and supercilious reporters, the place he lived in every day.

When Guy had finished his subsequent tour of Airport-ville—where the foul-ups were produced by computers instead of humans, and dingy peeling paint was fuchsia or chartreuse rather than Taxpayer Off-White or Civil-Service Tan—he carried his bag out of Boston's version of it with no fond looks over his shoulder. He took the subway into Boston because the library there was better stocked than Buxford's and its staff would not know his name, face, or occupation. Not all the books listed in the catalog under Leo Badge's name were in. And those that were had been, predictably, long since divested of their dust jackets, which might have exhibited a photo of the author. Guy selected, at random, one called *Nightmare in Town*. A piece of the dust jacket had survived, he found; pasted neatly inside the institutional cover was some of the promotional hurrah that had launched the book. Under a two-sentence summary of the plot, the first critic rejoiced that Leo Badge was once again exhibiting his mastery of the intricate puzzle which yet plays fair with the reader. A second quote directed itself more specifically to the book: only Leo Badge, the reviewer said flatly, could so skillfully insert exotic poisons into everyday small-town teacups. The third, a one-liner squeezed in at the bottom, mentioned Sherlock Homes.

Guy carried the book to the desk and checked it out. Outside, he stopped to open his suitcase and drop the book in on top of his pajamas. Then he went straight to his office, discovered with relief that his absence had not served as an excuse for dumping problems on his desk, and put in a call to Toots Cantor. Waiting, he extracted from his suitcase and coat pockets the newspaper clips he'd collected, Xerox copies of others, and a sheaf of blurry copies of the pertinent New York records of the Robinson case—each initialed by Delano Clemens, as was the transmittal slip.

The voice in Guy's ear was saying Lt. Cantor was off this Thursday but had left a number where he could be reached. With a clear sense of reprieve, Guy declared his business too unimportant for that and left a message for tomorrow. Then he gathered up the papers and jiggled them into a file folder. He resisted the demand of the folder's blank label for a while, but finally succumbed: he wrote "Elm Circle," remembered there already was such a file, and added "(Background)". He eyed that effort without satisfaction and then stowed the thing out of sight in the file cabinet.

The telephone rang as he was reaching tentatively for the maroon-bound book in the open suitcase. "Oh, you're back," the voice said. "I was going to leave a message. Just figured you'd like to know before you read it in the paper, maybe— we're picking him up now."

"Who?" Guy asked. He was aware of sudden, ridiculous panic.

"Your boy over at Elm Circle." The voice, faintly puzzled,

changed to a reading pace. "James Waterman, 27, student—"

"Oh, yes." Guy said he was sorry and explained that he'd been thinking of something else. Because he really didn't want to hear more, he asked no questions and refrained from comment when the other man guessed this Waterman would have no trouble making bail, not with the profitable line of work he was in; he'd be out by tomorrow, you could bet on it. Guy said nothing, and hung up as soon as he could. Then he shut the suitcase with more force than the task required.

When he opened it again some hours later, he was all out of work excuses and dinner excuses and down to confrontation time. He admitted it, struggling with the desire to keep stalling—while he went on stalling by putting his dirty clothes in the hamper and replacing his toothbrush with exquisite precision in the exact spot it had occupied before it left home. He was still wondering why he should be dragging his feet, at this point and after all his labors, when he settled down at last with *Nightmare in Town.* He thought of awarding himself a highball for that achievement, but he decided that constituted another stall. If it didn't, if it represented a need for Dutch courage, that was even worse.

When the telephone rang, Guy had gotten far enough into the story to become a reader rather than an exhausted fighter, and not yet far enough to be forced to answer the question knocking at his mind. He was still a little abstracted when he answered, so he jumped to conclusions when the operator said New York was calling. "Yes, all right. I'll accept the charges."

"It's a paid call, sir." She sound so reproving that Guy wanted to apologize at once. "Go ahead, New York."

"Lieutenant Silvestri, this is Clint Wetherby. Ru Spencer gave me your number. I don't know if you remember hearin' my name—"

"Oh. Oh yes. As a matter of fact, I thought it was Spencer calling."

"I know. But I reckoned I could afford to treat. My contri-

208

bution to the Berndt Edmondsen Memorial Fund, let's say."

"Ah." It was less a word than a sigh, marking the end of struggle. "I'm glad." That sounded strange even to Guy, but something about Wetherby's tone gave Guy the feeling he would be understood. It was a big voice, not youthful, its rhythms blunt and brisk; but it had warmed noticeably when it spoke the old man's name.

"Doctor Edmondsen brought out the best in people, maybe," Wetherby said. "Anyway, seems like Ru couldn't shake off the notion he was lettin' the old man down, but even after he slept on it he couldn't call to mind what it was exactly that Edmondsen was so sore about. Ru hunted up my story to see if I had anythin' about it. But he didn't allow for my gimmick—I collect the facts at the time of the crime, all right, but I don't write the story till the cops close the case. By the way, if you want the pub date on this one," he interrupted himself, "I have it right here."

Guy said he did want it, thanks. He scribbled *Amazing Detective* and the relevant numbers on his telephone pad.

"Well sir, when Ru couldn't find it in my story, he broke down and asked me. That's the power of Edmondsen, I guess —it comes hard to Ru Spencer to admit there's somethin' he doesn't know." The genial voice grew grave. "I remember that old man, Silvestri, like it was yesterday. I couldn't give his beef the play I'd have liked because by that time the public was gettin' kind of tired of variations on the Kitty Genovese murder. But I laid it on heavy as I could, hopin' somethin' could come of it somehow. That's what was eatin' Edmondsen, see—the way this feller next door got clear away with it. Not even his name in the paper."

In the Genovese affair there had been more than thirty culprits—if that was the word for the people who'd failed to act when a girl was being attacked in the street below their windows. Kitty Genovese had put up a long fight and done a lot of screaming for help before her murderer succeeded, but only after it was too late had somebody called the police.

Once the facts came out, the press and the airwaves were filled with the peculiarly American *ex post facto* breastbeating characterized by columns of depth reporting and hours of panel discussions; inevitably, at least one book was also written about it. In the course of all that, one theory was most frequently cited—that the watchers in their apartments high above the scene had tended to confuse reality with TV, where girls run, calling for help, all the time. Guy's own theory at the time had been a little different: he could understand that in some neighborhoods one did not lightly take part in a fight that might be gang-related. But also, one did not care to acknowledge that fact—which is what telephoning the police does. Therefore, the way to avoid danger and still be manly was to declare what was going on a non-event, to refuse to hear it or assign it a category—like a domestic quarrel, or "a bunch of drunks"—in which noninterference is okay.

The man whose behavior was reminiscent of the Genovese case, on the January night when Joan Robinson collapsed in the snow, seemed more likely to be explained by Silvestri's theory of inhibition than by a habit of watching TV dramas. "All I can remember is, he was some kind of visitin' scholar," Wetherby said. "Very quiet type—he'd been livin' next door at Number 140 almost six months and Edmondsen had only spoken to him once or twice, maybe."

"But surely Doctor Edmondsen knew his name?"

"Sure he did, but he'd forgotten it when the newsmen were there that night. You can understand that: you think of the house next door as the So-and-So's house, not by the name of the stranger they've rented it to. And the old boy certainly didn't want his buddy, the real neighbor, associated with what he considered the crime of the century. So—"

Guy asked suddenly, *"Was* it? I mean—"

"I know what you mean. I was afraid you'd ask me that."

"Well, clearly Dr. Edmondsen believed the neighbor could've made the difference," Guy said slowly, thinking

210

about the details Clint Wetherby had just supplied. When the old astronomer angrily told the full story to the press—too late, for Joan Robinson's murder had declined to a few impressionistic pieces by then—he insisted that the man next door was at a window, looking out, when he himself reached the girl. That was why he believed help would come—and went on believing it, assuming that when the neighbor disappeared from the window, he had gone to phone for an ambulance. That assumption had been slid over in the summary Guy read in New York: there, Edmondsen had been seen as hoping someone would come, rather than expecting it to happen. "According to Spencer," Guy said into the phone, "the doctor at St. Vincent's thought the girl was too far gone right from the start."

"I know, but he was discounting Edmondsen's statement that she moved, and even cried. I wouldn't, Silvestri."

"Hmm. It's true he was a scientist. With whatever that implies about a habit of making exact observations."

"Right. And these doctors don't know as much about some of the drugs as they ought to, or think they do. The young ones may be brash, but the older men admit their ignorance. So I add it up," Wetherby went on, "and I come out right close to Edmondsen's version. You know how those drugs act, generally speakin'—depressin' every body action, until they finally depress the breathin' enough to cut off the oxygen supply to the brain. Well, if you assume she still had some muscle action after she collapsed, she wasn't that close to the end. And it makes you wonder if artificial respiration, a heart stimulant, or any of what would've come with an ambulance and a doctor might not have done the trick. I mean, she was young and healthy." Wetherby paused. "I think you'd have to say she could've had a chance," he said sadly. "The hospital was right handy. And the ambulance got there ten minutes after Dr. Edmondsen phoned."

"I've never been good at the minute-by-minute stuff," Guy confessed.

"No? Well, I am. I operate at a distance, from secondhand material, so I have to be. And I make it a good—oh, twenty minutes'—difference, if you stick to the half-hour time frame the cops used. Figure Mr. Neighbor starts lookin' out around the same time as Edmondsen: why shouldn't he have been closin' up for the night, too? And then figure he doesn't think he ought to do anythin' when he sees the old man go out there, because maybe it'll turn out to be nothin'. So allow five whole minutes for watchin'—which is a hell of a long time to look at an old man out there without a coat in that weather and still tell yourself it may be nothin'. But okay, give Mr. Neighbor five minutes to make up his mind, and then let the ambulance take fifteen minutes, even, and that still brings you to no more than five-till-twelve. At the most conservative, mind you, that makes it twenty-eight minutes before Edmondsen's phone call was clocked in."

"Eight minutes for him to get back in the house and get his call through? I guess that's more than enough," Guy conceded. "You seem to have made your point."

"Well, if you want to know the truth, I could make a hell of a lot better one. Because I reckoned on eleven thirty-five for when Edmondsen went out there, but I bet it was five or ten minutes earlier."

"He said he watched the TV news, didn't he? Doesn't that end at eleven-thirty?"

"Sure it does." Triumph was clear in Wetherby's voice. "But the old boy said he watched the news, not the news broadcast. What do you bet he didn't give a damn about the basketball scores? And he was an astronomer, Silvestri—do you really think he held still, through the Lord knows how many commercials, so some clown could show him diagrams of cloud formations?"

"You think he—"

"Sure. He turned off the set when they got to the end of the straight news. I can't prove it, but I bet that's what he meant. So he was out there in the snow before that damn

212

broadcast was over, and when he saw Mr. Neighbor lookin' out, there's a good chance it was still only around eleven-thirty. If the girl didn't die till twelve-fifteen—if I'm right, Silvestri, the chances that the girl could've been saved keep right on growin'. I think they were always better than the doc said anyway," the writer added heavily. "Maybe better than he thought, too. It could be he was tryin' to make Edmondsen feel better, you know."

Guy said he was convinced; he had to clear his throat to say it. After that he wondered silently what all this left them with.

Wetherby seemed to divine the question. "I feel right bad about not havin' that name for you, but I didn't keep my notes, you see. Ru gave it to me for sure, because when he started rememberin', one of the things he remembered was Edmondsen hammerin' at the name. The old guy even tried to sic the cops on the bastard, but they told him it wasn't a crime. Anyway, I didn't use the neighbor in my script at all because it wouldn't have made sense to sidetrack the story that way."

"I understand. You shouldn't blame yourself."

"Well, I'd give a lot if I could remember. But I'm not empty-handed." Pleasure brightened Wetherby's voice. "When Ru and I got to talkin' about the gutsy old boy and how he tried to make things hot for that cat—well, we reckoned we'd help him out. So Ru looked up the property owner, meanin' to ask him who rented the house that year and so come at it that way. And then, wow! The owner of the house next to Edmondsen's is now right in your backyard. Good?"

Guy said happily, "Very good. Give." He recognized the name dimly even while he was scribbling the forwarding address in Trowbridge the reporter had obtained. Guy thanked Wetherby earnestly, asked that thanks be transmitted to Spencer, and then had a better idea. "Tell him I'll see that word gets to Goldberg."

"What does he do, give gold stars?"

"Sort of." Guy hesitated. "I don't know what I can do to repay you, Mr. Wetherby."

"Could you maybe find that lousy creep? I know you can't do any more than the New York cops could. But if the feller he rented from is up your way, maybe he is too. And maybe he puts his trash out an inch too far from the curb. Or spits in the subway. You know what I mean?"

"I know what you mean."

"For the old boy's sake," the writer said. "I never got over that gutsy old feller. I'd sure like to been there when he came out of the hospital and went callin' next door. You can bet he did, too."

Guy admitted it was a tantalizing scene to imagine, and wished he could be as free as Wetherby to stop at blissful contemplation of it. Edmondsen was an attractive character, but Guy had a hunch men like Dr. Edmondsen were more of a revelation to Wetherby than to anyone who'd spent much time in a college town: gutsy old men on university faculties didn't usually make news, but they were around. Guy remembered suddenly that one had made news recently—an Emeritus marching in a graduation procession had swung the ceremonial mace at a would-be disrupter. Maybe universities were still growing gutsy old men, he decided. But on the other hand it was the outside world that had grown Spencer, who worried because he couldn't remember a fact, and then did a lot of work for no visible reward. And Wetherby, an outside-world man if there ever was one, who'd remembered and served what he admired even when he knew about it only secondhand . . .

Just before they rang off, Guy remembered something he could do for Wetherby: if he ever needed anything from a Boston paper, Guy told the writer, call Frankie C. at the *Star* and mention Silvestri.

So it was with a feeling of good fellowship, and it should have been with a restored sense that things were going his way, that Guy returned to the quiet of his thoughts. If not to page 64 of *Nightmare in Town* by Leo T. Badge. He excused himself on what he could feel now were legitimate grounds. He studied the name of the peripatetic Lambert archaeology professor—one long look at the telephone pad and Guy had recognized the name fully—who owned a house in New York. The odds were that he wasn't in Trowbridge now, but it didn't matter: the good professor probably didn't even need to be bothered with inquiries. Guy tore the slip of paper from the pad and stuck it into *Nightmare in Town* to mark his place, then went to fix himself his long-delayed drink. In the morning it would be a simple matter to find out at Lambert whether Lowell Lester's address during his year of research in New York had been 140 University Lane. Doubtless one of Lambert University's services had found him the furnished house; another had surely mailed him checks, announcements of faculty teas, and whatever else a lad away from home would need. Lambert might not do too well *in loco parentis* for its students, but it took kindly care of its own.

And then, before Guy could possibly have consumed enough alcohol to explain even mildly odd behavior, he behaved not only oddly but quite inexplicably. The only reason he even offered to himself was not a reason but an excuse—that it wasn't really very late, and the lady in the next apartment shouldn't be hearing Lowell Lester's bath water running quite yet. Guy had driven most of the way to North Buxford before he tried offering himself a brace of explanations. One was that the spirit of Berndt Edmondsen had entered into him and was irascibly demanding prompt action at last; the other was that the click-click of everything falling into place had come back and it would be fatal not to move in some direction at least. Now. Right away.

He arrived at Lester's door, knocked, and presented himself demurely before the peephole.

"Lieutenant Silvestri?" Lowell Lester's voice, which had

probably been muffled since infancy, was rendered almost inaudible by the closed door. "Isn't it late to come calling? I'm afraid I—"

"I just want to speak to you a moment, sir," Guy said cheerily, thinking that it was rather later than Ell-Square guessed. "It's about a collection for a memorial."

"Oh, I see. Just a minute, please."

Guy listened to the chain being released and then the turning of a lock. Caution made sense for anyone who lived alone, and Guy knew it. Yet, unreasonably, all the unlocking made him feel justified in not having waited for tomorrow and an appointment at the Merritt Library. It seemed right, somehow, to get past the defenses Lowell Lester had erected and get him where he lived.

The librarian opened the door. He was wearing a smoking jacket—Come *on!* Guy said to himself incredulously—and slippers, and altogether the air of an English gentleman addressing a constable. "What is it, Lieutenant? Usually, for the Police Fund—"

"This is something a little special, sir. Selected prospects only." Guy filled the doorway. "May I come in?" His body stated its clear intention to do so; his voice was loud in the hall of the staid apartment house, and he was quite ready to make it louder if necessary. Anybody who cast him as a constable, he thought gaily, would get the bluff-and-hearty version.

Once inside, he went into the living room: it was only a step, and when he had taken it, Lester had no choice but to follow. "May I?" Guy asked blandly. He selected an armchair without waiting for an answer. And presumably without noticing that his host, who looked decidedly ill at ease, did not sit down.

"It's rather late," Lester ventured. "I was about to retire. So, this matter of a collection . . ."

Guy stretched luxuriously, making himself at home. He took out a cigarette, searched elaborately for matches, and was reaching for a cloisonné dish that might or might not be an ashtray when he said, "It's a memorial for Professor Edmondsen."

"I beg your pardon?"

Lester, thinking in terms of Lambert professors, had not recognized the name; his bewilderment was genuine. "Berndt Edmondsen," Guy said. "You must remember him—he was your neighbor in New York City about five years ago. University Lane?" He saw recognition. And, he was also certain, dread. He went on benignly offering aids to memory. "A radio-astronomer. Tallish, very thin man, with a lot of white hair? You were renting the house from Professor—"

"I remember Edmondsen," Lester said dully. He sat down. "But I don't see—"

"Well, this isn't your usual-type memorial. Fact is, some of us boys got together and decided old Edmondsen had been done wrong, and we ought to ride around the countryside, righting it."

"Lieutenant Silvestri, are you—intoxicated?" Lester glanced toward the telephone, on a small table in the hall. "I must ask you—"

"No, sir, I'm not intoxicated, but I am what you might call agitated. In a state of moral indignation, sir." He looked at the little man. "Were you going to call the police, Mr. Lester?" he asked quietly.

"Well, certainly I'd prefer not to. I'm prepared to overlook—"

"I'm not, Mr. Lester. So I suggest you call. Though from what I've heard," Guy said slowly, "it's hardly your usual practice. Or is it only New York police you can't bring yourself to call?" He paused, giving guilty memory a moment to stir to life. "Because frankly, Mr. Lester, when you saw that old man go out into the cold to find out what happened to the girl who fell, when you saw he was staying out there—you know, now that I think of it, it could easily have looked as

217

though Edmondsen had fallen, too. Well, but even anyone who still wouldn't go lend a hand would call the police at that point, Mr. Lester. Anyone who wasn't incredibly selfish, and self-serving, would do *something*. Don't you agree?"

"I don't know what you're talking about," the librarian said, his lips trembling in a face the color of cigarette ash.

"You *were* living at 140 University Lane when you had that research grant in New York?" Guy waited, and then said almost gently, "I can check it. Easily."

"Certainly I was. I don't deny that." Lowell Lester was visibly summoning his courage. "But I don't recall any such occasion as you describe, Lieutenant." His eyes surveyed the unwelcome visitor with growing hope. "I stand on that statement."

Unreasonably, Guy was smitten with pity: within Ell-Square's me-first limitations, it could be said that he was being gutsy, too. "Okay, look. This is off the record, and it doesn't really matter a damn any more, I suppose. And I can quite understand if you just panicked, or something like that." He hesitated, sensing nothing but opposition, and then tried again. "All I really want, Mr. Lester, is to understand. Edmondsen is dead, and the girl is dead." And Hilary Bridge was dead, too. But Lowell Lester was not dead. *Yet?* Guy wondered suddenly.

But that belonged to the official side of things—where Lowell Lester was somebody entitled to protection and it was nobody's business whether he was a good man or a bad one. But this, now, was unofficial stuff, was just Guy Silvestri wanting only a reason, whether a good one or a bad one. "I just want to know why. If you know. Or if you honestly don't, then that."

"I've told you, I do not recall any such occasion."

"I see." For a moment, Guy wondered: people did suppress memories, and this would not have been one for a man to cherish. "You do remember Doctor Edmondsen, though?"

"Yes. Slightly. I didn't know him well."

"Oh? Then have you any idea why he should have charged you with the—unfeeling, shall we say—behavior I described?"

"Edmondsen is dead. He can't charge me with anything."

Guy told himself he was imagining the gleam in the other man's eyes. But he knew he was imagining his own sense of freedom from the burden of compassion; doubtless there was a considerable gleam in his own eye. "Yes, he's dead," he said coolly. "But he was literate, you see. Not to say articulate. For a librarian, it shouldn't be news that death doesn't stop a man's words. But why should he have—"

"He was an irascible person," Lester said quickly. "A very quarrelsome temperament."

"Really? Remember—your landlord was his neighbor for many years." Guy left it at that; he didn't think he needed to lie directly.

Lester looked hounded, standing in the open space of the room but with an air of being backed into a corner. "Well, these things change. Perhaps Edmondsen had grown senile."

That does it. "I'm afraid that won't wash," Guy said without pity. "On that night in January, Doctor Edmondsen was seen by"—he stood up and walked toward Lester, ticking off the list on his fingers—"a squad of police officers, several doctors, a slew of reporters, and a ward full of nurses. In fact, Mr. Lester, I'd guess he talked to more people that night than you do in a year. And most of them were professionally equipped to detect senility."

"I have nothing more to say, Lieutenant. And I suggest that you are exceeding your authority."

Guy stopped moving, because Lester was backing away: he had little more to go before he really would be up against the wall, and Guy didn't want him to get even that much reassurance. "Let's not worry about that. Because frankly, my dear sir, you ain't seen nothing yet. I'll do it without exceeding my authority if I can, and I think I can, but I'm not about to let that stop me." He stared down into the

frightened face. "The reason I think I can is, you'd be amazed how difficult your life in Buxford can get, without my exceeding my authority or even stomping on your civil liberties."
Guy bowed, elaborately. "And now, if you'll excuse me, I'm off to study the statutes—which go back more than three hundred years, I remind you. You'll be enchanted to learn all the things that are illegal in this state, county, and city."
Lowell Lester made a small sound in his throat.
Guy ignored it and went on, now perhaps intoxicated indeed. "Next time we meet, sir"—he clicked his heels—"it'll be law books at twenty paces. In the meantime, let me give you a tip. Don't jaywalk." He began another, more sweeping, bow: he was acting like a tipsy schoolboy, and he knew it and it was wonderful . . . And then he caught sight of Lester's lips working, and abruptly all the fun went out of everything.
"What's the matter?" asked Silvestri. The real Silvestri, a man who knew revenge was not really sweet. "Look, don't be afraid. I won't—"
"Please. Don't," Lester said.
"No. I won't," Guy repeated. "I wouldn't. Not really."
The little man had clearly not heard. "I appeal to you. You'll know about it tomorrow, anyway. Everyone will soon."
"Know about what?" asked the big, stupid bully—formerly an overgrown undergraduate, drunk and disorderly.
"My contract. The university isn't renewing my contract."
Lowell Lester put both hands over his face and began to cry.
An hour and a half later, Lester, plied with medicinal brandy and all but tucked into bed, had finally been brought to believe that his last days in Buxford wouldn't be a series of relentless persecutions by a surrealistic Inspector Javert. But the *Les Miserables* bit had been a near thing, a shaken Silvestri told himself as he drove back across town.
Ell-Square, effectively murdered already, was guaranteed at least a decent burial. But Guy, sick at heart and no longer buoyed by a magic knowledge that the dice were hot, was

220

left to pursue a real hunt that could not possibly contain exhilaration. And to confront a worry—because maybe he was wrong and the situation wouldn't stay under control. He thought it would, at least until tomorrow night, when he could try heading off what he guessed was the next step in the design. But he was gambling—and after what he'd seen of himself in action tonight, he was no longer so sure of his ability to call the shots. Any shots.

By way of checking on the odds, he slid his car along the curb on Nathan Avenue opposite the front of the Experiment Perilous bookshop and waited, immobile in the darkness, until he saw Florence through the glass. He checked the time while he watched her come down an aisle between rows of books. She was wearing a brief dress, of some sort of lavender and white pattern, and she looked all right: she looked wonderfully safe and normal, and she would undoubtedly stay where she was until she went home to bed. Or almost undoubtedly, which was the trouble. Guy scanned the few other figures visible in the Perilous: the movie's last show must have let out not long ago, and the customers seemed to be routine Circle Theatre types.

It was the best he could do until tomorrow, so Guy started up his car and drove home to read *Nightmare in Town*.

13

Preparing the Turf

After the way he'd bullied poor Lowell Lester last night—and it *was* "poor" Lester even if he had made the difference between life and death for Joan Robinson: recognizing that was the hard part, the grownups' burden—Guy had this coming to him. At least, so he told himself morosely, while he stood in Ann Price's little shop being cast as the storm trooper he certainly wasn't. *(Not now. But what about last night?)*

"I mean it. Out!" Ann said fiercely. "Unless you've got a warrant, you can just remove yourself from these premises. I know my rights." Her lips tightened when Silvestri made no move to obey. "Listen, do you think I was born yesterday? Do you expect me to believe you couldn't at least *warn* Jim?"

"No." He looked at her flushed, angry face. "Do you expect me to believe I should have?"

"Oh for God's sake. I hope you didn't come here to give

me a lecture on the law. Because it's not holy to *me*. And as long as I obey it—which I'm doing, I remind you, and you're not—I don't have to think it's holy." She shook the small, pointed awl with which she had been working the blue leather in her hand. "Jim is a good man, and that makes you a louse. So beat it."

"And what does that make the poor slobs who die of what he sold?" Guy moved toward her, slowly. "If we go by moralities instead of law, what about them?"

"Get back. Or so help me, I'll stick this into your gut. And don't think it isn't sharp."

"I know it is. But I don't think you're going to use it."

She looked near to tears. "It isn't as if he did it so he could gamble in Las Vegas. All he wanted was money to finish school. Is it a crime to be poor?"

Guy shook his head No, though the question was clearly rhetorical. It always was, because the fashionable notion that those who had suffered injustices were then automatically above the law would not bear the weight of answers spoken aloud. They would lead to other questions—like, *Isn't it a crime not to prefer being poor to being some other things, assuming even the barest minimum of choice?* Also, freed of rhetorical flourishes, the observation might emerge that a habit of irresponsible charity, though it too was not a crime, was rather like driving at a crawl on a two-lane highway: it led you to feel personally virtuous while you were piling up the odds that somebody would get killed.

Guy took the little awl out of Ann's hand, laid it on the table that served as a counter, and went on wondering what to do about the fact that she would not change. She was the same, and would probably always be the same, as when she had taken Florence Hathaway in and then, after that brought disastrous results, taken her in again in another time and place—always rescuing, but never really helping. Guy rubbed both hands over his face and then smiled wryly as he heard Ann ask, with concern, whether he was all right.

If he was hurting, then—he saw—he was immediately not the enemy anymore.

"I'm all right," he said. "But I came because—well, Florence may not be all right."

"What on earth do you mean? If you're planning to give Florence the same treatment you gave Jim, I warn you to think again, Silvestri. I'm not without resources, and I—"

"Oh, shut up," he said quietly. "Is Florence hurting anybody? Well, Jim was." The trouble with Ann was, she was a well-wisher of only her immediate neighborhood. "I'm trying to protect Florence. Because somebody should."

Ann looked wounded, predictably. She struck back with the quick anger of one who has been dealt a blow. "Florence is a free person, an individual. She has a right to—"

"To another bad, sick year?"

"What are you talking about?" Ann's voice fell to a hush, the anger gone and some pleading added. "I mean it, Guy, what are you trying to tell me?"

"That it would be a good idea to keep Florence away from Mrs. Chandler's basement tonight. If your principles will allow you to mess with her freedom to that extent." He paused, and tried what he hoped was a meaningful look. "I'd tell her myself, but I just don't think she has enough sense to accept a tip and shut up. And naturally, I can't risk"—he shrugged, even more meaningfully. "My usefulness would be over if . . ."

"Pandora and Ken? And Dracula? Are you trying to tell me they're going to be—raided or something?" She peered up into his closed, blank face. "That's it, isn't it? Somebody's decided tonight is hassle-the-hippies night. You didn't warn Jim because you thought what he was doing was really bad. But you think Florence is just foolish."

"Isn't she?" he asked softly.

"If you mean all the witch-signs and the magic potions—" Unexpectedly, Ann giggled. "I have to admit she's a sight, pouring and mixing and muttering. If she'd studdied chem

224

half as devoutly as she hit those old books at the Merritt—oh, that's how you knew. Ell-Square. I *heard* he was finking far and wide. He's ugh, just ugh. I mean, there's never been anything anybody with any sense would get in a flap about. Some absurd little law . . ."

Guy waited till she had run down a bit and then advised her that Ell-Square, for reasons not known to the general public ("Ask yourself, what do you really know about his origins, his early years?"), was too pathetic to be picked on; short of openly assigning Lester status in some appropriate minority group, this was the most efficient way, in the circumstances, to arrange some relief for the Merritt librarian. Then Silvestri picked up what chips he had managed to win and left the game, feeling that he'd not exactly covered himself with glory but he'd probably come out ahead. He rather doubted that Ann would tell Florence directly about the "raid," because their culture made having a policeman-pal too risky—and Del Clemens' observations about the efficiency of the "regular rich kids" in protecting themselves applied to protection from the peer group as well as from society. But however Ann got the message across, Florence would probably be safe: she was not self-destructive, so she wouldn't go looking for the trouble that was reportedly about to descend on the hippies; and that strange, half-drunken middle-of-the-night phone call to Guy *could* be read as a hidden plea. The odds were, Florence would let herself be rescued.

Not that it wouldn't be safer, from the point of view of law enforcement, just to pounce—and, if everything went right, catch a murderer. The trouble with that, though, was that if everything didn't go right, some idiot kids would get picked up for smoking pot, and Florence, whether she got a jail sentence or not, would finally lose the last of her courtier friends at Lambert University. Hercule Poirot and Nero Wolfe and all that crowd could afford, maybe, to have everything hang on successful confrontations with murderers; but

Guy Silvestri, who was not a hero and not even a genius, had to consider, before he took off on his own, what would happen if he lost.

So he composed two documents Friday afternoon, typing them himself in his office. One, addressed to Lt. Harold Cantor, outlined a possible case—maybe enough to make a charge, maybe not—against a suspect in the murder of Hilary Bridge, the only murder in which Guy had any more than just plain hunch to offer. His second letter was to Tim Whistler, who Guy thought was probably telling the truth about the destruction of the scarf found in the Residence's yard. But even if he was, and the scarf thus could not be produced to test Florence's story that she'd seen "Jacques" coming from the garage, Tim Whistler's boys could be produced if he wanted them to be. Somebody had torn up the scarf and flushed it down the toilet, or burned it, or dropped it in the river—and that someone could so testify if Tim could be persuaded to give the white folks a break.

Guy did the best he could to be persuasive, and then he sealed the letter in an envelope addressed to Tim and marked "Important—Please Hand-Deliver." After that, he made certain small physical preparations he rather thought would prove useless, as no combat was likely to happen and he probably wouldn't need a weapon if it did. Finally, he picked up both envelopes and took them home. There, he propped them conspicuously against the telephone. If it was not Guy who came back here to the apartment tonight, it would be police officers—who would need to use the telephone, and then would know what to do with the letters.

The last thing he did before he left home was rove his bookshelves until he found a dust jacket that would fit over the library's *Nightmare in Town*. He carried the book out disguised as *Modern Verse in English: 1900–1938*, which had proved a tidy fit. Downstairs, he took his mailbox key off his key ring and locked the rest of his personal keys in the mailbox. Then he went out to the prowl car he'd checked out after noting carefully, "Will return before 2 A.M. Sat." He fished the car's keys from his pocket, unlocked the glove compartment, and tucked his mailbox key into the pad of official forms in there.

He drove up to Elm Circle and then kept circling the block patiently until a parking space appeared on Nathan Ave. He got out and locked the car, contemplating the location with satisfaction: it was not too far from the street light, and though some stores on the Avenue stayed open Friday nights until ten o'clock, soon after that the parked Buxford Police cruiser was likely to be alone and conspicuous. Then, having done everything he could think of to make life difficult for a murderer who might try to repeat what had worked with Adonio, Guy pocketed the car keys and carried *Modern English Verse* over to the Grotto.

He ate at a back table, keeping the book propped open. But it was not hard to avoid conversation anyhow, for this early, most of the diners were local—inhabitants of Elm Circle and its immediate neighborhood, rather than patrons of the Circle Theatre. And Guy was willing to admit he might be imparting significance to what could be just casual glances, but there were some he was sure about: a graduate-student couple who lived in the apartment house, for example, unmistakably felt that their Friday-night dining-out treat was all but ruined by the presence of this particular, particularly hateful fuzz. And the Lambert undergraduate who was helping out at the bar regarded Guy neutrally at first but then, after the graduate students had paused for a word while paying their bill, he took to staring the length of the restaurant with ill-concealed fascination. Only Gus George behaved normally. And he made his greetings brief, respectful of the open book.

Guy sat on, reading but also listening to the voice behind the words as the novel's amateur detective—one of those traveled exquisites with no job or relatives or bodily limitations—solved the murders before which official minds had

227

boggled. It was the combination of the words and the sound behind them, the diction and cadence of the prose, that Guy had recognized late last night and still thought he could. There was no way to prove it, or even anything specific enough about the similarity to make it viable in a court of law, but it was there: the brisk, light, half-ironic voice of Leo T. Badge was one Guy knew well.

When the Circle Theatre opened for the early show, Guy decided it was probably about time to begin. He paid his check, offering a blank face to the student who was staring at him with exactly the balance of fascination and revulsion cobras are supposed to provoke. He waved goodbye to Gus and went out into the Circle. The lights were on because it was not yet Daylight Saving Time and so this was officially night; in two days this would be officially daytime. It was a pleasure to belong to anything so wondrous as the human race, Guy decided, and suppressed a small tremor of advance self-pity.

Passing Mrs. Chandler's house, he noticed that the windows of the basement apartment, close to the ground, showed the bluish light the hippies fancied. Friday-night festivities had already begun, it seemed. Or maybe just the preparations for them—Pandora and Ken and Dracula, householders, getting ready for a visit from Libby and Bibby and Red Beard and Florence, putting out little dishes of this and that like suburbanites setting up the drink tray before the neighbors come over for the party. Earnestly, Guy hoped this Friday-night get-together would prove to be a dull evening, a real bummer.

14

The Fox

Guy stood in the doorway, hoping he didn't look as crushed as he felt: he had simply never thought of Kate's being a problem, much less of finding the Sterlings taking their after-dinner ease together while the dishwasher bumped and groaned in the kitchen. Kate saw his consternation but ascribed it to polite reluctance to intrude. She went to work on it promptly, with reassurances and invitations, and thus was too busy to observe Guy's further dismay when he learned that she would be right there until she and Elliott went out—together, for once.

"Please do come sit down, Guy." She nodded at the brandy glass on the coffee table. "Come and join me—"

"Or me," Elliott said genially, waving his cigar. "Or, if you're afraid of offending either faction, play it down the middle. Have both."

"But whatever you do, don't *lurk* that way." Kate got up

and succeeded finally in herding Guy into a chair. She didn't press a drink on him when he said no, thanks. "We don't have to leave for a while yet, anyway."

"I don't know why I assumed—I mean, all the couples I know have Friday and Saturday nights staked out in advance," Guy apologized. "But you people never seemed to operate that way."

"Well, we don't. But Ellie wanted to go to the Alcoholics Anonymous meeting tonight. And I haven't gone with him in ages, so I suggested that I put on a dress and come along."

"You do look elegant." She did, too, though it was just a dress—dark green, the color of grass under a tree, and pretty enough but not in any way fancy. Millions of women probably wore dresses like that on any ordinary day, Guy reminded himself. Nobody but Kate would consider it a special-occasion dress. "I like your hair, too," he said. It had been formed into dark, soft, vaguely Japanese-looking poufs.

"Oh, I went to trouble. But it seems the exertion exhausted me." She rubbed her eyes with the back of her hand, and the tired-child gesture promptly undid some of the effect of her finery. "I've been drooping ever since dinner."

Elliott glanced at her with mild concern and said she ought to lie down for a bit.

"Well, maybe I'll just put my feet up." She kicked off her high-heeled pumps, thus yielding still a little more glamour: Guy watched with genuine suspense this slow emergence, tantalizing as a striptease, of the everyday Kate. "The meetings don't start till eight-thirty, anyhow." She located her knitting bag and extracted a blue-wool something. This provided the final touch: Kate was with them again. "Why don't you come along, Guy? The meetings are open. I mean, you don't have to be an alcoholic."

"It's a bit dull," Elliott said. "Earnest narratives of how-I-was-beaten-by-booze. But that's only an hour, and afterward there's coffee and cake and talk."

"They go somewhere after that and talk some more, too

—Ellie doesn't get home till all hours." Kate smiled. "That's one of the classic hazards of A.A., a bunch of egotists being encouraged to talk about themselves. Naturally they go on till dawn." Kate yawned, and raised the hand holding the knitting to cover her mouth. A long needle poked out from her profile like a cat's whisker.

She looked beautiful, and absurd: Guy couldn't help smiling fondly upon her and he doubted that the rest of the world could either. But he knew by then, despite the domestic scene and all the hopeful signs of dress and shoes—and even stockings, he noticed—that she wasn't going to be seen by the rest of the world tonight. So he said merrily, "Well, you've hooked me. I'll come along" and watched the flicker of dismay Elliott Sterling couldn't control. "But listen, as long as we've got time, could we repair to your sanctum a minute, Elliott? I'm thinking of buying my nephew a telescope. And there's no sense getting him a toy—I mean, I might as well invest in something he can see something with. So I thought if I could have a look at yours—"

"Go ahead," Kate urged them drowsily. "I'll watch TV. Maybe I can get some news. I missed the seven o'clock."

There was nothing Elliott could do, and Guy knew it. He heard a TV voice begin as he picked up *Modern English Verse* and followed Elliott up the stairs to the third floor. He was going to follow Elliott anywhere, all evening, because, unlike Kate—who'd suddenly messed up the handy excuse of those A.A. meetings that allowed disappearance "till all hours"—Guy could not be unloaded.

He proved it, too, through nearly an hour of maneuvers —including hints, subtle at first and then rather frantic, that Guy was being the kind of friend who hadn't the grace to know when dropping-in unannounced isn't really a good idea. Bland, thick-skinned, Guy stayed and stayed, sneaking a look at his watch whenever Elliott did.

Because once they entered Elliott's third-floor sanctum, Guy was handed more nourishment than simple self-confidence could provide. The gods were good: as soon as the tilted telescope on its stand appeared in Guy's sight, so did a flashed memory, a sight stored in the brain although hardly registered at the time, of the telescope looking like a machine gun. Which was hardly a natural simile, for telescopes are usually pointed upward, but machine guns . . . What Guy had seen, he knew now, was a telescope pointed straight out or tilted slightly downward—in preparation for what had not yet happened at that time, but was being researched while Elliott played with his "hobbies" unquestioned and undisturbed.

"Where's the mirror that used to be here?" Guy asked suddenly. He gestured at the table to the left of the telescope. "Last time, there was a mirror on a sort of stand." He hadn't actually remembered it that well, not at first. Not until after he'd had a leisurely look at Elliott's meticulous "map" of Elm Circle, noticing with amusement the care with which this conscientious Detective's Sidekick had put in every tiny jog and jiggle of the Circle's property lines—and then seeing, suddenly, that it wasn't *every* jog and jiggle, and in fact the phenomenon was confined to the area between Number 5 and the Grotto. Which was odd because, if Elliott was simply putting in everything he knew, he must know just as much about the piece between the Perilous, which he also owned, and his own house; and yet that section, though neatly sketched in, paid only casual attention to whose lot ended where and no apparent worrying about square corners or the lack of them.

Elliott's reddish eyebrows had risen in elaborate surprise. "I do all sorts of things I forget about later, but I don't remember using a mirror for any of them. Kate has a makeup mirror on a stand, though: I bought it for her, to encourage primping. If that's the one you mean, it's in her bedroom." He smiled. "So you couldn't have seen it, could you?"

Lt. Silvestri, who'd managed compassion for Lowell Lester's fighting back—up to a point, anyway—was certainly able to shrug off this much assault from a desperate man. Or so he told himself, thinking determinedly about the primary purpose of the vanished mirror, which probably had become a present for a surprised Kate and doubtless *was* in her bedroom. But it had once been used to see the alley behind the Grotto and Ralph Adonio's beauty shop from the vantage of Number 5's slightly jutting third-floor back porch. Would it have taken more than one mirror? Guy wondered now, looking around the room. He'd noticed only the conspicuous one before, because he hadn't been conducting a survey.

Abruptly, he stopped conducting a survey and looked quickly away from what he had seen, the thing not a mirror and not looked for but found anyway. He smiled and said lightly, "The lesson of the purloined letter, right?" With luck, none of his sense of diving into deep water would be heard in his voice.

"What?" Elliott half-turned. "Listen, I hate to hurry you, but it's getting close to—"

"It's past time. And she's asleep, isn't she?"

Elliott shrugged. "I wouldn't bet against it. I've known here to fall asleep in front of the TV."

"Oh? I thought this was the first time she'd proved inconvenient." But this was no time for scoring debating points. Quickly, Guy reached up and pointed at—but without touching it—the thin, ancient book inconspicuous in a crammed row of books, all of them old and dusty. "That's the book from the Merritt, isn't it?"

"What're you doing, collecting library fines? How could it be from the Merritt?"

"Is it?"

"Take it down and see, if you like."

Guy suggested gently, "You take it down."

"You're being very mysterious. And I can't say I'm enchanted by your manner, either."

"Take the book down and show me. Then I'll apologize for not enchanting you." Guy waited. "No?"

"I don't know what you're suggesting."

"I'm suggesting," the detective said sadly, "that you didn't want to deface it if you didn't need to. It would've been insurance, but you just couldn't do it. Not if you could get Lowell Lester's hide without going that far. So you told Bridge the book had been defaced and then hid it among books, purloined-letter style"—it had probably been safe, at that: Kate's housekeeping was far short of a crusade against dust—"instead of doing whatever you were going to do to it and getting it back to the Merritt right away. Which is what any self-respecting professional crook would do—he wouldn't keep anything around that he didn't have to." Not only crooks, he thought, remembering the black students who had also learned not to keep anything around that could prove dangerous to them. "Well, you've succeeded in getting Ell-Square without going to extreme measures. So I guess the book would've been back in the Merritt, unharmed, by Monday." Via Florence, probably. Who, witting or unwitting, would probably also have been the way the book got out.

"Interesting," Elliott observed. "Apparently you've discovered that I complained about Ell-Square's management of the Merritt. And from that, I suppose, the rest of this twaddle follows. Conjecture upon conjecture." He looked at Guy happily, anticipation of the delights of winning debating points brightening his eyes. "I put it to you, the fact that I'm not unhappy about the departure of Lowell Lester is as far as you can legitimately go."

"I went farther," Guy said, aware of sorrow for the loss of innocence—of Elliott and Guy, incipient friends, beguiling an afternoon with mock battles. "I went to New York. Elliott," he said with pity, "I know about Joanie."

"Tony who?" Elliott asked smoothly.

It was quick, and courageous in its way. But it was also a line in a script written by a cool, alert man—and delivered by a man who was, suddenly, clearly not right for the part.

Guy unwrapped the false jacket of the book he'd brought

upstairs with him and held it up so Elliott could see the title and author's name stamped on the spine. "Weren't you a little transparent?" He moved in quickly, while the fuddled actor was still trying to find his place in the script. "Merritt, and Badge?"

"Well, it was only a *nom de plume*, and people didn't know about the Merritt. I'm sure you know I could have done better than that if I'd meant it for—" Elliott stopped abruptly, took a deep breath, and managed a smile. "Once again, it seems, it's vanity that proves the malefactor's undoing."

Guy put the book down and waited, silent and patient.

"All right," Elliott said briskly. "I'm pricked, but I'm not killed. In fact, I'm not even bleeding much. Vanity is not a vital organ."

"Oh, come on. Everything depends on Elliott Sterling having no motives." He had been sucked in by that brisk, everyday tone, Guy realized with something like horror: his own voice had held the mild impatience of a tennis player whose normally top-seeded opponent was off his game. "Leo Badge has motives, big clear ones." The note of *Game and set* flatly claimed was an improvement. But, *For God's sake, this is a murderer,* said an inner voice of Silvestri, and its tone was outraged.

Elliott smiled. "Are they really so clear, I wonder."

"Was Hilary Bridge Joanie's faculty advisor?" Guy looked at the smile and added, "I can check it at Merrivale, you know."

"Then check it, and to hell with you. Do you take me for a complete fool? Don't you think I know that if you had anything to deal a mortal blow with, you wouldn't have come here to fence with me? You can't get that much kick out of pricking my vanity."

"I'm afraid it's a matter of pricking my own vanity."

Elliott looked interested, but cautious. "What can that mean?"

"Oh, I guess an apology to the team, in a way. For playing fancy games with the murder of Hilary Bridge, instead of counting several sets of minutes and alibis. But I could see that everything would have to begin with Bridge. Because the others were here before he came, and nothing happened."

"He came to Elm Circle three years ago," Elliott pointed out. His tone was judicious: fox-colored head tilted, eyes bright, a clever man followed the making of an argument, prepared to give it a fair hearing. "And nothing happened then."

"No. I've been wondering why. Did it take a while until you knew who he was?" Even given the tragic circumstances, the name of Joanie's faculty advisor wouldn't have been printed on her stepfather's memory. Elliott Sterling, who drank official sherry at Lambert's English Department soirees, would have known that the newcomer Hilary Bridge had formerly been at Merrivale College. But it must have taken more than just that. "A remark over a bridge table?" Guy guessed. But not hopefully: it was impossible to imagine Hilary Bridge—who had made a valentine of Joanie Robinson's photo and kept it, who was almost undoubtedly sorry and maybe even felt a little guilt—making casual conversation about the tragedy; but it was possible that a maudlin moment when everybody had too much to drink . . . "Something he said made—"

"Not 'said.' He was doing it again, Guy. But not touting up the glamour of opium-eating, not this time—because the new thing is much too puritanical."

"Oh. Revolutionary politics."

"For everybody else. Hilary was at it all over again, the business of leading the student into danger and then ducking out." The reddish head tilted again, as though it was necessary to see—literally—both sides. "Of course, he didn't actually say, 'Go storm the Post Office,' or whatever."

"No." Guy remembered the Lambert administrator ex-

236

plaining Prof. Bridge's "scholar's interest" in the "literature of revolution." The scholarly Prof. Bridge, discussing an idea, had nothing to say to the students about what happened when the idea was put into effect; that was, after all, the business of departments like history and political science. "What it usually amounts to," Guy said, "is 'To the barricades!' shouted from behind the library wall. Then some poor kid ends up with a broken head and a police record." But Hilary Bridge would feel no guilt about that, for he thought of himself as a scholar. A teacher might have an obligation to consider a student's level of knowledge—to know what kind of soil he was sowing ideas in—but Lambert scholars like Hilary Bridge had no vocation for teaching: they regarded the need to lecture to students as mere wage slavery and spent large chunks of time and energy scheming to get research arrangements where they'd never need to see an undergraduate. Guy said, "The ideas you coddle, you have to take responsibility for, too." He looked up, saw Elliott's raised eyebrow, and apologized for the irrelevance with a gesture. "The point is, the day after the riot, when the students who listened to them are waking up in jail, types like Bridge are always back doing business at the same old stand. Right?" It was not really a question.

"Nobody could do justice, Guy. He was getting away scot-free again, slipping down the cracks in the structure. You couldn't have arrested him, could you" Elliott was not asking a question either.

"No, but we could've arrested Ralph Adonio. In fact, somebody was about to. I realize you couldn't know that. But what I couldn't bring myself to believe was that your system had no room in it for that possibility. That what you'd set up was not an auxiliary justice, but a competing one."

Elliott was stung. "That's not true."

"I thought it wasn't. I thought I understood you, so my vanity misled me; I dismissed what logic, or common sense, or whatever it was, was telling me. Because I couldn't believe

237

it of you—that there was Jim Waterman, plying his trade, and you let him. Is there only one crime in your code of justice? Because at the very least, you could've tried some version of calling the cops." Guy was scoring his point, and he thought he knew why. What he was using was genuine feeling, transferred from another situation: he was describing almost exactly the disbelief he'd felt when he'd tried to see Elliott planting the scarf on the Residence students. Finally, of course, Guy had seen that what he was looking at was the ironic end-product of true tolerance: color-blind Elliott, not guilty even of paternalism, had simply not thought of the black students as especially vulnerable.

"Dammit, I *told* you," Elliott said angrily. "I *said* I didn't have a very good telescope. I could see how it was done—the business of slipping out the back door of the Grotto and in the back door of Adonio's shop. But I couldn't tell who it was."

"I see." Guy said it apologetically. Elliott *had* complained about his telescope, quite markedly and specifically. And in being unable to learn more without revealing the fact of his surveillance, he'd had the same dilemma as the drug squad—which had also held off, letting the pickup man go about his business.

"I tried asking Gus George casual questions," Elliott went on. "As if I'd hoped to run into somebody and missed him. *You* know."

Guy did know: Elliott had begun hanging around the Grotto in the evenings—Silvestri himself had encountered him there, "anthropologizing." But it was useless because Jim Waterman was invisible in the same way Tom Carrothers was: like the detective, Jim was always around, here or there at Elm Circle, on some legitimate business. Gus George, when asked, would simply not remember seeing Jim at any specific time except when he reported to work as bartender; after that, neither Gus nor anyone else would take notice of

238

Jim heading in the direction of the men's room at the back of the restaurant. There, when the Plymouth Linen Supply package contained more than towels and when Ralph Adonio had duly collected his packet of currency, a key to the back door of Adonio's shop was left for the pickup man. It was a simple system, dependent exclusively on mutual self-interest to prevent abuse: the key was left only a short time before it was to be used, and the pickup man, when he had collected his goods and locked Adonio's back door behind him, dropped the key in the store's mail slot—if he didn't, or if anything else in the shop was molested, the key would not be waiting next time. The key, left in an old razor-blade box on a high window ledge in the Grotto's men's room, was not visible to the ordinary user of the room, but it was no problem for a searcher to find if he looked at the right time. The drug squad's persistent searches had included one performed at the right time: Tom Carrothers had looked into the razor-blade box one Thursday evening right after Ralph Adonio's car pulled out of the alley. But the drug squad, gambling on making a larger haul, decided to leave the razor-blade box unmolested. Carrothers, happening by the Grotto on an occasional Thursday evening—but not every one, lest his too-coincidental presence alert the pickup man—ascertained that the mechanism of delivery had not been changed, and the narcos let it go at that.

"As for your implied comparison of me with Lowell Lester," Elliott said stiffly into the silence, "I find that particularly odious. His sort of thing was the lowest."

"Well, I take that one back." Elliott wasn't the only one, Guy conceded, who could be betrayed by pricked vanity. "Lester was doing his sort of thing again, too, wasn't he?"

"I'd tried so hard to be fair—just because I never liked him, you know. He was the one I practiced forgiveness on: I knew he was here when I came back to Elm Circle, and I knew he always would be. I tried to learn to live with it." Elliott

239

shrugged. "But once I saw that Hilary had to be stopped, then I had a responsibility, didn't I? Ell-Square couldn't be allowed to get away unpunished if Hilary wasn't."

"You tried to tell me. Last Saturday, you even said you despised Lester because he didn't call the cops."

Elliott's smile was wry. "I got cocky. I didn't think you'd see a double allusion."

"I didn't. I got there by following old Doctor Edmondsen's trail. He's the one who really nailed Lester."

For the first time, Elliott looked defeated. "I should've been able to manage some reward. After all, it was because of Edmondsen that she—well, that she didn't die alone. Sometimes I think it was only that," he added quickly, hastening to put an analytic distance between himself and memory, "that little consoling fact, that made the difference between me and Mary. At least it was enough for me to hang onto. So I chose a slower form of suicide, and survived."

The matching tragedies, then, had brought together Elliott Sterling and Kate Cermak, another survivor of a broken life. Guy said, "You wouldn't hurt Kate." It came out with more plea than he meant. "If you've been dosing her—"

"Don't be silly. It hasn't happened often, this problem. Usually she's quite biddable, and anyway I know what I'm doing." Elliott grinned. "I'm rather a minor expert." He glanced across the room at the table near the door, where a wooden rack of test tubes and a covered microscope stood. "One of my hobbies. Or, now it is—it used to be research, for Badge's plots."

"Oh? Well, maybe you could lend the Buxford medical examiner a hand. They're still not sure what killed Ralph Adonio." Dimly, Guy remembered his dream of being chased by a pygmy with a blowpipe.

"Curare," Elliott said proudly. "If they keep at it long enough, they'll get there."

Right idea, wrong continent, Guy thought—and then caught himself in this lightmindedness and wondered, startled, what could be said to have him in thrall this time. Nevertheless, he still sounded insanely conversational when he asked, "But how? Was it a blowpipe?"

"A *blowpipe?* Merciful heavens! Why be elaborate when you can be simple?" Superior knowledge seemed to revive Elliott wonderfully; he was clearly enjoying himself now. "A needle. In my pocket, stuck in a ball of Kate's wool. Adonio did his best to send me on my way, but I just bumbled along and wouldn't take a hint. So finally he took off his smock and started to put his coat on. When he had both hands out of the way, it was easy."

"The stuff really works that fast?"

"Well, not instantly, if that's what you mean. He thought something bit him. He got one hand loose, reaching for the spot—the way you swat a mosquito. I asked him what was the matter, and then got all helpful so he couldn't reach it." Elliott assumed a look of mild, somewhat fuddled concern. "Was he having trouble getting into his coat? I came to his aid. The more he tried to get his arms loose, the more I helped him into his coat. And in a minute, all I had to do was get out of the way and let him fall."

Guy wondered fleetingly why he wasn't shuddering. True, Adonio too had simply gotten out of the way and let them fall. But still— "It must have been a bad moment," Guy said quickly, leaving his own bad moment to think about later, "when the fellow on Park Street saw you driving the car."

Elliott shrugged, smiling faintly. In some other context, it might have looked like modesty.

"You took a lot of risks."

"Well? Adonio did a lot of damage. As doubtless you know. Since you say your colleagues were about to arrest him." Elliott looked at Silvestri curiously. "You seem to have managed to know quite a bit without them, though. Would it be too utterly banal to ask how you—er—followed the trail? Broken grasses? A careless footprint in the mud? Or some other kind of sign a keen eye could read?"

Silvestri said to himself severely that *now* was no time to begin to shudder. "What I read was your metaphors, actually. They were—very neat."

"I think I'm supposed to simper somewhere around here."

"No, really. Look at Adonio: the drug had to be something available in nature, and it was—curare's what poisonous snakes get you with, isn't it? The drug had to be artificially introduced into the body. And the victim's attempts to get free had to be hampered by the same hand that gave him the drug. It was all—masterful."

"Come *on*, Guy. I've already told you, vanity is not a vital organ. The only thing I can't fathom is, is that all you're aiming at, or is it only what you hit?"

"Then there's the matter of Hilary Bridge." Silvestri had not been successfully provoked, he was sure. And he spoke calmly and without any change in his expression. "You made the punishment fit the crime there—so accurately that what he did can be read backwards from his death, as a matter of fact." But surely only a man who'd been provoked could have then gone on, speaking out loud and matter-of-factly what amounted to outright cruelty? "Because Hilary had the same reason to trust you as Joanie had to trust him: you were where you were, and you wore a label implying trustworthiness. Neighbor is to teacher as Hilary not expecting anything bad to happen from Elliott coming toward him in the garage was to Joanie not expecting anything bad to happen from taking her doubts to Professor Bridge. A ratio, right?" Guy could tell himself it was necessary, a means to an unquestionably desirable end—but it wasn't hurting him enough to be only that. An anger he didn't know lived in him was being somehow satisfied by the process, even if a necessary one, of inflicting pain. He thought it came of a sudden image of Hilary Bridge scrabbling at the inside of the car door in a desperate struggle to reach breathable air. But it was also possible, Guy knew, that he had summoned up the picture to feed the anger. Nevertheless, it was the agony of Hilary

242

Bridge, sentenced to death for vanity, that Guy was thinking of when he went on: "And it equaled the same kind of death—a slow loss of the ability to help yourself, a struggle to move, and then a struggle just to breathe—"

"Stop it. For God's sake, stop." Pain crackled in Elliott's voice. And then, visible in his eyes, an anger like Guy's. "You can't do justice, but you could at least try mercy."

Guy felt suddenly lighter, freer. And he knew the reason: it was a relief to be fighting, to have an identifiable enemy. "I *can* do justice. Me and my team. You've underrated us."

"Ah yes, the law." Elliott shrugged. "The law is welcome to do anything it can. But it can't."

"I wouldn't be so sure. There's the scarf, you know: the black students at the Residence found it." Guy examined his opponent's so-what shrug and decided it was a bluff. But there was also always the possibility that Elliott was really living within the Leo Badge plot in which Elliott Sterling was a character with no motive for murder. "It matters. Because it knocks out Florence's testimony that she saw Jacques coming from the garage."

"That's nice for Jacques, if you and your little team should ever be tempted to charge him with the murder. But if you were to consider trying to charge me, what do you think you could show?"

"Just what happened. You went back to the Perilous, ostensibly for a book, and stayed there till you saw Jacques leaving the house. Which Kate also saw, right? How come? You didn't need that, and it created a danger that she'd be called to testify."

"She just saw it, that's all. I couldn't blindfold her."

"Okay. You dashed into the shop, got the book, and told Florence to draw the curtain. You could be pretty sure she wouldn't do it right away, but just in case, you got to Number 20 by slipping out of the Circle—you went through along the Piecemeal furniture store, I guess: it was closed and there wouldn't be anybody around to see you—and walking behind

243

the houses on that side. You came through Hilary's garden and walked into the garage. It was taking a chance, but not much: if anybody saw you there, he wouldn't be so surprised that he'd necessarily remember it, and he certainly wouldn't look at his watch if he did see you. And that's what it would take, a minute-by-minute check, to cause you any serious trouble," Guy admitted. He paused for thought. "After you knocked Hilary out was the next risk. You put on Jacques's scarf, or one like it—"

"It's his. I swiped it when I was playing bridge there once."

"Okay. You closed and locked the garage door and walked up the driveway as Jacques, so to speak. I don't suppose you could count on Florence seeing you just then, but you had to come out that way so being Jacques reduced an unavoidable risk. Once up the driveway and out of the light, you ducked into the shrubbery and took off the scarf. Back the way you came—behind the houses, tossing the scarf into the Residence yard as you passed, and you materialized in the Circle, Elliott going home to report that Hilary's gone off and left him. That's about it," Guy said, "There are slippages in the times. But that's the idea."

"Very good. But to no avail, and I think you know it. Those slippages of time won't do a prosecutor any good. They could be explained away by my efforts to find out whether anyone was at home at Number 20—maybe nobody saw me ringing the doorbell, and so forth, but that doesn't prove I didn't. And I'm not the one who has to account for those slipped minutes and half-minutes, either. So what kind of a case would you have? Not terribly strong, I think you'll have to admit. Probably not even strong enough to make a charge, would be my guess."

It wasn't a bluff after all, Guy concluded: Elliott really had blinded himself to anything beyond the borders of Leo Badge's plot. "You forget something," he said flatly, almost coldly. "If there's any generalized suspicion again, any casting about for possible suspects, any kind of fresh start at all—well, from now on it would be without the presumption of Elliott Sterling's innocent-passerby status. Next time around—" He stopped.

Because Elliott saw the point now. Or maybe only conceded it—but if he had been bluffing, he was giving it up. He moved painfully, like someone who had suffered a literal blow, as he crossed in front of Guy. "All right," he said. He sat down on the straight wooden chair at the table. "You read a book and you recognized me. But you can't take that into court."

"Listen." This further blindness could be just a stall, but it did fit with Elliott's odd self-delusion, so Guy took it at face value. "How deep do you think that secret can be buried? Leo Badge wasn't really a separate identity, you know— many people would have known your real name. I don't have to torture the truth out of Hilliard Snowe." It seemed too obvious to need saying. But imagination, floating free of the real world, could produce incredibilities: in *Nightmare in Town* a detective had artfully deduced something a real detective would have simply looked up at City Hall. "In Merrivale College's records," Guy said patiently, "it wouldn't be Mrs. Leo Badge who was listed as Joan Robinson's parent, but Mrs. Elliott Sterling, right? An unshakable cross-reference. More than one, certainly. Like, surely you didn't pay Merrivale's whopping tuition in cash?" It came to him sadly, behind these explanations of simple reality, that Joanie, too, had floated free of the real world. She'd been, it seemed, truly the unreal Leo Badge's stepdaughter.

Elliott sat silent, his head bowed. For Guy, it was a profoundly shocking statement: it was more surrender than, even in the relief of doing battle, he would have asked.

And then Elliott looked up and asked "What did you come for?" And Guy knew the fight wasn't over yet after all.

It was a fair question, all right: if Guy was The Law, why had he come here tonight? Maybe it was true that Leo Badge made Elliott only just vulnerable enough to be charged with murdering Hilary Bridge and not enough for conviction, but if so, by-the-book Silvestri was obliged to settle for that—and if he was here at all, it ought to be with a warrant, and with Ptl. Donahue and a pair of handcuffs. So Silvestri was clearly not being The Law, and was in fact a man who only last night had sought revenge on Lowell Lester. For that reason, and maybe others, he owed at least an honest answer to this man who'd taken revenge on Hilary Bridge. A straight answer—there could be no hiding behind talk now. "I came for Florence," Guy said.

Elliott arched his brows. "I believe you. Also, I assume you do realize the implication?"

Guy kept his face expressionless: it was necessary to take the other fellow's blows, but there was no point in letting him see how solidly they'd landed. Silvestri, the erstwhile Golden Rule Kid, no longer sported the white trunks. For instance, he could not say—not any longer—*It was wrong, Elliott. Whatever Hilary did, whatever Adonio did.* Already bruised, and very much aware that he too could hit the canvas, Guy took a flat-footed stance, and put his faith in simply punching harder. "I won't let you punish Florence," he said. "Because she's innocent."

"The innocent are not necessarily harmless. As I'm sure you know. There are so many foggy idealists around who don't know. But you do, don't you." Elliott paused, though not for an answer. "She did what she did to Joanie," he said softly.

"You don't know. I admit you can guess, but you can't know. There's only confused talk, about people whose real names nobody knows.

"*You* can't know. You forget, I was there first." Elliott looked away from his hands suddenly restless on the table. His eyes avoided Guy's—as Guy avoided his, not wanting to watch Elliott remember. "I talked to Florence on the phone. I was Popsy, remember. Joanie—well, we really hit it off."

"I know. Everybody told me that," Guy said, hoping it helped.

246

"So she called me often. And once she was with this great kid she'd met in New York. She put the other girl on, to say hello to her Popsy. The girl was excited and bubbly, like Joanie: she did most of the talking, and I hardly said more than *Hello*. So she wouldn't remember me, but—"

"You could be mistaken."

"I'm not. Florence talks like—well, like Florence, not anybody else. She was already back at Lambert when I got here, and so far as I knew she was just another Lambert student —but I recognized her as soon as I heard her talk a couple of times." Elliott sighed. "I did check into it—I'm not that inefficient. But I knew before I found out that she'd been a dropout, and all the details."

Briefly, Guy hesitated: if Florence was safe, maybe there was no enemy? But Hilary Bridge had been safe for awhile, too. "You used your influence to get her taken back after she dropped out of Lambert again. Why? Why did you want her around at Elm Circle, Elliott?"

"Oh, for heaven's sake, do you think it was because I was cooking up a dire fate for her? I told you, I wasn't really sitting around spinning homicidal plots. You can see it for yourself: did I make a move, in any direction, until after I had to do something about Hilary?" Elliott smiled faintly. "I suppose I'll have to answer, because you'll think I'm evading the question. But it's embarrassing: the truth is, I had noble ideas—like people who endow memorial scholarships in the names of *their* dead children. I—oh hell, I wanted to help Florence, believe it or not. So she wouldn't be—so what happened to Joanie wouldn't—well, let's just say I wasn't about to do Florence any harm."

"No?" Fighting the impulse of sympathy, even of belief, Guy asked, "What *were* you going to do?" Because it was necessary not to be seduced: in the end, Florence would be safe where she had rights, not where she happened to find favor. That was what he had come here for—to claim Florence for the real world.

"You saw what I was doing. Trying to get her to see."

"I saw it wasn't working." Last Saturday he had thought of Elliott as a kind of sheep dog barking at a stray. Only, there'd been more of both desperation and authority in that performance, and now Guy could see why: Elliott had invested too much in the girl, had held off judgment and even offended his own system of justice on her account. So if she still insisted on her follies, Elliott would not be only angry or sad—he would be betrayed. That, Guy knew, explained both the peculiarly frantic note in Elliott's "operatic" scene with Florence and its oddly impersonal tone: whatever he felt about the girl herself, it was because she was a unit in a juridical system that he had to move her.

"I think," Guy said, "you'd given up on trying to turn Florence around." Elliott had been frantic because he knew he must decide—because if he didn't do anything about Florence, he lost his self-awarded credentials for "doing justice," and then the deaths of Hilary Bridge and Ralph Adonio, and the destruction of Lowell Lester, could not be justified. "You weren't going to an A.A. meeting tonight," Guy said wearily. The words helped to remind him: it was inviting to believe that Elliott had at least begun with a kindly impulse; but that Elliott would follow a kindly impulse to the point of his own immolation was impossible to believe.

"Well, I didn't actually go anywhere tonight," Elliott pointed out. "So we're being rather hypothetical, aren't we?"

Guy stood up. He hesitated, but it had to be said. "Come on, Elliott. Let's go."

"Am I arrested? If so, what for?" Elliott's objection was only verbal: he rose obediently as Guy approached. "Shouldn't we give a moment's thought to the Bill of Rights and all that sort of thing?"

The Bill of Rights had gone out the window long ago, though perhaps Elliott really didn't know that: he did seem to think of the law less as philosophic furniture than as an appliance, to be pulled from a cupboard when wanted. "I've given a moment's thought to the fact that there's an A.A.

meeting every night of the week," Guy said. "I can't nurse-maid Florence full-time. And I'm just not convinced she won't need it. So I'll have to think of some charge, won't I?" He put a hand under Elliott's elbow, urging him forward. With no reluctance, for leaving that room, even if without a clear victory, had certain advantages: it was full of potential evidence, most of it easily smashable. Elliott had appeared unaware of that, but Guy's muscles ached from constant readiness.

Elliott asked politely, "I take it you'd like me to go first?"

"Please," Guy said, warily remembering Adonio, who had turned his back on Elliott. He followed Elliott down the stairs, keeping a safe distance that still could be closed in time to avert a successful dash for the front door. If you were tired enough, and all out of ideas, it was a comfort to have training to fall back on.

But nothing in Guy's training had prepared him for the moment when, as they reached the downstairs hall, Elliott stopped, turned, and mutely held up the small vial he had concealed in his hand. Abruptly, Guy's mind contained noth-ing but a huge, useless *How . . .?* But his trained muscles proceeded without wondering: his body tensed for a spring and then held motionless, waiting for the brain to click on. And then he stayed that way, frozen, immobile—because *Nitro?* was the first message his brain sent.

"I only want to go in and see Kate," Elliott said. He in-clined his head toward the doorway to the living room. "She'll be asleep. If we're quiet, she won't wake up."

That nitroglycerine was colorless was one of the two facts Guy remembered about the stuff; the other was that it ex-ploded if you so much as jostled it. Would *anyone* be foolish enough to keep it around his house? Maybe—if he thought himself God. The idea of carrying danger *toward* the sleep-ing Kate clashed with both instinct and learned methods of handling terrorist threats, and thus set up a furious reaction in every cell of Silvestri. But he struggled for self-control: the front door was too hopelessly far away to promise success in a go-for-broke plunge, and besides, there were innocent people out there; if Silvestri made a grab for the vial here, a couple of yards' distance and a plaster wall would hardly protect Kate. "All right," he told Elliott, feeling faintly surprised that his voice had appeared on demand. "Go ahead."

"Just for a minute. I promise." Elliott led the way into the quiet room, moving very slowly. "Let's just sit down for a minute, okay?"

Guy nodded, looking at Kate asleep on the sofa. Her right arm was flung up to shade her eyes from the light. Guy watched her for a reaction to their entry, but her slow breathing never altered.

"Please," Elliott said. "She's all right. Please sit down." His hand moved in a host's gesture, indicating an armchair. It was the hand that held the vial. Guy's jaw clenched at the motion, and his fascinated gaze followed it helplessly while he sat down in the chair.

It was only then, with the alteration of the light and his point of view, that he saw the vial was *not* full of a colorless liquid. It was empty. Again the trained muscles worked first: Guy was up, standing between Elliott and the door—Immobilized, this time, to keep from slugging Elliott—before he recognized that he'd been tricked but not in the way his clenched fists thought. Elliott, slumping in his chair, was frighteningly pale. And he was, most certainly, not planning to run.

"What the hell?" Guy said. "What was in that thing?" His eyes measured distances—from Elliott to Kate, from himself to the telephone in the hall.

"Please," Elliott repeated. "Please don't. I promise you, it wouldn't do any good at all. There's nothing they could do."

"I don't believe you." Guy started for the phone.

"Stop. I mean it—if you don't stop right there, I'll wake Kate." Elliott smiled faintly, peering up at the figure silhouetted by the doorway. "I know you can execute a perfectly

250

beautiful flying tackle or something. But whatever you do, I can make enough noise to wake her."

It was possible, Guy calculated. Unquestionably he could grab and immobilize Elliott, but not soundlessly. Besides, Guy had been too hasty with his disbelief, he thought now: with Elliott, *Schrechlichkeit* was always a possibility; but that pallor—the skin so utterly white and bloodless that a few heretofore invisible freckles on his forehead stood out like decorations—could not be achieved at will. The realization made Guy, first of all, angry. "I resent the implication that I can be twitched around that way. You misunderstand," he went on, speaking slowly because it was somehow important that the point be understood. "I admit to covetousness, or lust, or whatever it is. But if you think I'd let you get away with murder because—"

"I'm not getting away, you know. If you don't believe me, all you've got to do is wait—about five minutes now, maybe less. All I'm bargaining for is that, the way we spend the five minutes." Elliott closed his eyes and laid his head back against the chair. "It can't make any difference to me, actually. But what I was trying to indicate is, it can make an enormous difference to Kate."

Guy looked at Kate, sleeping peacefully, and noticed that she had extraordinarily shapely legs; he caught himself thinking that and realized he was doing much the same kind of psychic dodging he and Toots Cantor had seen in civilians suddenly confronted with death. He forced himself then to look at Elliott, to focus on this impossible, ridiculous, mind-boggling thing. "Why?" His voice came out hoarse and thready. "Why did you do it?"

"Well, it would've ended with me in the funny farm, probably—unsound mind, all that sort of thing. And then Kate would be trapped for fair. Unless she either admitted not being married or waited seven years or whatever the stupid law says, she couldn't possibly live here anymore. Not with you, and this is where you live." He seemed somehow

251

to hear Guy's protest, though it had amounted only to a small involuntary movement. Elliott opened his eyes and said softly, "If you alarm me, it speeds the absorption. Please. I need the time." He waited, perhaps resting. "But if Kate is a proper widow," he went on, "you can marry her. After a respectable interval, in maybe another state. And who'll check to see whose widow she was?"

"Elliott—"

"You can do it if you want to. If you can get her to want to. Try."

"For God's sake," Guy burst out, "will you stop writing the script?"

"What else makes sense? Should I have asked you in advance?" The familiar wry smile appeared, and Elliott opened his eyes and it was there, too. "Now you'll never have to know what you would have said."

"The stuff you took. What is it? How did you—?"

"Oh, I had it ready up there. Among a bunch of others. Purloined-letter style, remember?" Elliott was not interested—he was looking at Kate. "Her hair is in her face again. Too bad. But better leave it. If you touch her, she wakes up."

"Elliott, listen. I didn't even have the scarf, you know that?" A knot of pain, or guilt, or something less identifiable, was all but blocking Guy's throat. "I was bluffing. The Residence kids thought somebody was trying to frame them, so they got rid of it."

Elliott went on looking at Kate. "It doesn't matter." His voice sounded drowsy.

"But it does, dammit. You've—executed yourself—for something nobody could have convicted you . . ."

Elliott closed his eyes again. "It doesn't matter, Guy. It's really very simple: I know I'm terribly touching at the moment, but the fact is, I did kill them."

It's just not that simple, Kate had said once, and Guy had scoffed. But that was before, when he was—different. When he never would have thought of coming here alone, without leaving anything but the barest just-in-case record of what he knew: portrait of a separate-type man, with only fringes of groupness. Where was the self-professed team man now? Standing by through suicide was in fact a crime—which Elliott, always weak on the realities of life and law, maybe didn't know: his plot, with Guy and Kate strolling off hand in hand to a happy ending, seemed to have no room in it for a scene where Lt. Silvestri, an officer derelict in his duty, faced the consequences of personalizing the law. What it came down to, really, was letting Elliott make all the choices, by Elliott's Leo Badge rules and with Elliott's lordliness that maybe really was grounds for the funny farm.

Elliott said, "The point is, I *decided*. Incorrectly, it seems, about Adonio. But—"

"Adonio would've gone to jail in any case, whether you got into the act or not. Because he was guilty as hell."

"But he could have come out changed, couldn't he? I know they mostly don't, but it was—possible." With apparent difficulty now, Elliott opened his eyes. "A factor I—didn't allow for. Decided—on ins'f'cient—inf'mation. Major crime. See?"

Guy saw: if you made all the rules, elected yourself God, you foreclosed the right to fall short—of perfect knowing, of perfect justice, of in fact being like God. But that included also some very painful obligations: to be godlike, you maybe had to do some things you didn't want to do. "Elliott, wait," Guy said, suddenly sick with pity now that he thought he saw what Elliott had really pronounced himself guilty of.

"Can't—very—well." The thin lips twisted. "Old boy."

Guy was across the room and crouching by the chair. He took the hand that was trying to touch something.

Elliott's eyelids fluttered. "The—red—beard." He stopped to summon strength, and his voice came out with sudden clarity. "In with the—garden tools. So Kate—wouldn't find—"

Red Beard, who came to the hippies' pad but never spoke, who probably was seen only in that dim light and in some exotic costume. And who had probably stuck a needle into the neck of a doll, thus "proving" his magic powers when Ralph Adonio died, but also making Florence nervous enough to call Lt. Silvestri in the middle of the night. Guy realized, with an absurd pang, that he had forgotten all about Red Beard. But Leo Badge had tied up the strings of the plot.

"Elliott," he said gently. He could see the vial glinting in the depths of the chair, where it had fallen from Elliott's hand. It had been so conveniently at hand that even the presence of a policeman—though admittedly an insufficiently observant one—in the same room had presented no problem. *I had it ready.* Red Beard had not gone to join the hippies tonight, but he'd meant to, and he might well have had a "potion" ready for Florence, who would certainly swallow anything labeled "magic." But on the other hand, wouldn't Elliott, who wrote all the scripts and planned everything in advance, also have on hand something for himself, for the emergency of discovery? "The stuff you took," Guy said urgently. He gripped Elliott's shoulder hard to rouse him because he knew he'd know—if he got one chance, one good look—which "potion" had been in that little bottle. And he had to know, right now, from Elliott himself. "Elliott, tell me. Were you going to give that stuff to Florence tonight?"

Elliott's eyes opened. "Yes," he said. And then he made a major effort and added, "Of course."

It was his last mistake. Guy saw the glint in the eyes so close to his, and recognized it as triumph of Elliott's characteristic kind, a gamesman's delight, a debater's score. Guy had seen that look in a hundred arguments—it was Elliott seeing a chance for an across-the-board coup. And it was that: to assure Guy that he could live happily ever after because the man he'd hounded that night had really been on the point of murdering the innocent, and at the same time to prove that when Elliott Sterling elected himself God he really went through with it all the way—to establish all that with a single word would be a coup indeed. But Elliott, reaching for it, had

254

overreached—had, at the very last possible minute, blown it all by going beyond the single word. Guy had just enough time to recognize that "Of course" for what it was, a boast. And then Elliott was dead.

Guy let go of the thin hand. Remembering Edmondsen putting Joanie's body down in the snow, he knew he'd been right to behave illicitly: Elliott was entitled to die not alone, or among strangers. He stood up, giving himself a minute before he had to do the things that would have to be done. Easing his cramped muscles, he told himself it was much too soon—and would be for a long time yet—to begin to unscramble all this.

And to deal with, among other things, the knowledge that if Guy hadn't come here tonight on an illicit mission—if he had protected Florence the way he was supposed to, by wielding the law and letting the consequences fall where they must—Elliott would not be dead. Because Elliott Sterling had preferred to die rather than admit the implications of the fact that he had not been able to harm Florence. A fact that Guy Silvestri would somehow have to find a way to live with, though his friend had tried to spare him . . . But on the whole, he decided—for now, at least—if you had to manage to come to terms with the knowledge that you really could love a murderer, it was just as well if you didn't also owe him the rest of your life.

Guy went to stand beside the sofa, looking back over his shoulder to be sure he would be blocking any immediate view of the figure in the chair. Then he leaned and brushed Kate's wandering strand of dark hair away from her face.

He did it very, very gently, but she woke at once. Elliott, who was always right and thought of everything—Elliott, friend and enemy, yet never wholly either—had been right again. S,

Rennert, M.

Circle of death